Praise for Gravediggers

"An engaging mystery that leaves you guessing until the very end. This should be used in classrooms. It appeals to both girls and boys of all ages. I guess it's really for everyone. I could easily picture the characters and felt like I knew them. They were so real."
-Elizabeth Baker, reviewer

"Powerful story. This will stay with me for a long time."
-Becca Lever, reviewer

"Billy finds out there are more secrets in his small hometown than just his father's unsolved murder. *Gravediggers* is an intriguing mystery filled with suspense, humor and romance that readers of all ages will find hard to put down.
-Cindy Anderson, reviewer

Gravediggers has everything. It is a mystery wrapped with suspense, action, and heart.

-Mindy Holt, minreadsandreviews.com

"This was a great mystery! I loved how the author made the characters' emotions so real. And the ending—it is so fulfilling!" -

Elizabeth Ashby, reviewer

"Amazing Read! Didn't want to stop reading and couldn't wait to find out how everything turned out. Amazing job being inside a boy's head...and dealing with emotions."

-Parker, reviewer

"Oh, the ending! Wow! Riveting. Superb mystery. I had no idea what would happen."

-Calin Pale, reviewer

"Nice mix of mystery, suspense, and romance. I want a guy like Billy next to me."

-Stephanie Mann, reviewer

GRAVEDIGGERS

CINDY M. HOGAN

Hannah,
forgiveness is
always the answer!

C. M. Hogan

Other Books and Audio Books by Cindy M. Hogan

Watched

Protected

Created

Watched Trilogy

Adrenaline Rush

Confessions of a 16-Year-Old Virgin Lips: First Kiss

Stolen Kiss

Rebound Kiss

GRAVEDIGGERS

CINDY M. HOGAN

O'neal Publishing
Layton, UT

Gravediggers
Copyright ©2013 by Cindy M. Hogan
First Edition
Cover design by Novak Illustrations
Cover photography by Still Memories by Tomi
Cover models: Jason Anderson and Gabrielle Hutchison
Edited by Charity West
Formatted by Heather Justesen

Layton, UT.
ISBN: 978-0-9851318-4-5
Library of Congress Control Number: 2013915129
Visit her at **cindymhogan.com**
Facebook- watched-the book
Twitter-Watched1

This story is for you, Bill
I love you

Chapter 1

Why did people have to die in June when it was so dang hot? I jumped on the top edge of my shovel, forcing it into the ground, the metal pressing into the soles of my feet through the holes in the bottoms of my shoes. The muggy late afternoon air sent sweat dripping into my eyes. I wiped my sleeve across my face.

Henry, my best friend since forever, and I had dug three graves in just over two weeks. The average for the Halls, Tennessee cemetery was only one grave a month for the six years we'd been working there. It was hard to believe it would be my last year of digging graves, but I was totally excited about going away to college. Even though I hated sweating to death and would rather be playing baseball, I was stoked about the one hundred bucks I'd earn. I'd finally have a few extra dollars to buy new shoes. I'd seen an awesome looking pair of Nikes at the thrift store just the other day. They had probably belonged to Mikey, Mayor Clement's youngest son. I didn't want to have to wear *his* cast-offs, but I needed every penny for college. Mikey tended to wear something only a few times before tossing it aside anyway. No such luck for me. *Use 'em up and wear 'em out* was our family's adage.

Across from me, Henry grunted with the effort of throwing the dirt he just dug up into the small pile to the side of us. He leaned on the big, leafy tree next to him. "I bet when Mr. Wallstrom picked this site, the tree was only a foot high. He probably had no idea how hard it would be for us to dig with all these roots everywhere when it came time for him to kick the bucket." He took a sharp intake of air before stepping forward and slamming the blade of the shovel back into the dirt.

"Yeah," I said. "I bet Mr. Wallstrom's watching us right now from his perch in Heaven, feeling just terrible." I snickered.

He snorted. "Didn't your mom say he was the strictest teacher she ever had? He's probably up there critiquing our work." He chuckled and I did, too, as I abandoned the shovel for the pick. Henry preferred the chainsaw for big roots, but there was something liberating about swinging that pick behind me and throwing it hard. I'd gotten good at it over the years, and it usually only took me two hits to annihilate a nice big one. In a cemetery this old, there was no escaping the roots. I thought of it as an extended workout—bonus time.

The hard work helped me clear my mind. As the tenth anniversary of my dad's death approached, I needed that release more than ever. July eighth was only thirteen days away. I hated this time of year. The painful memories were almost unbearable. The worst part was that I couldn't do anything about it. At least, not yet.

GRAVEDIGGERS

"Did you hear how Wallstrom died?" Henry's voice cut into my thoughts.

I grunted as I heaved a shovelful of dirt. "Yeah, Henry." I kept my back to him, trying to indicate I didn't want to have this conversation.

"It was a hit and run. And you know what? That coward left him on the side of the road to suffer and die. Just like—" He stopped abruptly, realizing a little late that some sensitivity was in order.

I sighed. The guy could be an idiot, but he was still my best friend.

"Just like my dad. You think I forgot or something?"

Henry looked abashed. "I'm sorry, Billy, I just..."

I stopped working and leaned on my shovel. "Forget it. I know you didn't mean anything by it. It's just not my favorite subject, you know."

"Well, it just kills me, that's all. I mean, this guy—if he'd stopped and called 911, Mr. Wallstrom might still be alive."

I spat. "I heard the guy was drunk, out of his mind."

"Just a stupid seventeen year old kid. Hard to believe someone our age could do that. Guess that's the bright side, though—they found the guy."

"Some bright side. I guess they're better at finding hit and run suspects in Dyersburg than they are here in Halls."

"Doesn't it make you want to go after the guy that killed your dad?" Henry huffed as he dug.

I sighed. We'd been over this. "It was a hit and run, Henry. If the police couldn't find the guy when the evidence was fresh, what am I supposed to do about it now?"

CINDY M. HOGAN

"You could get Chief McKnight to show you the evidence—maybe you'd see something he missed. He was *your* dad, after all."

I grimaced. "I've tried—Bud promised Mama not to involve me in the case. He won't let me anywhere near it. But just wait until I'm in the FBI. He'll have to give me access." While I loved that Bud acted like my dad, it bothered me more than I could say that he wouldn't talk to me about the evidence from my dad's death.

"You think once you're a big shot FBI agent they're gonna let you come home and search for your dad's murderer? That's just nuts. Now's the time. It could be years before you make it into the FBI, and by then all the evidence could be gone."

I picked up my shovel again and jabbed at the dirt in frustration. "There's nothing I can do about it now! Mama made me promise not to get involved in the case. Bud won't give me any information. Once I get into the FBI, though, I'll have clout, authority. Then, maybe I'll find the guy that hit my dad."

"You mean the murderer, Billy. Call him what he is."

"It was an accident. My daddy wasn't murdered." A ball of heat seared into my gut.

"The second that scum drove away, he became a murderer and you know it. Chief McKnight even said so."

I sighed.

"It's time for you to man-up and put an end to your misery." Henry shook his head, looking me dead on. "Find out who did it."

"I'm not miserable."

"You're not? You mean you don't get up at the crack of dawn every day to work out and study your butt off so you'll be the perfect candidate for the FBI, just so you can uncover who it was that hit your dad? If you figured out who killed him, you'd find closure and be able to move on. I'll help you. Your mom doesn't need to know."

I glared at him. "First off, I'm training for the 5K on July fourth. Second, you know Mama would find out, and I won't break her heart like that."

"Fine, Mama's boy." He smirked and threw a shovelful of dirt at me. I retaliated and threw a mass on him. It ended after that. By some miracle, we both knew when to stop. The topic of my dad seemed to put us pretty close to the edge, though.

"Do you think Sarah Ann will come to the funeral?" Henry sighed and got that faraway dreamy look people get when talking about someone they like.

"If you'd ever talk to that poor girl, she just might let ya look at her up close and personal every day." I switched the shovel for the pick. "Besides, has she ever come to a funeral?"

"No." Henry threw a load of dirt behind him. "I think I'll have to be satisfied with a look here and there. You know how sweaty I get when she's around. I'd die if she knew. It's better just to have you talk to her for me."

"What? Are we in second grade? Asking girls if they like my friend? I think you should just go for it. She likes you already." I swung the pick hard into a root. The impact jarred my elbows and a raw wood smell wafted into the air. I raised the pick for another blow. "She always asks if you're going to be around when I invite her to come to things."

I stopped to remove the root, brushed the dirt off my gloves, and then took hold of the shovel again. After the first six inches, the dirt usually hardened. It helped that we were under the canopy of the tree, and we lucked out still hitting soft dirt at six inches down. The shovel sank into the earth without much effort, and I was able to get five good shovelfuls deeper before I hit a rock. Henry was steadily digging behind me.

"Why don't you just ask Sarah Ann to the Fourth of July picnic and dance?" I started digging around the rock, slicing at the dirt. It didn't take long before I realized the object wasn't a rock. While the surface was hard, it gave slightly when the shovel clanged against it. I bent over to examine it. Army green looked back at me, a metal handle taking shape as I brushed away the dirt with my hands. I looked back at Henry, who was taking a swig from his water bottle while surveying the cemetery. I realized he hadn't seen what I'd found.

Was this an ammo box from World War II? I'd seen boxes like this on display at the war museum. He would love this.

"I don't know," Henry said, digging again at the opposite end of the eight foot long future grave.

I turned to see if he was looking over my shoulder. He was still staring off into space, dreaming about Sarah Ann. "I could never spend the whole evening alone with her. You'd have to ask someone, too and we could–"

"Uh, uh! You're not dragging me into–"

At that moment, I heard yelling. The anguished bellow sounded like the cry of someone who was hurt or scared. I

6

stood up quickly, letting the shovel fall to the ground. Pastor Higby hobbled toward us, his wispy grey hair flailing in the wind.

"Stop! Stop that right now!" he hollered.

Something terrible must've happened to get that man to yell. I'd never heard him raise his voice, ever. I'd heard a lot about preachers who talked the talk but didn't walk the walk, but not Pastor Higby. He was as gentle and kind in his regular life as he was as a pastor. He never stopped doing good and never spoke a cross word. At the moment, he didn't look sick or in trouble, he looked furious. He was almost upon us, his finger wagging.

I looked back at Henry wondering what we could've done to bring out the bear in the man.

"What are you doing?" Higby cried, closing the gap between us and looking the ground over.

He was definitely mad.

"We're digging the grave you asked us to, Pastor," Henry said quickly.

"No, no, no," he said, stomping his foot a little bit. "I told y'all to dig under the hickory tree way over there." He pointed to a different tree. "Not the pecan tree!" His eyes searched the ground. As he did, his frenzied attitude along with his red face seemed to leave him.

He must have noticed that we hadn't dug more than a foot and it wouldn't be hard to cover the hole back up. "Don't worry, Pastor Higby," I said. "We'll put all the dirt back. The tree will be fine." A few years back we'd made a similar mistake, and the tree died a few weeks later. He had good reason to be upset. Pastor Higby had mourned that tree. I hoped this one wouldn't die, too.

I watched the anger partially drain from him although he still seemed a bit jittery. He patted me on the arm and said in his familiar docile tone, "I'm sorry, son, I didn't mean to lose my temper. It's no excuse, but I'm not feeling well. Can you forgive an old man?"

"Of course, sir, I apologize for digging in the wrong spot. We'll head over to the other plot and get busy."

"No. No." He took a step back, removing his hand from my arm. "Your mothers would tan my hide if I kept you here past supper. You'll just have to get here bright and early and dig the hole before nine when we need to set up for the funeral."

"We'll get this all set first, Pastor," Henry said, taking a shovel-load of dirt and spreading it over the area. "I thought it was weird that you wanted us to dig under this tree," Henry mumbled.

The pastor grunted. "I guess I'll need to start marking the gravesites for y'all again. Thank you, boys, I don't know what I'd do without ya." He turned and headed for his little house that stood next to our white, small-town-Tennessee church.

"Probably buy a backhoe," Henry said under his breath, lifting another haul and spreading the dirt.

"I heard that, Henry," the pastor said. "Just because I'm 72 don't mean I'm deaf, and just remember, I can get that backhoe at anytime. Don't tempt me." He chuckled. "Don't worry about Ol' May. I'll get some water on her tonight."

"Ol' May?" I mouthed to Henry.

Henry shook his head. "He named this tree May."

GRAVEDIGGERS

I laughed. I hadn't picked up my shovel yet. A part of me wanted to continue to dig and pull out the box I'd hit, but I couldn't start until the pastor was long gone. He'd notice if I was digging instead of filling.

"There's something about this tree he loves. Sometimes when we surprise him with a visit, we'll see him sitting or lying on a blanket under it, praying or reading the Bible or something. It must be his special place. I was shocked he'd sold a plot under here, but then I thought maybe it had been sold a long time ago." Henry's mom had been close with Pastor Higby's wife, and after she'd passed nine years ago, Henry's family had kind of taken special care of the pastor. They spent a lot of time with him and watched out for him. That's how Henry'd ended up working for him, and he'd pulled me in right along. Henry was that kind of friend. He could have kept the job and the money for himself, but he wanted me to benefit, too. I was lucky to have a friend like him.

I grabbed my shovel, exposing the army green again. "That was kinda scary. I've never seen him mad about anything." For a split second I wondered if Pastor Higby knew about the box. If he'd put it there, I shouldn't dig it up. I'd have to get permission first. I decided I'd ask Pastor Higby, and then Henry and I could dig it up together. I grabbed a shovelful of dirt and started filling the hole back in.

"My mom says he used to be scary, but not anymore." His eyes lit on the fading figure of the pastor for a second.

"Really?" I said. "Scary how?" I watched Pastor Higby go into his screened in porch, the door squeaking as it shut behind him.

"I guess he used to yell or something, I don't know, Mom doesn't say much. She's just always going on about what a changed man he is and how he shows the power of the Lord to change the sinner, you know—all that Bible talk." Henry shrugged.

"Huh." I frowned. "You don't think he'd really get a backhoe, do you?"

"Naw. My parents said he wouldn't be buying one until you and me stopped wanting to dig. He thinks he's making men out of us." He sighed.

"Good." I needed that money. I'd been busting my butt to get perfect grades so I could not only get into college but get a bunch of scholarships to pay for it. Once there, I had to make the FBI notice me before I could formally apply.

We finished scattering the dirt over the area. Henry jumped up and down over it for good measure. Before we walked away, unable to stop myself, I kicked a fist sized rock over the spot where I'd found the box.

"I can't ask Sarah Ann out unless you come with us on the date," Henry said, picking up the thread of our earlier conversation. "You could prevent me from spazzing out."

"No way. All the girls around here are crazy." I swiped at the sweat on my forehead. The scraping sound of my sleeve catching the hair on my face reminded me that I hadn't shaved today.

"Yeah. Crazy about you." He kicked at an empty plastic bottle in the ditch.

"Very funny."

"You know it's true. All the girls love you, Mr. MVP pitcher, and Mikey, and the rest of the jocks. You're crazy not to hang out with all of them."

GRAVEDIGGERS

"You know I don't like silly girls. All the ones I could stand have graduated and moved away from Halls."

He kept wearing on me, trying to get me to agree to a double date the whole mile back on Tigrett Street to our area of town. We passed Arnold's Drugstore on Main, and I wished we could get a Coke. It was so hot still, but Henry'd forgotten to bring any money today and of course I didn't have any.

We had to take our ritual detour past Sarah Ann's house. We walked on the opposite side of the street. Henry never took his eyes off that girl's property, unless she was outside, in which case he wouldn't look that direction at all until we turned the corner onto Church Street.

Henry lived in the newer section of town, where brick homes were going up with nice lawns and flowers. They even had sidewalks. It was a pretty small town and there wasn't much going on around here, but Halls had been named one of top ten safest cities its size in the United States, so people wanted to live here and there were actually quite a few new people moving in. Two bigger towns, Dyersburg and Ripley, were only fifteen minutes away anyway. Rumor around town was that Coffco, a big coffee company, was thinking about building a new big factory on the outskirts of Halls. If that happened, we'd see all kinds of new building going on.

My house happened to be on the east side of the tracks, the poorer side. No one with money would ever have a house over there. My mom insisted we keep our home, really just a rental property, looking as nice as possible. So, she had me either fixing something, gardening, or mowing all the time. It was the nicest of the run-down properties, I had to admit.

11

But, watching Henry turn and saunter down his street to Beautifulville, while I had to continue another few blocks down and over the tracks to Scaryville, rotted—every time.

When I got home, I found a note attached to the fridge,

Took some overtime. I fried up some of that fish. Check the front bushes for weeds. And fix the planter box on the west-facing side of the house under the window. It looks like it's about to fall off. I love you more than a thousand millipedes. See you around 9.

I chuckled. Henry's response had always been to roll his eyes whenever he overheard or read an exchange like that between Mama and me, but for me, it held special significance.

When I was almost eight, Daddy, Mama, and I sat out on our deck at our old house on the outskirts of town, and a bunch of butterflies had glided around our rosebushes.

"Look at those beautiful butterflies," she had said. "Aren't they the most beautiful things you've ever seen? I love them."

I had looked at her with every ounce of love I could muster in my little body and said, "I love you more than a thousand butterflies."

The smile on Daddy's face was engraved on my mind. I knew I'd pleased him. He adored Mama and he expected the same of me. Luckily, it wasn't difficult to love her.

Daddy had died the next day.

Seeing how devastated Mama had been with the loss of him, I was determined to love her enough for the both of us, and that was the best way I knew how at the time.

Ever since then, we never left each other a note without picking something and inserting it into the saying.

Today it was millipedes. I always felt completely accepted and loved when we played that game. It was almost like Daddy was still around.

I hurried out to the yard and found no weeding to be done. I made quick work of fixing the loose planter box and then dug into my supper. We didn't have cable and our rabbit ears only picked up a few stations and nothing good was ever on them, so instead, I picked up a book about an FBI agent and read for a couple of hours. I spent every Wednesday during the summer helping out the librarian. She made sure a good history or science book landed in my hands just about as often as a good mystery or thriller.

"That planter box looks great, sweetie, thank you," Mom's voice filtered in from the front door. I put my book down and greeted her as she came into the living room. She gave me a quick peck on the cheek, then eased down into our creaky old rocking chair. "How was your day?"

While I talked, she took her hair out of her tight bun and it fell over her shoulders in brown curls, the smell of her shampoo wafting through the air. She leaned her elbows on her knees, cupping her chin in her hands, and stared at me. "Were you able to finish digging the grave then?"

"No. We actually started digging in the wrong place. Pastor Higby even yelled at us." I leaned back in the couch. My mom mirrored me, leaning back too.

"Really? That doesn't sound like him." She pressed her lips together as she looked up at the ceiling, then said, "We should paint the ceiling soon, don't ya think?"

I wasn't deterred by her obvious attempt at changing the subject. She hated gossip. So I pretended she hadn't mentioned the paint. "That's what I thought, but Henry said that when he was younger, the preacher used to scream a lot." I let my eyes go wide, hoping she felt the sensationalism in the statement.

"I can't imagine it. I guess that was a stage in his life he had to go through to become the gentle, kind man that he is now. Not all bad experiences yield bad results. We can learn from the hard things in our lives and become better people because of them. We definitely shouldn't gossip about them."

My mom loved to throw in words of wisdom when she talked to me. It could be annoying, but I'd never let her know that.

I could tell she was thinking of my dad, the way she started wringing her hands. She always did that when she thought of him.

"You're right, Mom," I smiled at her.

She leaned over and squeezed my hand, then slapped her hands on her knees and said, "I'm beat, and I have to be at the store by six-thirty so that I can go to the funeral during my lunch hour." She stood up.

"You don't need to go to the funeral, Mom. I'll be there to represent our family." I figured all the talk about what had happened to Mr. Wallstrom would bring back terrible memories of that horrible night with Daddy ten years ago even more.

She ruffled my hair and said, "Thanks for looking out for me, Hon, but I have to go. He was one of my favorite teachers ever. He was strict and not always the nicest man, but I owe him a lot. He brought the best out of me."

14

GRAVEDIGGERS

"Alright." I stood up. "I think I'll go to bed, too. Maybe I'll catch a ride with ya and get an early start on that grave. It's under a hickory tree that probably has roots the size of my thigh to cut through." It felt good to exaggerate like that.

She grabbed my bulging upper arm and said, "Shouldn't be difficult with these." She waggled her eyebrows at me. "It's going to be nice to add good money to your college fund this month." She sighed. "Three digs. The Lord is blessing us mightily right now."

I guess he was. Unfortunately, our blessings seemed to come at a steep price—someone else's death. The more money I saved for college, the less likely I'd have to work while at college and the more time I'd have to study. My mom wanted me to graduate from college more than anything. She hated that she never got her degree, which made it hard for us to live a comfortable life. I had to get into the FBI.

I went to my room and she to hers.

No matter what I tried, I couldn't sleep, and it wasn't the humid night air keeping me up. The memory of that object under the pecan tree kept popping into my mind. I tried to forget about it, but I couldn't. I had this strange feeling that I should go dig it up. I kept thinking I'd better ask for permission, but every time I thought about that, I got a bad feeling. When I really thought about it, I realized he probably wouldn't let me dig there again. He'd about had a heart attack seeing us dig there. The feeling that made my chest rock finally won, and I gave up and climbed out of bed.

Chapter 2

I slid back into my jeans and put on my shirt and shoes. Grabbing a flashlight and a hat, I headed for the window. I pulled the screen inside and climbed out. The air smelled damp and moldy, the humidity raging.

After replacing the screen to keep the bugs out, I stood still by the wall of the house and surveyed the area. My heart pounded hard against my rib cage, but seeing that I was alone, I began walking away from the house as if I was just going for a little stroll in the moonlight like Patsy Cline sings about on my mom's old-time CD collection. The grass softened the sound of my shoes. I stayed on lawns as much as possible.

I crept along, occasionally ducking behind bushes, trees, cars, and anything else I could find when a car came down the road or I heard what I thought were voices.

From behind the trunk of a large tree, I watched Lee, the town drunk, sway all over the sidewalk and run right into Mrs. O'Toole's mailbox. He fell to the ground and after he said a few choice words, he stood back up and staggered two houses down to his own home. His front door opened without much effort. It was common knowledge that he left his door unlocked at all times because he either went home without his keys, lost them, or couldn't see well enough to use them. He'd ended up sleeping on his porch or lawn and embarrassing his dad, Mayor Clement, too often.

The police had an almost permanent holding cell decked out for Lee like Otis had on the old Andy Griffith show. They tolerated him because he was the mayor's son and hadn't ever really hurt anyone. I always wondered what the chief, our family friend Bud McKnight, would do when he did. Since the chief was appointed by the mayor, I wondered if Bud felt pressure to do whatever Mayor Clement told him to do.

Once he was inside his house, I continued on my way. The closer I got to the cemetery, the shadows seemed to leap out to grab me, so I ran the last of the way there. The full moon cast large, menacing, areas of light and dark. I easily hid in the gloom but my heart raced the whole time. I silently reprimanded myself. If I wanted to be an FBI Special Agent, I'd have to get over my silly fear.

The church loomed in front of me, covering me in darkness. I shivered and decided it would be best to make a big circle out into the cemetery, stopping by the shed for the shovel and come back to the tree where the box, or whatever it was, had been buried. That way, I wouldn't have to walk too close to the parsonage and risk waking up the pastor. I'd hate to have him discover me and be disappointed in me—or worse, fire me.

I stayed in the darkest areas using the moonlight in lieu of the flashlight. A dim light shone in the corner of the pastor's small house, and I didn't want to bring any attention to myself in case he was awake. The ground was soft and the faint smell of roses from the graves drifted by every now and then.

After grabbing the shovel and a pair of gloves, I made my way back to the tree and, putting the flashlight as close to the ground as I could, I searched for the rock. Though I was slow and careful as I searched, I found nothing. The ground was moist. Pastor Higby must really have watered the tree after we'd left. The greedy ground had soaked most of it up, and my feet only sunk slightly into the drying mud.

I guessed the approximate area I'd left the rock and started to dig. When I didn't hit the metal box where I expected it to be, I moved my search and dug some more. I dug all around the area, and I was sure I'd excavated deeper than I had earlier. Frustrated, I abandoned my caution and shone the light wildly all over. Nothing.

I didn't believe the old pastor could have dug up the box. He was far too feeble. I remembered the way he'd hobbled out to us earlier. Maybe spraying the area down had exposed the box and he had pulled it out. I pressed the shovel into the earth and leaned lightly on the handle, trying to remember how far out of the ground the large roots had come before we started to dig.

I filled all the holes, clicked off my flashlight, and then stood under the cover of the tree in the shadows for a little while longer, trying to figure out what could have happened to the box when I heard the screech of a rocking chair from the pastor's covered porch.

I froze, cringing as I waited for the sound of the pastor's voice. He'd been where he could see me the whole time. He must have seen me. What would I tell him? I couldn't think

18

of any good excuse. I watched Pastor Higby stumble out, the flimsy screen door slamming behind him as he muttered to himself. Was he drunk? One of the pastor's favorite sermons was on the wickedness of the evil drink, but next thing I knew, he was bent over, puking. My first instinct was to go help him, but then I remembered it was the middle of the night and I shouldn't be here. And the pastor appeared to be drunk. He wouldn't want to be seen like this. I felt an odd pain in my gut.

After he stopped throwing up, he rolled onto his back and said, "Please Lord, take this affliction from me. I am needed tomorrow." Then he started to sing the hymn, *More Holiness Give Me*. Pastor Higby was just sick. The odd feeling left me as I remembered him mentioning he wasn't feeling well after he yelled at us. That was why our digging in the wrong place had set him off so easily. I hummed along with the hymn, finding comfort in it. My dad had loved that song. I didn't think it right to leave a man so vulnerable alone, especially in a cemetery. I would wait for the pastor to go inside before I left. I sat with my back pressed up against a neighboring tree, watching him, singing along in low tones with the songs I'd sung on Sundays since I could remember.

At some point, I must've fallen asleep. I woke to a slightly lightened sky. Startled, I popped to my feet and scanned the area. The preacher no longer lay on the ground and instead of moonlight illuminating the area, it was now the sun casting a small glow, as it tried to peek over the horizon, banishing the thick darkness. I took off for home in a rush, hoping Mama hadn't come in to wake me yet. It was almost six according to my watch.

When I got there, I could hear her in the kitchen cooking her Saturday morning special, pancakes. I knew she hadn't already come to my room, otherwise she would have been in a panic and not continued to cook for me. My stomach growled at the thought of eating a tall stack dripping with her homemade raspberry syrup and melted butter. It would have been nice to have a side of bacon, but it wasn't something I could hope for this time of year until Aunt Jamie slaughtered her hogs at the end of summer.

I made my way to the back of the house and climbed through my window, tore off my clothes, put shorts on, and jumped into bed. I figured it would only be minutes before she came to rouse me.

Sure enough, I heard her faint steps on the wooden floor of the hallway coming toward my room. I feigned sleep, closing my eyes and breathing lightly. She silently opened my door and tip-toed to my bedside. A rush of strong pancake and fresh egg smell followed her in. After putting a kiss on my forehead, she whispered, "Wake up sleepy head. It's pancake Saturday."

I let my eyes slowly open and gave her a huge smile. She smiled back and said, "I'll beat 'cha there."

"Only because you're already dressed," I called after her, sitting up in bed and throwing some clean clothes on. I'd shower after digging the grave.

After I'd eaten my fill, I asked, "Has the preacher lived here his whole life?" Something about seeing him last night out in the cemetery didn't sit right with me. I had no idea why. Had he eaten something bad or was he really sick and tried to hide it from everyone?

"He sure has," she said, standing to clean the dishes.

I joined her, bringing the rest of the dishes to the sink. "People are always comparing him to Pastor Paul. What happened to him, and when did Pastor Higby take over for him?"

"So many questions this morning," she said. "Why the sudden interest in the pastor?"

"I don't know," I said, turning my face away from her so that she couldn't see there was more to it. "I realized yesterday that I've worked for him for almost six years and don't know much about him. I mean, he treats me like his own grandson. I guess I was curious, that's all."

"As long as you don't have gossip on your mind—"

"Oh, no ma'am," I interrupted. I had to stay clear of sounding like I was looking for gossip. This time, she must have believed me.

"Well, Pastor Paul got old and retired. The Lord must have been looking after us, though, because only two years earlier, Pastor Higby had decided to give his life to God and become a man of the church. God prepared him to be ready for when Pastor Paul left us. Of that I'm sure. He couldn't have replaced him with a better man, don't you agree?"

I nodded and started drying the dishes. "He's not sick, is he?"

"I don't think so." She held onto the *so* a bit longer than normal.

"He said he wasn't feeling well. I just wondered if he was seriously sick and trying to hide it from everyone."

"If there was something the whole congregation should know about, I'm sure he'd tell everyone. Don't you think?"

"Yes, ma'am." I got the feeling she was hiding something from me, but I knew better than to ask about it now. I got my hands wet and brushed them through my hair to style it. There was no need for a shower before a dig. I met Mama in our old, green pickup. It had definitely seen better days, but I couldn't complain. At least we had a car. I wished I could fix that ol' truck up. It had a great engine. I could pull out the dents, get some nice rims and tires, dual exhaust, the works. All I needed was a bit of money. Money seemed to get in the way of most things I wanted to do.

I jumped out at my mom's work at Town and Country grocery store. The air was thick. I could smell the diner down the street already cooking up bacon and biscuits. I took my time getting to the cemetery. While the sun wasn't high in the sky, the landscape was completely visible now, the scary shadows chased away.

I rushed over to the hickory tree and started the dig there. Four distinct, bright orange stakes stuck out of the ground at the four edges of the soon-to-be grave. Pastor Higby really didn't want us to dig in the wrong spot again. It was far enough away from the tree trunk that I figured I wouldn't need the pick much.

I dug with zeal, enjoying the time I had to myself, but I was unable to stop thinking about the box and its possible contents and wondering if I'd just imagined it. The ground was softer here and wet. Pastor Higby must have put a touch of water on the area to help us out. I'd managed to dig about three feet deep by the time Henry showed up. Only one foot to go. It was nice not having to dig six feet like used to be required.

GRAVEDIGGERS

"Dude, when did you get here? You've done a ton." He dropped the snack bag his mother always sent next to the tree.

"Where have you been?" I stabbed the ground with the shovel and leaned on it, grinning. Henry jumped into the hole, then pulled his shovel in, as well as a small step ladder. In truth, I would have completed digging the grave for him anytime and still let him take his full cut. He paid for me to do everything all the time since my mom wanted me to find stuff to do that was free and discouraged me from spending money.

"Some of us need sleep, ya know?" He slammed the shovel into the dirt and, after jumping on the shovel's edge, threw a large scoop out.

About a half hour later, I climbed out using the stepladder and had Henry hold the stick in each corner and the middle to be certain it was at least four feet deep. I had dug so many of these, I knew it was right and didn't really need to measure, but Pastor Higby insisted on it and asked each time if we had, so we made sure we did. When finished, we leaned against the tree and ate our snack. Today it was four pimiento cheese sandwiches with a package of Oreo cookies and four juice boxes.

"You'll never believe it." Henry scowled, pulled his knees to his chest, and chomped on an Oreo.

"What?" I turned to him, taking a bite of my sandwich.

"Remember like five years ago when my cousin from Florida came and stayed with me for the summer?"

"The one with the braces and stringy brown hair?" I bit into a double stack of Oreos.

"That would be her." He rolled his eyes and grunted.

"Mandy or something like that?"

"Yep." He smacked his lips together, emphasizing the "p" with a popping sound. "*Amanda's* coming tomorrow to spend the next six weeks here. Her parents are going on an extended tour of Asia, and so she's staying with us while they're gone." He shook his head in disgust.

I groaned. "Little Miss Know-It-All returns." I made sure to have a nice coating of Oreos on my teeth and grimaced at Henry.

He made a gagging noise. "She's going to ruin our summer. My parents are insisting that I take her wherever I go."

"All you'll have to do," I said, "is bring her here to the cemetery once and she'll head for the hills. She'll think you're crazy to work in a cemetery and want to stay with your mom or little sister from then on. It won't be hard to get rid of her at all. Not at all." I wondered if she'd changed for the better or the worse. Did know-it-alls ever stop being know-it-alls? I doubted it.

"I haven't even talked to her since she left. I can't believe my parents are doing this to me. Ugh."

I chuckled some more and ate some more Oreos. "We better go help the pastor with the other prep work. I'm glad Wallstrom only wanted a graveside funeral."

I stood up, taking a big swig of water and sloshed it around to clean my teeth, then helped Henry to his feet. He was much taller than I was, but I was by far bulkier. He wasn't weak, just slimmer. I'd go early to school all year to rock the weight room, wanting to keep strong for the FBI. Henry thought it was boring. In the summer, I'd do tons of sit-ups and pushups as well as run as much as I could. Henry never worked out. Even when he'd come over to my house and I was working out, he'd just sit and tell me stuff until I was done.

After using the small tractor to lower the cement casing into the hole, we got the big hammer and spikes as well as the thick, outdoor carpet that would be lying on the ground underneath the mourners' feet and around the grave. Everything would look peaceful and beautiful before the lamenters arrived. We set the scene. We were very important in creating the right atmosphere. As a kid, I didn't realize what a big difference that carpet made, but after digging a hundred graves, I'm glad we didn't have to watch my dad's coffin get lowered into a dirty hole. We set up the lift that held the coffin above the grave, level with the ground and covered it with the grass carpet. Once the pallbearers brought out the casket, it gave the illusion that the coffin sat softly on the ground before the bereaved guests.

We found Pastor Higby and told him we were finished, then walked back with him to the grave. After he gave it a cursory once-over, which was unlike him—he liked to look over every little thing— he nodded and handed us each $100.00 for our work that day. He looked pale. I guess he was really sick.

I always felt rich for about half a second until I mentally tallied up where the money would be going. Ten percent back to God. Ten percent to long-term savings—yeah, Mom wanted me to retire in style. Twenty percent into my short term savings for things like shoes and a laptop. Thirty percent into school savings. And finally, the rest, thirty percent, went to household expenses. Mama always said that that last thirty percent was mine to spend how I chose if I wanted it, but I almost never took her up on it. I wanted to help out with living expenses. It killed me to see her work so hard for us.

You'd think I'd be used to it by now since we'd done this with all the money I'd earned my whole life, but it was still hard. I stared at the money, a longing, deep in my chest burned to have more of it. And I would. I would be successful and rich and get my mom out of that run-down house.

For now though, there were few jobs available in town, most reserved for family or relatives, or the older crowd. To get a good paying job, we'd need to go to Dyersburg, about fifteen minutes away. That much driving required a better car, which also required more money. My mom always told me that I did plenty, that my job was to hunt, fish, help the elderly in town, and get good grades to get scholarships. College was the key to success, she liked to say. I did want to follow in my dad's footsteps and graduate college for sure. I did catch some seasonal jobs like planting and staking tomato plants at a farm nearby, but they were always short lived.

"Boys, please stick around and help Pastor Stanley when he gets here. He'll be covering for me today. I just can't seem to get it together." Pastor Higby started to shuffle away.

"You look sick, Pastor." Henry took a few steps and put his arm around him. "I'll help you back to your house. You need rest." He turned and nodded to me, so I made my way to my father's grave.

I smiled as I sat down on the soft grass next to his gravestone, excited to talk to him about the box.

GRAVEDIGGERS

"I found something really cool yesterday while digging a grave. At least, I think it was cool. I think it was an ammo box from WWII. You see, we were really digging in the wrong spot and Pastor Higby stopped us right after I found the box. So, I had to cover it back up. Don't get mad, but I snuck out last night to come out here and dig it up without the pastor knowing. The crazy thing was, it wasn't where I remembered it being. I couldn't find it. I sure would have liked to have dug it up and looked inside. I would have given it to him. I just wanted to see what was in it, ya know?"

I started whistling, imagining the possible contents of the box. Being so close to my dad made me happy. I could work out my problems sitting at his headstone, leaning up against it. All my problems except one—who had run over my father with a car. I wished he could whisper from the grave and tell me. Really, I wished he were here, so I could have a conversation with him. I tried hard to follow my mom's advice and let my dad rest in peace, but it was hard sometimes. I often lost track of time, sitting, chatting with my dad, and when I saw Henry jogging my direction, I knew this was one of those times.

He waved me to him. I stood upright, said goodbye to Daddy, and hurried over.

"I got Pastor Stanley all set up. The funeral starts in five minutes. Your mom just got here. She's waiting by the car for you. You better hurry—she looks a bit agitated."

She may have looked a bit agitated to Henry, but when I saw her, she was anything but. She had a habit of changing her demeanor when I was around. She wanted me to be happy and never stressed. I'm sure today was really hard for her to retain her composure.

"Hey sweetie! Sorry I'm late. I'll wait for you to get dressed." The only thing that hinted at a bit of anxiety was the slight wringing of her hands. I don't know why she insisted on attending all the funerals of anyone she knew. They always made her think about Daddy. Her face remained a mask of calm.

"No, Mama. You go ahead. They'll be starting any minute."

Her face washed with a mix of appreciation and anxiety.

"Go, Mama. Don't worry about me." I reached into our old truck and took hold of my clothes and the bag with all my essentials.

At my comment, her expression shifted to complete appreciation, and she hurried off to the hickory tree.

I rushed into the church, entering from the front near the organ. As I passed the pulpit, on the way to the restroom at the other entrance to the chapel, a flash of army green caught my eye. Curiosity tugged at me, but I ignored it. I was late already and Mama was counting on me. I'd just have to hurry and get dressed, go to the funeral and then check the pulpit. It was probably nothing, anyway.

I used a towel from my bag with water and soap to quickly clean up and after putting on some deodorant, I dressed as fast as I could. I almost left immediately for the graveside, but a glance back at the pulpit changed my mind. It would only take a second to take a look after all. What could it hurt? Still tucking in my white shirt, I sped over to the pulpit and looked behind it. I gasped. There, on the second shelf, sat an army green ammo box with a light dusting of dirt around it, little clods of dirt sprinkling the shelf it sat on.

Chapter 3

I looked around the chapel. No one was there. Curiosity burned in me. I had to know more about the box. Who knew how old it was? It could have been buried out in the cemetery since WWII. People in town found all kinds of things from the war since we were so close to an Army Air Base that was used back then to train pilots to fly B17s. I scanned the room again and then went for it.

I didn't dare take it from its spot, so I kneeled down. I had no idea what I might find, but I had to know. My hands were sweaty and my breaths, quick and fast. The lid wouldn't budge. I eyed the doors of the chapel. I found a latch on one of the narrow sides of the metal box. I unhooked the latch, dust puffing into the air as I did. I pushed up with my thumbs on the narrow lip of the lid. It still wouldn't lift. I'd have to move it to pry it open. I needed leverage. I pulled it out, leaving a trail of fine dirt and pea-sized dirt clods behind. I sat down cross-legged, cradling the box in my hands.

I pressed hard into the green metal as if I could divine what was in it before I opened it. Nothing came to mind besides an excitement to discover. I pushed extra hard on the lid. It popped open with a metal clang.

A mass of dazzling jewelry, red, gold, white, blue, and green splashed out onto my lap. It sparkled in the light as if the jewels were excited to be released from their own little grave. I peeked around the pulpit to make sure no one had entered. The room was empty. I exhaled loudly. Had anyone come in, they surely would have heard the loud clatter when the box popped open. I scooped the jewelry off my lap, piling it on top of the rest of the jewelry that hadn't been disturbed by the violent opening of the box, and I stood. I poured it all out on the slightly angled pulpit. It glittered in the light. A few pieces slid to the bottom edge, hitting into the lip, a prelude to the thudding of bundles of money tumbling out of the box.

I dropped the box and it hit the corner of the pulpit and then slammed onto the floor. I couldn't help but call out, "Uh!" My eyes darted about the room, but still, no one was there. My whole body seemed to vibrate as I looked back at the loot. All the money, the jewelry—they could be the answer to my prayers. The greedy part of me longed to grab it and run. I had been the one to find it first, after all.

Just then, I heard voices outside coming closer. I snatched the box from the floor and shoved all the jewelry and money back inside. It didn't fit right. The box was the size of a small shoe box, but it wasn't big enough anymore for what had been inside somehow. I glanced at the back of the room near the bathroom. The main door to the church started to open. Panicked, I jammed the box and its abundant loose contents into my bag and rushed back to the bathroom to hide. I leaned on the door and looked down at my bag, a big lump at my feet. I breathed deeply, trying to calm myself.

GRAVEDIGGERS

As soon as the person left, I'd just put everything back in the box how I'd found it and return it to the pulpit. I couldn't keep it. That would be stealing for sure.

I set the lid down on the toilet and poured the contents of my bag onto it. I put the money in the box first, pressing hard on it and then, trying to recall the order it was all placed inside, I put the jewelry inside, one piece at a time, trying to hurry, so that my mom wouldn't start to worry. I couldn't make it all fit. Just as I was about to pull the jewelry out and try again, someone knocked on the bathroom door. I started and a piece of the jewelry flipped out of my hand and clattered as it hit the floor. Sweat poured down my back. I grabbed the errant piece of jewelry as fast as I could, squeezing it hard in my fist and looked at the door.

"Is anyone in there?" A woman's voice.

"Mommy, I've got to go!"

"I'll," my voice cracked. "I'll be right out."

I scrambled to put the items back into the box and shoved it into the bag. I flushed the toilet for good measure and then washed my hands, leaning my forehead on the mirror as I dried them. Stupid. Stupid. I was so stupid. I berated myself. I'd have to put the box back on the shelf in the pulpit, open and in disarray.

Hearing the child whimper just outside the door, I threw the paper towel away and opened the door. I smiled and stepped out of the child and mother's way. Unfortunately, a line of children and their father sat on the back pew watching me. There was no way I could put the box back now. I'd have to do it later. My chest tightened, and I had this sudden urge to keep touching my face.

"Sorry I took so long," I said. "I had to change."

The woman smiled. "No problem. We're late for the funeral as it is. Kids, you know."

I nodded repeatedly and headed for the door, hurrying out, carrying the bag with me. The air was thickly humid, and I found it hard to breathe. My bag seemed to weigh a thousand pounds. After setting it in the truck under a folded tarp, I looked around to make sure no one had seen me and then hurried to the gravesite. I slipped in next to my mom, trying not to make too much commotion, but everyone stared at me anyway. A man was speaking about the deceased.

"That's Mr. Wallstrom's son," Mama whispered to me. "He reminds me so much of Mr. Wallstrom when he was younger."

I tried to imagine the younger man speaking to us right now as Mr. Wallstrom, all wrinkly and stooped over, gray eyed, and slow. The only thing that reminded me of him was his prominent chin. I got the gist that he was talking about his dad, but I couldn't concentrate. All I could think about was the bag and the box. My heart pounded furiously. I had to get the box back before someone noticed.

I looked around, wondering if one of the people attending the funeral had unearthed the box and turned it in. The speaker sat down, and a woman, who I figured to be the man's sister, stood.

She started in on a story about her dad, but my thoughts were elsewhere until she said the words, *hit* and *fled*. "When I first heard that a drunk teenager hit my dad and then fled, I was angry and I wanted revenge. Over the next week, talking it out with family and a grief counselor, I was able to find it in my heart to forgive the boy. It hasn't been an easy path, but the second I decided to forgive, peace filled me, and I swear I could feel my dad cheering me on. I guess my dad felt vengeance wasn't the answer. He wanted me to feel that sweet feeling that comes with forgiveness. It's so nice to have closure."

I needed closure. I wished I had been able to release the pain like Mr. Wallstrom's family seemed to have done. It burned inside me, and I was glad when Mr. Wallstrom's daughter stopped speaking and a tall woman with pitch black hair stood and sang a bright, sunny song of hope. Bud showed up and sat down next to me. I wondered if he'd been taught by Wallstrom like my mom had. Maybe he was here on police business. Or had he come to support my mom and me? He was probably here for us. He knew it was getting close to the anniversary of my dad's death, and I'm sure he recognized that the way Wallstrom died would make it hard on us. He put his arm around my shoulder and asked in a whisper how I was doing. I gave him a quick nod, trying to let him know I was okay.

The singer ended her song. Pastor Stanley made his way to the coffin to give his oration. I'm sure his words were full of wisdom, but I didn't hear them. Pastor Stanley said, "Let's commence with honoring this man with flowers. If we could have the immediate family members first, please."

After several minutes, my mom nudged me to stand and handed me a red rose to place on the casket. She followed me, and I followed Bud. I put the rose to my nose and breathed in before setting it with care onto the casket and moving forward. Anger filled me. Bitterness pressed down on me.

Why? Why were they able to find the closure and peace I so desperately sought? The feelings of the day my dad died crashed into me, and I could hardly breathe. I felt alone, sadness enveloping me. My dad needed to find justice just like Mr. Wallstrom had. It wasn't fair. I watched as family members gathered to reminisce even more about their dad and grandpa, anger raging inside me.

I suddenly realized that Mama and Bud had left me there. I thought I could see a part of Mama's skirt peeking out from the side of the church. I made my way over, and was about to call out to her to wait for me, but the sound of angry voices held me back. I stopped at the corner of the building, afraid to interrupt.

"We had an agreement," one of the voices growled. "You leave that family alone—you know what you could lose."

It was definitely Bud, though I'd never heard him sound like that. I knew I should walk away, this was none of my business, but I was frozen to the spot.

"I don't care about you or your threats," a reedy, nasal voice spat back. "I'm not hiding anymore—I'm going to get what's owed me, one way or another."

The voice sounded vaguely familiar, though I couldn't place it. It sounded sinister, threatening. My muscles tensed. I knew the chief could handle himself, but I wanted to be ready to step in should he need me.

"You get what we agreed on, Jack, or you get nothing. You just stay away from the Howards."

My breath caught in my throat. They were talking about us! I crept a bit closer, trying to hear more.

GRAVEDIGGERS

"Maybe that Howard kid wouldn't mind a visit from old Jack. Maybe he'd like to know what I know about his Daddy's murder."

"You don't know nothing about nothing, you old drunk."

"I know what I know."

"You just keep your lies to yourself, Jack, or you'll answer to me."

"You pal around with that kid, let him follow you around like a bum dog. You ever tell him what we found that night? You ever tell him it was someone from town who ran his dad down?"

"That's speculation—"

"It's what *you* believe. But you never did tell him that, did you? Well, maybe I'll just pay him a visit—" There was a sound of scraping, bodies slamming together, and the voice cut off in a grunt. It was silent for a moment, and I had to strain to hear the low voice of the chief.

"I said, you leave that family alone. You're not going to squeeze any more money out of me, so you let it alone, or I swear you are going to regret it."

There was a grunt, and the choked sound of swearing, then what I was pretty sure were Jack's footsteps fading away. I had to get out of there before Bud saw me.

Chapter 4

I backed away from the building, trying to be as silent as possible. Blood rushed in my ears and I couldn't focus. What I'd heard thudded in my brain with every beat of my heart.

What we found that night. Someone from town. Murder.

I felt a hand on my shoulder and whirled around, nearly stumbling to the ground.

"Billy! What's going on? I've been looking all over for you—are you all right?"

I steadied myself. "I'm fine, Mama. It's nothing."

She pursed her lips in concern. "It's been a hard day. For me, too. Let's get home." She pulled me into a hug, then led me toward the parking lot. Without even being aware, I found myself in the truck.

"Why the scowl?" my mom said. She started the truck but didn't start driving, yet.

"It's nothing," I said, turning my frown into a fake, but hopefully convincing smile. Unfortunately, she could always see right through me.

She started wringing her hands and turned to me. "Baby, you know that's not how it is between us. You got something to say, you say it before it eats you alive from the inside."

"I don't want to talk right now, Mama. We better get going or you'll be late for work."

Mama pursed her lips. She turned away, but still kept the truck idling. "Billy, I know you miss Daddy. I miss him, too. But I don't want this funeral to get you depressed. You gotta focus on the future, not the past."

I tried to nod and keep silent, but the conversation I'd just heard pressed on me. I realized now who the voice belonged to. It was Jack Pitt, but everyone in town just called him Old Man Jack. He was just an old crazy guy; kids in school told scary stories about him during campouts and sleepovers. He wandered around aimlessly and acted weird, but as far as I knew he'd never been a threat. I couldn't figure out why he'd be talking to the chief about me—and about my dad.

"Mama—what do you know about Old Man Jack?"

She blinked. Obviously, she was not expecting that line of conversation. "Old Man Jack? You mean Jack Pitt? You know I don't approve of you kids calling him names and treatin' him badly." She gave me a sharp look.

"Sorry, Mama," I sighed, trying to keep the impatience out of my voice. "I'm just wondering, you know, cuz I saw him at the funeral. I thought maybe he was one of Mr. Wallstrom's students, too."

Mama's expression softened. "I don't know. Jack was a bit older than me—I didn't even know him until, well—until what happened with Daddy. He was one of the detectives on the case."

My breath caught in my throat, and I coughed to try to mask my shock. So Old Man Jack could actually know something—and Bud had asked him to hide it!

I tried to keep my voice even. "He was a detective? What happened to him?"

"Now, Billy, you know I don't stand by gossip," she held up a hand to silence my protests, "but I'm going to tell you this one thing I know about him, because I think you could do with a little compassion toward him. Jack was one of the officers that helped with your father's case. I think it must have been just one sadness too many for him—it's not an easy job, protecting people from the evil in the world. I don't know exactly what happened, and I'm not one to speculate, but the case hit him hard. After they'd done all they could and they still couldn't solve it—well, he started acting strange. Eventually, he got so bad Bud had to fire him. Now, Bud wasn't cruel, don't go thinking that. He paid him a severance package and tried to help out where he could." She sighed and shook her head. "I don't think it's helped him any, in the end. He's gotten in a whole heap of trouble ever since then. We shouldn't judge him, Billy. We should be kind—but keep our distance, if you understand me."

I sat back in my seat, processing this information. That explained what Bud had said about Old Man Jack not getting any more money from him—didn't it? But still, Jack's nasal voice echoed in my memory *You ever tell him what we found that night? You ever tell him it was someone from town what ran his dad down?*

"Do you ever wonder—what if it was someone we know that killed Daddy?"

"Billy," Mama's voice held a warning note. "I've told you again and again, you've got to let the past alone and move on. You've got a whole lotta living to do."

GRAVEDIGGERS

"Don't you miss him, Mama?" I exploded. "I mean, really, you act like he was here for a little while and that was great, but now he's gone, and we can forget about how he died."

She looked stricken. "I've never told you to forget about him."

"Not him, but his killer!" It had slipped out of my mouth before I could stop it. Now that my mouth was going, the dam was open and gushing. "You just forgave whoever it was that killed him without one ounce of effort to find the killer. Don't you think Daddy deserves justice?" I wanted to sew my mouth shut seeing the look of horror on her face, but I'd worked myself up and I needed the answer.

The revulsion digging into her face dissolved into a look of love and pity. "Son, it's like I've told you a thousand times. I couldn't do anything. The police assured me they were doing all they could. And more than that, I decided that your dad wouldn't want anger eating away at us for the rest of our lives. He would want us to live and not only live, but be happy. The only way to do that is to frankly forgive and move on."

"What if it wasn't just a hit and run? What if he was murdered? He needs his murder solved so he can find peace."

"Billy! There's no murder—it was an accident. There's nothing to solve. Honey, can't you understand, your daddy wouldn't want this for you. He would want you to move on and live your life and be happy."

I shook my head. "No. No. He would want us to find who did this to him and get justice. It's the only way to bring peace to his soul."

"Or do you mean *your* soul?"

I paused. Could she be right?

"Where did this come from anyway? I thought this whole thing was settled a long time ago." Her forehead creased with worry.

"Well, it's not! Okay? I'm not like you, Mama! I can't forgive so easily, not when I don't know the truth. I need closure. Did you ever look at the evidence? What if it was someone from town, and they're just living their lives as if nothing happened while we're barely scraping by? They shouldn't get away like that. They should pay."

She was shaking her head. "Please don't talk like that. Bud cleared everyone in town—they didn't have any suspects! But Billy, it hardly matters. The person who hit your dad was also a son, a daughter, a child of God. We must forgive and forget."

"Mom, he hit Daddy with his car and drove away. There was no looking back, no remorse."

"You don't know that." She was frantically wringing her hands now. "I trust Bud, and I know he did everything he could to find the person who hit your dad. There are just some things in life we're not meant to know."

"I don't understand how you could forgive them." I persisted. "I'll never forgive them for what they did to us. If Dad were still alive, you wouldn't have to work. We wouldn't be living in a crappy house and have a crappy old truck. And, I'd have a dad to talk to."

"You have to find a way to forgive. There is nothing worse in life than a bitter, resentful person. I don't want that for you. Let it go. Be at peace. Please let it go."

"I'm not like you, Mom. I can't. Until we know who it was, how can we forgive? No. I can't."

"So what exactly are you going to do about it?" Her voice was challenging, but I could tell she was scared.

"I want to find out who killed Daddy."

"And when you find this person, whoever it is, are you dedicated to forgiving them?"

I paused. "Probably not...Mama, help me find whoever did it."

"Please, son, let peace wash over you. Let it go. Let it go. Let it go." She wrung her hands with an intensity I'd never seen before, and it kind of freaked me out. "Do you really think that finding this person and punishing him will give you the satisfaction you crave? I'm telling you, Billy, seeking revenge only hurts the person seeking it. It eats away at your soul. Let it go. Please."

The way she looked at me almost persuaded me, but the idea of finding the killer had become a ball of fire that I couldn't extinguish, so I lied. She couldn't know I was going to find whoever it was, and I wasn't going to wait. I had to look out the front window in order to do it, but I did.

"I'm trying, Mama. I'll try harder." After turning to her, I said, "Sorry. I get carried away sometimes." I gave her a rushed smile and turned away again. When I discovered who the coward was that hit my dad, I'd make him pay. He should suffer like I had.

She smiled, trying to make me feel more comfortable. "I only want what's best for you. For you to be happy."

"I know, Mama, and I am happy." That was a blatant lie. Revenge ate at me now.

41

She reached over and mussed up my hair. "Stay that way, then."

She pulled out of the parking lot and took me home before returning to work. Mama hummed the tune to the song the lady had sung at the funeral the whole way home, never looking my way. It gave me time to think about what I'd overheard. It was a murder. Old Man Jack had called my dad's death a murder.

He'd said there was something they found at the scene. What could it have been? He'd also said the killer was someone from town—and that Bud believed that, even though he'd always told me it had to have been an outsider. That was the worst news of all. Could it all be true? And what Bud had said about money—did it mean he was bribing Old Man Jack to keep information hidden or was it part of the settlement he'd gotten for leaving the police force?

We pulled up to the house, and I hurried out of the car. As I turned to walk away, I remembered the box in the back of the truck. Crud. I had forgotten about the box. Now it was at my house. I turned and knocked on the truck window before Mama drove away. I grabbed the bag from under the tarp and took it inside.

Trying to get my mind off my dad, I sat on the floor next to the bed and opened the bag. The smell of dirt and metal floated into the air. The contents of the green box lay in the bottom so I dumped it out, the heavier jewelry falling out first, and, after a firm shake of the box, the bundled money, last. I put the ten pieces of sparkling jewelry into a surprisingly large pile and then did the same with the money. My hands shook as I counted over five thousand dollars. Six of the pieces of jewelry were bulky, while the rest were gold or silver chains with some sort of charm on the end. One gold chain had two keys attached to it. One was fat and old, it reminded me of a treasure chest key, and the other was a little silver key that could fit in a small lock. I thought about all the dirt and dust on and surrounding the box when I found it. Whoever found it must not have had the chance to look inside. If they had, the dust would have been absent, and besides who would ever have turned it in knowing what was inside? The box also had a layer of dust and small dirt clods on and around it, making me think someone had put it there in haste.

My first thought was that I had to figure out a way to stuff everything back into the box so I could put it back. I moved the bills over to the box, ready to put them in first, when I noticed there was still something stuck in the bottom of the box. I pulled it closer. Paper was stuck to the bottom inside of the box. The paper was browned with age and dirt and was difficult to read, but it looked like a newspaper article. When I tried to pull it out by one corner, the paper crumbled away in my hand.

I carried the box to the bathroom and grabbed tweezers. With extreme caution, I pulled, but the paper just crumbled some more. If I destroyed the paper, I'd never know what was written on it. I took the box with me into the kitchen. I went to the junk drawer and grabbed a mini magnifying glass. I sat right under the light that hung over the table and peered through the magnifying glass at the bottom of the box. Light glinted off the metal. A newspaper article that had been folded to fit the cramped space peered up at me

CINDY M. HOGAN

Fall Takes A Life

By Jay Heath

Mrs. Maybelle Higby, 60,...dead in her home in...essee yesterday. Her husband...orty years, Mr. Charles H... ned home from a shopping t...his wife dead after an apparen...It appears Mrs. Higby was chan...ht bulb while standing on...r before she fell.

While no one was allowed o...ises, Detective Jack Pitt was...nswer questions. "All evid...cted at the scene confirms dea...dent. No autopsy...ormed." Her body was whi...y to be cremated.

"Your home is supposed to be a...even a refuge," Mark M...bor, commented...

Mr. Higby will not be return...ir home of thirty years. He w...ing with a brother nearby un...a new place to live. There a...y memories in that place,"...when asked why it w...returning.

hile the neighbors expr..., shock, and a true deep sa...news of Mrs. Higby's death...Mrs. Higby has found some re...from the depression she had suffered from since the big storm...

"She hasn't been herself, no wher...her happy self since she was hit...weather vane that fell from...uring that awful thunderstorm," daughter said. She hopes her mothe...lly found the peace she craved.

I wished I could see what was beyond the folds. The article had to be talking about the pastor. No other Higbys lived anywhere near here that I knew of, and Pastor Higby's wife had died many years ago. But what did this have to do with the jewelry and money? Where had it all come from? I read through the article three more times before wandering back to my room and looking over the loot again. Could it belong to Pastor Higby?

GRAVEDIGGERS

A buzz filled my ears and time seemed to stop. Why was this box buried in the church cemetery? What could it all mean? Jewelry, money, and a newspaper article about the accidental death of Maybelle Higby. Did they have something to do with each other? Why didn't whoever buried it come back for it? I glanced down at the box and wondered who had dug it up. Who had buried it in the first place?

Maybe the person who hid it was a local, just like the person who hit my dad, and out of the blue decided to come dig it up and put it in the chapel so that Pastor Higby would find it. Maybe the contents were stolen but the criminal's guilt never let them spend the money or sell the jewelry. Maybe they wanted to finally make amends in some small way by giving the money and jewels to the church. Or maybe the pastor had buried it to honor his wife when she died. Maybe her ashes were buried there and he buried some of the things she loved next to them. Maybe that's why he loved the tree.

The fact remained that this money and jewelry sitting on the floor in front of me belonged to someone, and I had to get it back to that person. I never should have opened the box in the first place. But maybe I could find the owner of the contents and get it back to them. I eyed the stack of money. Five thousand dollars. Pastor Higby'd just give it all away to some charity if I took it to him. I really wanted to find the owner.

I would put the box back when the time was right. I couldn't stand the idea of the pastor finding out that I'd taken it in the first place. I'd return it at a time that I wasn't supposed to be at the church so it couldn't be traced back to me. Chances were that the pastor hadn't even seen the box.

For some reason, someone must've put it there for him to find and the funeral had prevented it. Then I had prevented it.

I closed the empty box and then put it, the money, and the jewelry back into the bag, pulled the drawstring closed, and shoved the whole thing under my bed. Jack Pitt kept turning up today—I wasn't sure what it meant, but I was going to find out. I picked up the phone and dialed Henry's number.

"Hey Henry, how 'bout we go shooting today.

Chapter 5

Jack Pitt's younger brother Elijah had a shooting range about a mile away—the best around in fact, which is why I knew Henry'd be more than happy to go with me and I wouldn't have to explain why I wanted to go. We loved the small gun club because Elijah had a pulley system to move your targets, eliminating a ton of walking. I was hoping to get a glimpse of Jack while there.

Once at the firing range, Henry plopped his plastic tub with lots of ammo in it on the ground by our feet. We sent out our targets, acquired a good sight picture, and after taking a few deep breaths, we both shot. We liked to bring the target in after every ten shots when we were using rifles. We'd bet on chores, since I didn't have anything tangible to put up.

At first, I looked around eagerly for Old Man Jack, but before long I settled into the fun of shooting with my best friend. After the first ten shots, the targets showed we hit in almost the exact same spots. We laughed and went for it again. It took five tied rounds before Henry came out the victor.

"Yes, sir!" Henry yelled, making sure I could hear him despite my ear protection. "Someone's washing all the

windows in my house Thursday, and it's not going to be me."
He used his index finger and thumb to create a loser sign on
his forehead, grinning from ear to ear.

I put him in a headlock for several seconds then pushed
him away from me, laughing. He couldn't give me the loser
sign. I'd win next time, and I'd give him a crap job to do.

"Good shooting, boys," Elijah Pitt came over, giving us
the thumbs up. "Not many kids your age have tight groups
like that." He had such a narrow face, he looked comical with
his ear protection.

"Thanks, Mr. Pitt, sir. It helps that we get to use your
range—it's sure nice of you to give us a discount," I said.

He smiled at us. "I'm just grateful for your help cleaning
up all the brass before you go. We reload all we can these
days."

We packed up our guns, gathered all the shell casings,
and headed back to the pickup truck. As we neared the lot, I
caught a glimpse of a figure walking toward the house. It was
Old Man Jack—his figure was hunched, and he seemed to
sway a bit as he walked.

Without thinking, I called out to him, "Hey! Hey, Mr.
Pitt!" I started toward him but he threw a hasty glance over
his shoulder, scowled at me and ducked in the door.

Elijah sighed heavily beside me. "Sorry, Billy. He doesn't
really like to talk much these days."

I turned toward him and saw that his face was troubled
and sad.

"There was a time when Jack was the biggest draw to this
place—he'd come out and help you with your aim, or suggest a
certain load of ammo depending on what you were going to

use it for. When he wasn't busy with his police work, of course. We really thought he'd go far on the force, maybe even be the chief one day, but now..." His voice trailed off.

"What happened?" I asked.

Elijah shook his head. "He won't talk about it. Won't talk about anything really. Just drinks. Disappears for days at a time, holed up in some bar somewhere. He's never given me an explanation, but I think what happened was he saw something. Something no man should have to see, and it's been haunting him ever since. He never should've become a police officer—should've just partnered up with me on the range, like I wanted him to. Guys like us, we're not made for all that law enforcement stuff. We were meant to work with guns, targets and non-human animals." He looked up then, seeming to realize who he was talking to. "I'm sorry, boys, I shouldn't be loading you down with all our family business." He managed a tight smile. "This time of year is just a hard time for us, is all."

"Really? Why?" Henry piped up.

"Just a sad kind of anniversary, I guess, of when I lost my brother. It was right around the time of the first Independence Day dance and picnic—it always reminds me, every year, of when he started drinking and hiding from the world."

My heart raced, "Ten years ago?" I blurted out without thinking. Did the change in Jack have something to do with my dad?

Elijah looked at me sharply, confusion or maybe suspicion in his eyes. "No, nine—why?"

"Oh, nothing," I said, feeling dumb. I kicked at the dirt at my feet.

49

We stood there awkwardly for a moment, before Henry ventured, "Well, maybe we'd best be going." I nodded and held out my hand to Elijah.

"Thanks, Mr. Pitt. And sorry."

Elijah nodded and walked away, and we climbed up into the cab of the truck. Henry pulled his door shut and turned to me.

"What the heck was all that kind of talk for? Why'd you want to talk to that creepy Old Man Jack, anyway?"

"Nothing, man. I'll explain later."

Henry seemed happy enough to shake off the odd conversation. He was eager to talk about another subject entirely.

"Listen, I heard Sarah Ann talking to her friends about going bowling today—don't you think bowling sounds fun?"

I groaned. "Fine. We'll go bowling. Try not to drool all over the lane, though. You'll look like an idiot in front of Sarah Ann if you slip. I just need to stop by the mini-mall first."

Later, sitting on a chair outside the mini-mall, next to a funny looking cigarette collector that had a sign tacked to it that read, *No If's or Ands, only Butts*, I wiggled my toes in my new shoes. When I stood up, I felt like I was walking on a cloud. These were the best shoes I'd ever had. I snatched my old holey ones off the sidewalk and tossed them in the nearest trash can. "Hasta la vista, baby!" I then jumped off the curb and said, "Race ya to the bowling alley, last one there has to clean Elvis' bodaggits," and took off. Henry almost never beat me in a foot race, even when I wore old, worn out shoes. The new shoes did help me to beat him by a greater margin, though.

"No fair," he said, when he caught up with me, leaning over and grabbing his knees. "You got a head start."

Henry said that every time we raced even when he got the head start. I opened the door to go in and he said, "Wait! I need a minute to catch my breath."

I let go of the handle. Sarah Ann would be inside and Henry had to look composed and impress her. He couldn't do that breathing like a dog running after a coon. I was sure he'd be making a run for the restroom before we entered the actual bowling alley. Sure enough, once his breathing had returned to normal he headed straight for the restroom. When he came out, we walked back into the lobby, and Henry paid for our shoes and our lane. He asked in a low voice if we could get the lane next to Sarah Ann's group.

That's when Henry turned into a different person. He was no longer cool and collected, but fidgety and spastic. He went from Jekyll to Hyde—minus the meanness of course, in the moment Sarah Ann came into view. He simply couldn't hold it together around her.

"This is it, Scotty," he yelled, turning around in a circle and waving the ball above his head. "Watch as I beam those pins away. Behold the King of Bowling." I did my very best not to roll my eyes. Poor guy. And all he did was prove he wasn't the King of Bowling. His score went from 160 average to 80. When the ball guttered, he flailed on the floor saying, "Beam me up Scotty! I'm done for. Aliens have taken over my human body." Yeah. It was embarrassing.

I stuck by him. He was my best friend. I tried to make up for his total lack of suaveness by being ultra cool myself and making sure Sarah Ann knew that he wasn't normally like

51

that. She would always giggle and laugh and slap my arm. I knew she understood.

Once Sarah Ann's group was done, I invited her to join us, but she just giggled and hurried out to join her friends. Then Henry slumped into a molded plastic seat and sighed. "Oh I made such an idiot of myself. I acted like an idiot, didn't I? Was it Star Trek this time?"

It was my job as Henry's best friend to assure him that he'd done nothing that made him look anything like an idiot. "No way. She couldn't take her eyes off of you. She was checking you out. She loves you." I was sure that if I could only get the two of them to talk, just once, it would all be over, and they would never look at another person, ever. They would get married, have six children and live happily ever after. Too bad he turned into a total dork around her.

We heard a laugh. "Was that Sarah Ann's laugh?" He perked up. "Go look and see if they're still here."

I rolled my eyes.

"Hurry up. You owe me."

"So, if I do it, am I off the hook for the windows?"

"Yes. Yes!" he said, an anxious look dominating his face. Then he pushed on my arm, urging me to go.

I stumbled up to the eatery across from the bowling alley cashier. Their specialty was pizza, and they made a good one, but they also made all kinds of fast food like corn dogs, fries, BLTs, fried chicken sandwiches, and the like. Sure enough, Sarah Ann was sitting at a table with the six other girls in her group. I was about to turn and go back to Henry when Sarah Ann called out to me.

"Billy! Where are you going?"

I turned around. "Sarah Ann."

She barreled toward me. "Are you spying on me?"

"Maybe." I chuckled. Her fruity perfume slammed into me.

"Why don't you just spy yourself over to our table, there." She pointed. "I'm sure we've got enough pizza for ya."

Fat chance. They'd ordered one pizza for all six of them, and I needed a whole pizza for myself. "Na," I said, feeling my stomach twist with hunger and noticing she kept blinking the whole time she was looking at me. "Henry and I are in the middle of a game. Why don't you come join us after your snack?"

"Come on. You never want to come play with us. Why not?" She pushed her bottom lip out and frowned.

"It's not that I don't want to, but you've got to understand that I can't just drop what I'm doing to join you. I'm bowling with Henry right now, and I'm always working or doing something else when you invite me."

"Like spying?" She tilted her head and tapped her finger on my chest.

"Very funny." I took a step back, and her hands fell to her sides. "I've got to get back to Henry. Come join us."

She grabbed my arm. "I can't promise anything." She looked back at her group, who were all staring at us.

"Understood. But Henry would love it."

"Would you love it?" She kept blinking, in slow motion.

"I think it would be fun to have you."

She smiled a brilliant smile, and I pulled away. "See ya in a little bit, then?"

"Maybe. We'll see." She raised an eyebrow. Everyone at the table giggled.

CINDY M. HOGAN

So immature. I turned the corner to an anxious Henry.

"What did she say?" Henry's foot bounced a mile a minute.

"She said she might come over after they eat their pizza, but she can't promise anything."

"Did she really say that?" He repeatedly looked in the direction of the diner.

"Yeah. But I wouldn't count on her coming."

He looked hopeful despite my news.

"Let's wrap this game up so that if she comes, we can start fresh."

"Sounds good to me."

He rallied. When that girl wasn't around, he was a freaking bowling machine. I wasn't on top of my game because I was preoccupied, thinking about who in town could have killed my dad.

Once we were done, he sent me to find out what was going on with the love of his life. I told him just to come with me.

"No way. I'll wait here. I don't know what I'd say if we ran into her."

I stalked off and as I'd silently predicted, they were gone.

I didn't understand girls. They were a mystery to me. They seemed like a bunch of squawking ducks running around in a flock and making all kinds of noise. I vowed never to be like Henry and lose my head around them. Sure, there were pretty girls around, but I couldn't see myself with any of them. They were crazy.

Henry's shoulders slumped, and he mumbled something when I shook my head at him and waved at him to come join me. After we returned our shoes, we walked outside right into Sarah Ann's group.

Henry stopped in his tracks.

"Stay calm," I hissed under my breath. I grabbed his upper arm to encourage him, but I could tell I was too late. My hand slipped from his sweaty arm. He was preparing to say some super stupid stuff. I had to get him out of there before he made even a bigger fool of himself.

Sarah Ann grinned her big grin at us and after I wiped my hand on my jeans, I grabbed Henry by the shirt and dragged him away. He called out, "Help me Obi-Wan Kenobi. You're my only hope."

Henry fought me off once we were near my truck. "What are you doing?" He looked longingly over my shoulder.

"I keep telling you we need to get her away from her friends. When we do that, you can take all the time in the world with her. Until then, I will save you from yourself. Now, open the door."

He seemed to reflect for a bit then came to himself. "Did I really just say what I think I said?" He absently grabbed his keys from his pocket.

I took the keys and pushed the unlock button. "It was only a dream, man. Only a dream."

Chapter 6

"You've got to be honest with me, man." His eyes pleaded in the waning light. "Do you think I have a chance with her?"

"I do," I said it firmly, making sure he understood that I believed in him. "You just need to get her alone. Believe me. She always talks to me about you."

He sighed.

"I think you should ask her to the celebration. I'm not kidding. I'll help you."

"I can't. My cousin will be here, and I'm being commanded to spend all my time with her, remember?" Henry jerked his head up. "That's it! You can take Amanda and I'll take Sarah Ann."

"Whoa! Back up, Dude. I'm not taking your know-it-all cousin to the celebration. I'll go by myself. But you should definitely go with Sarah Ann."

"I'll make a total idiot of myself without you. You have to bring a date. Besides, you might like her. She's not from around here, and she's definitely not immature."

"Yeah. But she's so annoying, and I already told ya I'm not taking anyone, but I'd be happy to escort ya both. Let's give her a call right now."

He backed up and held his cell away from me. "I'll let you help me call her in just a minute, but first, I want you to hear me out."

Now, I was the one raising my eyebrow.

"You have to ask Amanda. She's a smarty-pants and won't giggle and laugh and all that stuff you hate. She won't want anything from you because she's only here for six weeks. And, I'm your best friend. Just do it for me."

I pushed out air between my teeth and scrunched my eyes up. "Are you kidding me?"

He looked smug and said, "To infinity and beyond and nothing less." He raised his arm in the air, and I rolled my eyes.

"Fine, but you owe me man. You'll owe me big time for this one."

"Of course."

"Call her, then." I smirked.

"No way. No way. I can't. You do it for me." Henry took several steps away from me and shoved the phone into his pocket.

"She doesn't want to talk to me. She wants to talk to you. You need to ask her out. Give me your phone. I'll dial the number."

"No way," he said, moving away.

I tackled him, getting the cell phone from his pocket and rolling down a slight incline. He chased after me but didn't have a chance of catching me. Once I was far enough away

57

from him, I clicked through until I found Sarah Ann's number and dialed it.

"Hello," Sarah Ann answered.

"Hey," I said, just as Henry caught up to me. "Sarah Ann, this is Billy."

Henry stopped in his tracks, eyes wild with anticipation.

"Billy? I was hoping you'd call." Sarah Ann's voice was smooth as silk.

"Well, I have Henry here and he has a question for you." I pushed the phone toward Henry but he put his hands up and crossed them and uncrossed them while backing away from me.

I squished my eyebrows together and put the phone back up to my ear. "Sarah Ann?"

"Yes?"

"Uh, Henry can't get to the phone right now," I walked away from Henry who was now sitting on the ground. "But he wanted me to ask you to the Fourth of July picnic and dance."

She screamed. "I'd love to go with you."

"No. No. Not with me, with Henry." I looked back at Henry, a good fifteen feet from me. "I'm already going with someone else. But we'll be double dating." I'd almost blown it. I had to be careful with girls.

"So, you're asking me to go with Henry?" Confusion infused her words, maybe even sadness.

"Yes."

"But you're going to be with us?"

"Yes."

"Well...I guess so."

GRAVEDIGGERS

Was that disappointment I heard in her voice? It seemed to weigh on her words. Did she not like Henry at all? Had I misread the situation? I decided to pretend I didn't hear it. "Great! It's going to be a lot of fun. Henry will let you know the details tomorrow."

"All right. Don't be a stranger." The words slid off her tongue.

"I won't," I said.

I turned to Henry who was now on his back looking up at me.

I kicked his leg. "It's done, you coward. I told her you would be calling her to give her the details tomorrow. Get up, you dork. Let's go home."

He extended his hand upward toward me. I grabbed it, leaned back and pulled him to his feet.

"Dude, you're a life-saver."

"Whatever."

The phone rang and his eyes went wide. He motioned for me to answer it. I did.

"No, sir. Here he is." I handed the phone to Henry. It was his dad.

"No, sir. I didn't—But I-I—Fine. I'll go do it." He hung up the phone and turned to me.

"I've got to go home and do the dishes. Want to come?"

"Yeah. That's exactly what I want to do right now."

He rolled his eyes.

"Really, I have some things I need to finish up, too." All I could think about was looking at the contents of the box.

Once home, I hurried to my bed and pulled out the box. While I searched the jewelry, the conversation between Bud and Old Man Jack kept playing through my mind. Why was I thinking about solving the mystery of who owned this box when my father's killer was still on the loose? I needed to talk to Jack. He had the answers I needed, I could feel it. I went into the kitchen and pulled out the phone book. Once I'd found Jack Pitt's name and number, I started to dial it. I paused several times, my insides freaking out on me. What if he came after me for asking questions? What if I became a target for him? He was scary. Despite my fear, I pushed the last number.

"Yeah?" I assumed the voice was Jack's.

"Hello, this is Billy Howard."

The line went dead. He'd hung up on me. I considered calling him back, but wondered if I should wait and get Henry involved before I did. I'd talk to him at church tomorrow and see if he wanted to help me.

Preacher Higby talked directly to me in Sunday's sermon. At least it felt that way. The sermon was about loss.

"We all know," he bellowed. And then there was a long pause. Too long. "That loss hits us all at one time or another. No one is exempt. We lose our keys, our job, a pet, a loved one." Then he paused again, his head hanging. I could swear I heard him mumbling to himself. Then he raised his hands in the air.

"Yes! We have all felt loss!" He shook his hands in the air and the whole room filled with *Amens* and *Uh huhs*. "It takes faith, my brothers and sisters to make it through those times of loss. We look to Job to instruct us. To lead us. Job's loss was great. Greater than any we shall experience. All his earthly possessions taken, then his family, and finally his health. And did he curse God? No! Should I curse God for the loss of my beloved Maybelle? No! Should I seek revenge for the wrongs others have perpetrated on me? No!" The audience murmured, *no* along with the pastor. "Just as Job held fast, I must also. You must also. And what did the Lord do for this man? He restored all that he had plus more than he could have ever hoped for."

He looked to the ceiling as if he could see the Heavens and mumbled again. The pause was so long that when one woman called out a hallelujah, echoes of the same word rang out through the crowd. He stared over the congregation.

I wondered what really happened to the preacher's wife. That article seemed to say she'd died of a bad fall. But how did she fall and from where? I looked at the pastor with sympathy. We had both shared a deep loss. It connected us, now more than ever. No, we'd never become friends like Bud and I had, but I respected him and what he did. I made a point of staying awake during his sermons even if I was dog tired. It was easy because he treated me like his grandson. I trusted him like I would a father.

"We must be as Job, brothers and sisters," Pastor Higby continued. "We cannot fall into the trap that Satan wants us to fall into. We must praise God when it seems our loss is too great. And if our loss comes because of our own sins or mistakes or those of others," his voice cracked and turned quiet. It was almost a whisper when he spoke again. "We must praise Him even more."

Amens and *Hallelujahs* filled the air. Pastor Higby turned to the choir, and they quickly stood and started singing.

I thought of the box, the money, and the jewelry and felt all squirrely inside. Why was the article about his wife's death included with the jewelry and the money? Was there even a connection?

After the choir finished singing, Pastor Higby gave a prayer praising God, and we made our way outside to eat.

Mrs. Adelay made sure everything was organized and in its proper place at the weekly potluck lunch after church. Today, there was a plethora of amazing offerings: green beans with bacon, cornbread dressing, fried okra, fried chicken, Ms. Pennybacker's famous mashed potatoes—and pies galore.

Mama expected me to wait until all the older folks and young children were served before I made my own plate. Sometimes I had been so hungry, I about died helping old Mr. Hilliar and Mrs. Bay get their food. On occasion, I'd have a chance to grab a roll or muffin and sneak bites while serving them. My mom caught me doing it once and made me clean the entire cellar, ceiling joists to dirt floor, and all the stored jars of fruit and vegetables. She didn't want me looking like some beggar child when we had been so blessed since daddy died. I made sure she wouldn't catch me ever again. I couldn't stand the look of disapproval on her face.

She had said, "Your daddy probably turned over in his grave seeing you do that. You are in control of yourself, and if you can't control your appetite for a few small minutes, you'll never survive real temptation."

What did eating a roll—because I was starving—have to do with being tempted? I didn't get it, but I had pretended to. "Got it, Mom. Control. I'll work on that," I'd said. Then I'd set to work on the cellar for four straight hours, guilt that I'd let Mama down weighing on me the whole time.

GRAVEDIGGERS

"Billy!" Mrs. Macon smiled at me as I held out her plate. Her hand shook a little as she took it from me—she was getting on in years. She often hired me to help her out with stuff she couldn't manage anymore. "Any way you could stop by and pick the cherries off my tree tomorrow? I know it's almost July, but the cherries needed more time this year to ripen due to the lateness of the spring. I only need to put up about thirty jars this year, with Jenny and the kids gone. You could take home the rest. What do you say?"

"Could I come on Tuesday, Ma'am? Henry and I are heading to the Memphis Airport to pick up his cousin tomorrow. It's kind of an all-day thing, but I'd love to help you out on Tuesday if you can wait."

"I guess the cherries have waited this long, what's another day?" She smiled warmly. "You're such a good boy. Remind me so much of your daddy." Her look pierced me before she turned and slowly made her way to a table with a bunch of the oldies.

I overheard her telling everyone at the table that I would be coming on Tuesday instead of Monday to pick all those beautiful cherries of hers. My mom would be ecstatic when I told her. We were running low on jars of cherries. Last year's crop had been a bit meager. Hopefully, Mrs. Macon's tree was loaded this year, then my mom and I would be able to make some jam, too.

Once the elderly were taken care of, I filled my own plate and found a seat next to the Haslams, a family that would be moving here if Coffco, that coffee roasting and packaging company, built its plant here. Mr. Haslam was one of the CEOs and the final say in choosing Halls as the town to

63

expand in. They'd been visiting all the different churches in the area for years. It seemed like they visited ours most often.

Pastor Higby walked up to the end of the table and talked to the Haslam twins, a girl and boy only two years old. He seemed overly friendly and loud, "How are these little youngins today?" He tickled Suzanna, who squealed with delight and then played peek-a-boo with Sam, who mimicked his actions, covering his eyes with his own hands. He then moved on to the father. "I hear you're getting closer to making the final decision, Jake."

"You know how much I love this little town, Pastor Higby," Jake replied. "There's enough room to grow here and a solid work force between Halls, Ripley, and Dyersburg. Even Memphis isn't too far away to pull from."

"You've got that right," the pastor said.

"What attracts me the most is the safety record here. You've been on the FBI's list for years and years now. I really like that. And while your mayor won't budge with tax incentives like Dyersburg and Ripley have done, I think we'll be able to attract great workers to this nice little town."

"So. It pretty much sounds like a done deal then."

"Let's not say that, but we should have definite plans before the end of the summer."

"That's really good news," Higby said.

While I loved all the new people coming to town, it bothered me that the new housing development was on the land Mama and Daddy used to live on and farm. People were buying up the newly developed land like there was no land left anywhere in America.

"And you know we'll welcome all the newcomers with open arms." I noticed Pastor Higby's hands were shaking by his sides and his eyes darted about the picnic area while Mr. Haslam spoke. His attention wasn't what it usually was.

"You feeling okay, Pastor Higby?" My mother interrupted. "You still look a bit under the weather."

There was a paleness to his skin that wasn't exactly normal.

He jerked his head toward her, a strange, scared look in his eyes that flitted quickly away as he drew his lips into a smile.

"It's not that noticeable is it? I've been fighting something off the last few days, and I just can't seem to shake it." He looked around again, and I thought he looked a bit nervous.

I wondered if worry about the box had anything to do with it. Had he seen it after all? I hadn't brought it today because I knew too many people would be around and someone might catch me with it.

"I'll bring you some of my famous chicken noodle soup tonight." My mom stood and put her hand on his arm. "It's sure to kick whatever's chasing you away."

I loved my mom's soup, but it hardly sounded good when it was so hot out.

The pastor took a deep breath and appeared to be back to his old self. "Nah, Sylvia. I don't want you going out of your way for me. But, thank you."

"I'll bring it by around six." She winked and, after squeezing his arm, sat back down and continued to eat.

Pastor Higby shook his head and, addressing no one in particular, said, "When that woman gets something in her mind, there's no changing it." He then walked away, his hobble appearing more exaggerated than usual.

I glanced around at all the people enjoying the Sunday picnic. These people had looked out for us after Daddy died. They'd known me my whole life and had always been there for me. Suddenly I realized something. They'd known me my whole life—they'd also known my Dad. Maybe someone here would know something more about what Old Man Jack had hinted at. If my Dad was murdered, that meant someone had hated him and wanted him dead. As hard as that was to imagine, maybe someone here would know something about it.

I quickly formed a plan in my mind. The tenth anniversary of Daddy's death was coming up; it would be a natural time for me to start thinking about him and it wouldn't be so odd if I wanted to collect stories about him to honor the date. If I talked to enough people, I might be able to learn something about him that would lead me to whoever might have wanted him dead.

"Mama," I said, putting my fork down and swallowing my last bite of chicken. "I think I want to write Daddy's history."

Her forkful of mashed potatoes hung in the air as she said, "Really?" Her brow furrowed. "Do you think that's a good idea?"

"I do. I really don't want his memory to be forgotten and I'd like to learn more about him. I should be able to collect all kinds of stories since he was born and grew up here. The hardest part will be finding information about him while he was away at school." I smiled brightly at her. "I bet we could even make his history into a book."

She bit her lip and started wringing her hands. After clearing her throat, she said, "Maybe that would be a good idea." She smiled at me but her smile held no mirth. "I guess it wouldn't hurt you to collect stories about him."

"Great, Mom." I gave her a hug and said, "No time like the present," and headed over to collect stories.

I went straight over to the old-timer's table and pulled up a seat. "Hi everyone."

"What are you doing sitting here with us fuddy duddies when you could be hanging out with your friends?" Mrs. Hanney asked.

"You know how much I love a good story, Mrs. Hanney, and I'm after a bunch of them."

"What kind of stories?" Mrs. Macon asked.

"About my dad. This July will be the tenth anniversary of his death, and I thought I'd honor him by writing his history." I smiled showing all my teeth, trying to hide the ache that was building up inside me.

They all seemed eager to talk and share what they remembered about my dad. They liked talking anyway, and the idea that it was going to help me seemed to put a fire under them.

"Your dad was the optimist of all optimists. Yes, siree," Mrs. Pennybacker said. "He vowed he'd get his degree and come back and buy up hundreds of acres of land to farm in order to keep out the greedy developers and help provide jobs for people in town."

Mr. Miles said, "Son, we all figured your dad would end up discovering the world when he left for college and decide he was meant for bigger things."

Mrs. Hanney said, "But he showed us, he came back and showed us all."

"It's just a shame that some developer bought up that land that he was trying so hard to save." Mr. Miles tsked.

"Harris sure was pleased though," Mrs. Hanney chimed in, a bit of wicked glee in her eye.

"Oh you hush, Mama," her daughter scolded. "Don't you say nothin' bad about the Harrises! You're just still mad at them for not picking your pie at the county fair."

"No, I swear, it's God's own truth!" Mrs. Hanney insisted. "Frank Harris was after Nick for years to agree to sell that land. His own land weren't worth a dime without Nick's going, too. Can't have half a subdivision now can ya? After Nick was gone—" she looked at me, suddenly remembering my presence, "So sorry Billy, it's a real shame, but after your Dad passed, the land went real cheap, and now that Coffco's fixing to move in, well," she shrugged, "Things are looking up for the Harrises, that's all I'm sayin.'"

My heart squeezed, and I took in a sharp intake of air.

"Don't you listen to her, Billy, she's just an old gossip," her daughter said, leading the old woman away, back toward the food. "Come on, Mama, I think your blood sugar's low. It's making you cranky."

"I'm not cranky!" The old woman growled, but allowed her daughter to lead her off anyway. Mr. Miles excused himself as well.

I watched them go and thought about what Mrs. Hanney had said. The Harrises had been our neighbors, back when we'd lived on the farm, and for as long as I could remember they'd hated us. They had three boys, Jeff, John, and Jamison, all right around my age, but their dad never allowed them to play with me or come near our property. I knew they didn't like us, but was it possible that Frank Harris hated my daddy so much, he'd actually killed him? Old Man Jack's words rang in my ears. *Did you tell him what we found that night?* I'd have to find a way to figure out what he meant. Maybe they'd found something that would indicate Frank Harris?

For some reason, my thoughts drifted to the ammo box. Why had I found it? It seemed like I was meant to have it. I'd found it digging a grave I shouldn't have been digging. Then, when I thought it was gone, it had turned up again, almost like it was calling to me—begging me to find it. Now I had it, but I had no idea what it meant or what to do next.

I grabbed the pitcher of water and poured myself a glass. Just as I was about to drink it, Mrs. Hanney grabbed my arm and stopped me.

"You don't need ta be drinking from that nasty pitcher, son. Look at all those fingerprints all over it. You don' know if they're on the inside or outside." She moved in close to me. "If you brought the chief over here, we could have him get the fingerprints and we could arrest the silly person who was too lazy to properly clean it before today." She raised her eyes to me in all seriousness.

A heat spread through my chest. Fingerprints. I could take fingerprints from the box and its contents. I should and I would.

"Hey man, what's the deal with hanging out with the geezers all afternoon?" Henry said as he sidled up beside me.

I looked at him, unsure of my next move. I needed help—I had two mysteries on my hands and no clear path to figuring them out. Maybe Henry could think of something I hadn't.

"Henry, I got something I need to show you."

Henry faked a jump shot with an imaginary basketball as we passed the hoop and headed for my house.

Once there, I took him straight to my room and pulled out the bag and handed it to him.

"Thanks," he said, his face questioning. "But what is this?"

"Just open it up. I found it yesterday in the church."

His eyes seemed to pop out of his head as he peered into the bag. He sat on the floor and dumped it out. "What the..." He reached for one of the bundles of money.

"Don't touch it. I'm going to fingerprint it."

He pulled his hand back. "What is all this stuff? That's a lot of money."

"I know." I went over to my dresser and pulled out my fingerprinting kit. I then took out two pairs of latex gloves for us to put on.

"Did you steal this?" He looked alarmed, but also slightly awed.

"I guess you might say that, but it wasn't intentional. I just wanted to see what was inside. I intended on giving it to Pastor Higby, but it didn't work out that way."

After we tugged the gloves on, I picked up the box and handed him the magnifying glass. "Check out what's stuck to the bottom of the box. We've got ourselves a mystery to solve."

"What? This article has to do with Mrs. Higby's death? What is it doing in this box with this money and jewels? Do these things belong to her?"

"I have no idea. Let me start from the beginning." I had his rapt attention for the next twenty minutes describing what had happened in the last twenty-four hours. I told him about hitting the box under the hickory tree and coming back to dig it up and how it was gone and finally how I found it on the pulpit in the church.

"It's like someone wanted you to find it," Henry said, shaking his head. "It's kinda creepy." He grinned widely and then said, "I love it."

"We'll see if you still love it once I tell you what happened after the funeral."

"Get on with it already." Henry picked up several pieces of jewelry and looked them over while I talked.

"I overheard the chief and Old Man Jack arguing behind the church. They both know something about my dad's death. I guess the chief is paying Jack to keep quiet about something they found that night at the scene, and he believes it was someone from town. Old Man Jack was threatening my mom and me somehow. It came to blows until Jack took off."

"No, way." Henry's jaw dropped.

"Yes, way." I nodded.

"My mom told me that Jack used to be an officer and was paid some kind of settlement to leave the police force about nine years ago when he went a bit crazy."

"Well, that would be a year after your dad died."

"And about the time Mrs. Maybelle Higby died." I raised an eyebrow. "I thought there might be a connection—suddenly I'm finding out stuff about my dad, and now this box mysteriously shows up, and Jack Pitt's name is involved in both? It was too suspicious—I decided to call him."

"Are you serious? You freaking called that whacko?"

I nodded.

"What'd—"

"He hung up on me right after I said who I was."

"Huh!"

"I decided to talk to as many people as I could at the picnic to see if I could find out if my dad had any enemies and who they were. That's why I spent so much time with the oldies. If Jack thinks there was foul play in my dad's death, maybe it really was murder—premeditated murder."

"This is crazy, Billy. Just crazy." He shook his head quickly from side to side. "Did you get any good info at the picnic?"

"Actually, yes. It turns out the Harrises wanted my dad to sell his land to some developer and he refused. That's why there's all that bad blood between our families."

"It's sold now. Have you been out there lately? Must be ten houses up already. I heard Coffco is looking at the Harrises' and Primly's property to build on now. Just think if he owned your dad's land, too. He would have made a killing."

"If Coffco buys his land, he'll make a killing."

"You're probably right. But, do you think that dispute was big enough for him to kill your dad? And how would he have known your dad was going to be out in the street right at that moment?"

"I don't know. Maybe he was lying in wait. Who knows?"

"Do you really think the deaths are connected?"

"No idea, but I think Jack Pitt has the answers we need."

"I doubt he's with it enough to tell us anything. Besides, he's freaking scary. Maybe we should start with that article. If we could find the original—"

"That's it, Henry! There's that new library in Memphis. We should go there tomorrow and see if we can find it. We could get a copy of it." And I could also see if there was any information on the land dispute.

Henry grinned from ear to ear.

"What about your cousin? You think she'll tell your parents what we're doing?"

"We'll just keep it from her. She'll probably jump for joy when she hears we're going to a library." He got this silly look on his face and clapped his hands pretending to be Amanda. "Yay! A library. I can't wait to get my hands on the newest encyclopedia."

I busted up with him. "And you want me to take her on a date?" It was going to be awful. I hoped she wasn't even worse now than she was then. What would I do with her the whole time while Henry and Sarah Ann go goo-goo over each other?

"I already told you I owe you. It was the only way."

I pushed air through my nose. As Henry took off, I couldn't help but feel totally lucky that I had a friend to help me sort through all the mess with my dad and Mrs. Higby. While it would be annoying to be with Amanda, I would do it for him, because he would do it for me.

I looked over the spread-out contents of the army box deciding which object to fingerprint first. I had handled each piece. I was such an idiot. I never should have touched them.

I knew that. Bud had taught me that along with several investigations books I'd read. He'd be so disappointed in me if he knew I'd made this blunder. I had been so freaked out about the box when I'd found it. I hadn't been thinking straight. Maybe I was being stupid and should just pile everything into the box as well as I could and take it to Pastor Higby. His face during his sermon today flew through my mind. No. I would first try and find out what the stuff in the box had to do with his wife.

Bud had given me the fingerprinting kit for Christmas a few years back. We'd had such a good time going around lifting fingerprints and running them. After Bud had told me I was an expert finger printer and the novelty had worn off, I'd tucked the kit away in my drawer and effectively forgotten about it. Thankfully, it was still in pretty good condition. I pulled out the things I would need and went to work dusting all the items in the box. First, I dusted the items, slowly, carefully. Next, I put the tape with precision on top of the prints I found. And finally, I stuck the tape to an index card. I repeated the process for each print I found. I worked methodically, set on finding what Bud would need to find who this stuff belonged to.

I was able to lift several good prints from the chunky pieces of jewelry and a few partials from the money. I berated myself for ever touching the items. Even though I knew the prints I'd found were most likely mine, I forged forward. What if I could get a break in this case? Maybe that would soften the blow that I'd taken it in the first place. Maybe Pastor Higby would finally have closure.

GRAVEDIGGERS

I now had a bigger problem. I'd have to find a way to get Bud to run the fingerprints for me without knowing the truth about them. It'd been so long since we'd played with the kit, I wondered if he would be suspicious if I suddenly handed him a pile of fingerprints. Maybe I should tell him about the box and have him do the fingerprinting. But after the conversation I'd heard between him and Jack, I just wasn't sure I could trust him. Besides, he'd said I was a pro. Once we got the results and they told us who the fingerprints belonged to, I'd tell Bud all about the box.

Too bad I couldn't take it to him tomorrow—I was stuck going to Memphis with Henry to pick up Amanda. I sighed. I wished it could be just Henry and me this summer, instead of having her as a tag along. We had a lot to do, and she was only going to drag us down.

Chapter 7

When morning arrived, I was already up, unable to suppress the excitement that rushed through me. I felt like I was on the edge of something big—I was about to get some answers.

Dressed and waiting on Henry, I pulled out the bag, scattering its contents on the floor. I examined the newspaper article in the box and wrote down the name of the reporter and the title of the article. That would help us find it again—since we didn't have the date. I re-counted the money, pushing the jewelry to the side. My heart pounded hard at the sight of it. There were so many things I could do with even just a little bit of this money. I thought of all the repairs the truck needed, not to mention the house, and my meager college fund. Something deep inside me started to ache. The excitement faded and I shoved the money and box back in the bag and then examined the jewelry. I couldn't help thinking about my mom teaching me about temptation with some rolls at the church picnic. I thought I understood now. I held up the chain that the two keys were attached to and inspected them. If the box had all this stuff in it, what would these keys open?

GRAVEDIGGERS

Someone banged hard on my window. I jumped and dropped the chain. I looked over the bed at the window. Henry's face was squished up to it, his nose and cheeks flat. I stifled a scream that turned to a laugh. I made a face at him. He pointed to his watch. I stuffed the jewelry back into the bag and shoved the whole mess under the bed. I slipped on my dad's old snakeskin boots, grabbed my empty wallet and scooted out the door.

We made it to the airport just as the sign said the flight from Florida had landed. We pulled around to the pick-up curb and tried to find Amanda. I jumped out onto the sidewalk wanting to stretch my legs. No one looked anything like the girl I remembered. There were a couple of tall, very hot girls waiting on the sidewalk with their luggage. Definitely not Amanda. I only glanced quickly at them—several times. I didn't want them to think I was staring.

"Maybe she got lost in the airport," Henry called out to me from the driver's seat.

"I doubt Amanda-know-it-all would get lost." Right after I shouted that at Henry, a beautiful brunette with striking brown eyes moved purposely toward me. I couldn't help but stare. I kept telling myself to avert my eyes, but I couldn't. My brain wouldn't respond. She was too much. I was on sensory overload.

"Billy Howard?" the girl asked...I realized my mouth was hanging open, and I snapped it shut like a turtle, my teeth clattering together.

She stared at me like I was crazy. "Are you okay?"

Still entranced, I couldn't move. It was like my whole world altered in that moment. There was something in the way she held herself—so self-assured and downright confident. I'd never seen anything so beautiful in all my life.

Henry hollered out the window, "Hey, Amanda!"

For some reason beyond me, my knees gave way, and I almost fell off the curb as she continued to the car.

Her smooth and sun-kissed face shone in the morning light as she recognized Henry. Her pressed lips started to curve into a slight smile. When I tried to smile back, instead, a strangled laugh spurted from my mouth. What the freak? By that time, Henry was out of the car and steadied me, then opened the front door for Amanda to climb in. He then shoved her luggage in the trunk. No matter what I tried, I couldn't avert my eyes. I watched her climb in the car and shut the front door. In my peripheral vision, I could see that Henry had taken his place in the driver's seat. I was stuck—in complete awe.

"Billy. What's up?" Henry called out to me over his shoulder.

I couldn't stop staring at the back of her head. I couldn't get my body to open the back door and climb in. That's when Amanda climbed out of the car and said, "You were supposed to help me in the car, not vice versa." She smiled, genuinely it seemed.

When her hand touched my arm, something electric shot through me, and I came to my senses. Her face was only inches from mine, and I had to resist the urge to move even closer. It was all so ridiculous.

"Just take a step back, and I'll open the door." She reached for the handle.

"N-N-No. I g-got it," I sputtered out. "Just having a mental breakdown. Sorry."

"What was that?" Henry asked as soon as I shut the door behind me, his face squished up in confusion.

I gave him a dark look. "I'm not sure what happened."

"Maybe you had an aneurysm or something. Should I take you to the hospital?"

"Don't be stupid. I'm fine now."

Amanda had pulled her visor down and was applying a fresh coat of lip gloss. Her eyes weren't on her lips, however, they were on me. I thought I would die, my heart pounded so hard. That time, I had my wits about me and looked away. My stomach rocked and my heart raced. I had to win this girl over and she must think I'm a total idiot.

My mom always said that when she and daddy got together, it was like fireworks. There was no way of getting out of it because they loved each other right from the very start. I couldn't help but think that was what was happening between Amanda and me. I was no fool. I knew most people don't think about love at first sight or believe in it. I'd never really believed in it either. But this—it was just like how my mom described it. It was amazing. The most beautiful girl and she somehow invaded my soul in less than ten minutes.

We drove twenty minutes to downtown Memphis, Henry talking to Amanda the whole way. What was up with that? He couldn't talk to Sarah Ann, but he could talk incessantly to the most perfect girl in the world? Sure, they were cousins, but still.

I had teased the snot out of Amanda the last time she'd come for not having a southern accent. Now, the soft sweet tone of her voice sent a peaceful wave through my body every time she spoke.

When we exited the freeway, Amanda said, "Where are we going anyway?"

"There's a new library not far from here, and we wanted to go check it out," Henry said, just like we'd planned.

Instead of being thrilled like we'd thought she'd be, she said, "Seriously? I came here for vacation not school. Can we at least get something to eat first? I'm starving. They had this super fancy yuck for breakfast on the plane. It reminded me of intestines, and I couldn't eat it." She pulled out her phone. "In fact, we could grab something at the Peabody Hotel after watching the ducks march to the fountain."

"You know about that?" Henry asked.

"Of course I do. It's like one of the things you have to do if you come to Memphis. I read about it in a travel guide book. I've wanted to see it ever since and it happens in less than twenty minutes. Can we make it?"

Henry rolled his eyes and looked at me through the rearview mirror. I nodded. I wanted to make this girl happy.

"Yeah. I guess," Henry said grudgingly. "But, it's to the library after that."

"Fantastic." A playful sweet smile slipped over her face.

Once we pulled into a parking spot, we hurried into the hotel and up to the roof. It only took the ducks five minutes to make the daily march from their castle up there down to the first floor. The view on the roof was spectacular. We could see for miles and miles in all directions. I tried to stay right next to Amanda the whole time. I loved how she smelled so fresh and flowery. She snapped a bunch of pictures, and I made sure to be in as many as I could and also took several of her.

GRAVEDIGGERS

She talked about how cool it was that they were able to train the ducks to stay in the fountain with all those people coming and going all the time. Somehow she told us about it without sounding like a know-it-all. I just thought she sounded smart. I liked it.

The interior of the Peabody was amazingly lavish. I didn't want to touch anything. A man played the piano and customers sat at tables eating all kinds of decadent food around the fountain where the ducks stayed during the day. When Amanda turned quickly, a strand of her hair flipped across my face. She continued to snap picture after picture with her iPhone.

"Thanks so much for taking me here. That was so fun."

I'd always seen beautiful girls like Amanda be extremely high maintenance, demanding and expecting certain things. Amanda's excitement at seeing something so simple as ducks marching from their home on the roof to the elevator of the hotel and then to the fountain on the main floor made me smile.

We made our way to a nearby café and had a quick snack of croissants. Amanda added on a hot chocolate to her order and bought a hot pink T-shirt with a cartoon-like duck in a castle. In small letters it read, *Wish I were a duck*. It was cheesy, but she seemed to love it.

"You know, it's already ninety degrees outside," I said when the waiter brought out her steaming mug of cocoa.

"It's never too hot for a hot chocolate," she said. "The world would be a better place if everyone, everywhere had a hot chocolate for breakfast every day."

"Isn't that coffee's job?" Henry asked.

"Nah. Coffee just helps people stay awake. Hot chocolate makes people sweet." Amanda smiled.

I sat across from her thinking about how sweet I thought she was.

"I need to put your numbers in my phone," Amanda said.

Henry rattled off his number and she punched it into her phone.

"Billy?" She cocked her head to the side and looked at me with one eye.

"Oh, I don't have a cell phone. But my home phone number is—"

Her eyes lifted as she interrupted me. "Are you serious? I don't know anyone who doesn't have a cell."

"Well, now you do. I'm just holding out for the iPhone 6 to come out, ya know." Heat rushed through me. I did my best not to look embarrassed. I'd never felt this way about not having a phone before, but boy did I wish I had one now. To think I could have put her phone number in mine was blowing my mind. Henry's parents had offered to put me on their plan because it would only cost ten dollars a month, but mom refused, saying we couldn't accept such an offer, that we needed to live within our means. I was suddenly tired of living within our means. Maybe I could get Henry to have them offer again, and I could pay the ten dollars a month. Then it wouldn't be charity. It was only ten dollars. Do-able.

Just as promised, we headed for the library as soon as we were finished. I felt a little bad making Amanda come with us.

"It's summer, Henry," Amanda said. "I mean, I like a good book just as well as the next person, but we're only in Memphis one day—"

"It's a brand new library with brand new toys. It will be awesome." Henry was good. I shot him a look of appreciation. Normally, he hated libraries.

"Well, there is a book I've been waiting to get my hands on. Maybe they have it," Amanda said.

"You can look and even read while we're there, but keep in mind that you can't check it out," I said.

"Got it. You don't have a card to this library." She nodded her head.

"Yep."

After we parked, we walked inside.

"Do what ya want, y'all," Henry said, veering off toward the restrooms once we'd entered. "I'm about to do some crop-dusting magic."

"Gross, Henry, really. I'll find a book and sit on those comfy sofas over there," Amanda said, pointing to a grouping of chairs to our right.

I wished I could go with her and just sit beside her, but I ignored the urge and went straight for the reference desk. Henry would catch up with me. I asked about using the periodical searches and how to optimize my chances of finding the articles on my dad and Mrs. Higby. Luckily, most newspapers had put all their back issues into electronic form. Access to the files required a paid account, which the library had. The bad news was that all the articles weren't indexed, yet. That meant that they weren't totally searchable. Since I didn't know which newspaper it was, I had a hard time finding any articles I needed. My local librarian was old and wasn't very tech-savvy. I needed this librarian to teach everything so I could not only search the archives today, but at home, too, just in case I didn't find what I needed while here.

The excited, new librarian gave me a few good hints about six newspapers that would most likely have carried the stories back then and how to quickly search from article to article. That would take a lot of time off my searches. I also had her look up recent releases in the FBI arena real quick. Then I had her show me how to look up land deals, but warned me that I'd have to find recent land deals at our county recorder's office. I paid the twenty cents to have the list of FBI books printed and then went to work searching the newspaper archives.

I found several articles that were written about Halls about the time of the murders just as Henry joined me.

"All these articles are about Halls and its distinction of being in the FBI's top ten safest towns. None mention the murder," I whispered. It hit me that this year would make the tenth year in a row Halls had won that distinction. We were probably one of the only towns where its citizens regularly left their doors unlocked. If I were Coffco, I'd want to build my factory there, too.

We finally hit upon an article—not about Mrs. Higby, but about my dad. We read through it and then I hit *print*. Henry walked up to the reference desk, paid twenty cents and picked up the copy.

"I found and started my book," Amanda said, startling me. "I'll have to order it once I get to Henry's. What are you all doing over here all secret like?" She looked at the computer screen, and I panicked and hit the back key so she wouldn't see what we were doing.

"Nothing."

She raised an eyebrow. Henry walked up waving the article until he noticed Amanda. Then he folded the article and tried to shove it in his pocket. Amanda grabbed for it. He wasn't expecting that, and she easily took it from him.

"Nothing, huh?" She unfolded it and read as she backed away. Her face turned from one of triumph to one of concern. She held it out and walked back toward us. "Sorry, I thought you guys were researching something else."

I felt bad for her. We'd embarrassed her. "No," I said in a rush. "It's okay."

Henry's eyes went wide and he shook his head almost imperceptibly. He must have realized that I was about to clue Amanda in on what we were doing. I didn't want her to feel bad.

"It's okay, Henry. Amanda won't tell anyone." I turned to her. "Will you?"

"Uh, I'm not sure I know what you're doing."

"We should keep it that way, Billy," Henry pleaded. "What if she tells someone? It would ruin everything."

"She won't tell," I said. I don't know why I was so sure about it, but something about Amanda made me believe my words. I trusted her already.

I turned to Amanda. "If we let you in on our little mystery, do you swear not to breathe a word of it to anyone?"

"I guess."

"You can't guess, Amanda," Henry said with a huff. "See, we can't tell her."

"Hold on," she said, "Is it something I'm going to be obligated to tell someone? Did you guys do something terrible? Hurt someone or something?"

I raised my eyebrows. This girl had morals.

Henry bristled.

"Of course not. We're trying to solve a couple of mysteries. The problem is that they involve people from Halls, including my dad."

"A mystery, huh?" I saw a spark in her eyes. "I always love a good intrigue. You have my word." She rolled a chair closer to us and took a seat.

I filled her in on what we knew and what we hoped to find out. Henry listened to the story again without a sound. He must have been totally fascinated by the whole thing.

"Incredible, Billy. Simply incredible. If we can figure this out..."

I nodded. "The problem is we haven't found the article about Mrs. Higby, only my dad."

"I thought you said you had it?"

"We still need to find the actual article. I mean, most of it was readable, but what if we missed something behind the folds?"

"Let me try," she said. I stood up and traded spots with her.

I was about to tell her I'd already searched that paper, but she typed Halls+Higby+Heath in the newspaper's search bar and the article popped right up.

I grinned. She was amazing in every way.

"Is this it?"

We both nodded, speechless. We all read through it several times before hitting print. Henry picked up the copy and we all pored over it again.

GRAVEDIGGERS

Fall Takes A Life

By Jay Heath

Mrs. Maybelle Higby, 60, was found dead in her home in Halls, Tennessee yesterday. Her husband of forty years, Mr. Charles Higby, returned home from a shopping trip to find his wife dead after an apparent fatal fall. It appears Mrs. Higby was changing a light bulb while standing on a tall ladder before she fell.

While no one was allowed on the premises, Detective Jack Pitt was there to answer questions. "All evidence collected at the scene confirms death by accident. No autopsy will be performed." Her body was whisked away to be cremated.

"Your home is supposed to be a safe haven, even a refuge," Mark Mathis, neighbor, commented.

Mr. Higby will not be returning to their home of thirty years. He will be staying with a brother nearby until he finds a new place to live. There are too many memories in that place," Higby said when asked why it was he wouldn't be returning.

While the neighbors expressed surprise, shock, and a true deep sadness at the news of Mrs. Higby's death, they hope Mrs. Higby has found some release from the depression she had suffered from since the big storm last year.

"She hasn't been herself, no where near her happy self since she was hit by a weather vane that fell from her roof during that awful thunderstorm," her daughter said. She hopes her mother has finally found the peace she craved.

"So, she fell from a ladder? That's terrible." Amanda sat back in her chair. "It's so sad that her husband never returned to their house after that."

"I know what the article says, but don't you think he had to go back to get his stuff?" Henry asked. "You wouldn't just leave it all behind to rot, would you?" He looked perplexed.

"I don't know. It's kinda sweet, ya know," Amanda had a sad, endearing look on her face. "He tried to protect her, never leaving her alone and then she dies from a fall when he leaves her, just once. Maybe his love or guilt wouldn't allow him to return. Heartbreak changes everything." She spoke like she knew where he was coming from. Had she lost someone she loved?

I turned back to the screen and pored over the article again, then finally sighed. "Well, that was a bust." I leaned back and put my hands behind my head.

"I disagree," she said.

"We already knew all this stuff," Henry said.

"Yes, but what if we could find Jay Heath?"

"Jay Heath?" Henry asked, completely confused.

"Do you think we can?" I asked. Why hadn't I thought of that?

"Why not?" She started typing on the computer.

"Who's Jay Heath?" Henry asked.

"The reporter who wrote the article about Mrs. Higby."

"Ohhh," he said, finally understanding.

She searched for a reporter named Jay Heath and results filled the page. It seemed Jay was a pretty well-known investigative reporter. He had tons of articles published. It wasn't difficult to find his number. Seemed he was aching for people to get in touch with him.

Without a thought, Amanda pulled out her cell and dialed his number. She apparently got his voice mail because she left a detailed message for him. We waited a good twenty minutes, but he didn't call back. With a few more searches, Amanda was able to find what she believed was his address. "If all else fails, we could go visit him. He lives right here in Memphis."

We laughed. "Alright!"

We all walked toward the exit, Amanda laughing the whole way. Strands of her hair blew across her face as we opened the door to leave.

"I never saw you as the bookworm type, Billy. Glad I'm not the only one."

I snorted. All I could think about was her nerdy little self the last time she was here. The change in her had been astounding. I hoped I was better in her eyes, too. Smells from a nearby restaurant filled the air.

"And, I'm relieved that you guys didn't want to go to the library just to check it out. I plan on leaving school, my friends, and everything to do with Florida in Florida. This mystery is just what I need."

We'd spent several hours at the library, and my stomach growled. "Let's grab some lunch before we go looking for Jay's house. That'll give him some more time to call us back. Besides, I'm starving."

We headed to Gus's for the best fried chicken around. The place was packed. We jostled our way to the back and claimed a table in a far corner by the jukebox and the Coke bottle placard. We had to talk loud to be heard. I couldn't help but notice Amanda wore only a tiny bit of makeup. It looked like she'd only put on a little bit of mascara and lip gloss. I hated it when girls slathered so much makeup on you couldn't even tell what they looked like. Amanda didn't need any makeup at all.

The waitress, Cindi, wearing a T-shirt that said, *If you haven't eaten at Gus's, you haven't eaten fried chicken*, took our order. She came back in no time with plates of chicken along with baked beans and slaw. She plopped down a bottle of ketchup and hot sauce and told us to enjoy it. I watched Amanda take her first bite of chicken. "You're right, you guys! This is the best fried chicken I've ever had. It has a slight spicy kick to it." She immediately took another bite. This girl knew how to eat.

Henry blurted out, "Alright, Amanda, while you're here, you'll have to lose the 'you guys' and say 'y'all.' We don't want people mistaking you for a Yankee."

"Alright. It'll be fun to talk hillbilly while I'm here."

We both gave her miserable looks, mouths hanging open, and she just grinned and then like she hadn't just insulted us said, "Once, when I was in L.A., we went to Roscoe's House of Chicken and Waffles. While the chicken and waffles combination was good, this chicken is way better. Y'all were right." She emphasized the *y'all*.

Case closed. We were hillbillies, and we had no defense.

Just as we started to go over the mysteries again, Amanda's phone rang. She looked at the screen and nodded at us. She rushed outside to take the call where it was quiet, and Henry and I waited on pins and needles. She came back soon with a triumphant smile on her face.

"He was in a meeting when we called. He said he has meetings the rest of the afternoon, but he can see us around six at The Arcade diner."

GRAVEDIGGERS

We had two hours to kill. Amanda suggested we go to Graceland. She'd always wanted to go there even though the guide books said it was underwhelming. I'd driven past Elvis' house and his plane, but I'd never gone inside. Lucky for Amanda, Henry's parents had sent him with enough money to go there.

"I had to do some major convincing to get my parents to spring for Graceland." Henry said after hanging up the phone.

"We bow down to your cleverness, Henry," Amanda said. "I've always wondered how the really rich live."

I thought she was one of those really rich people. Maybe really rich people didn't consider themselves rich. Once inside, we had to laugh. The place was crazy, psychedelic and wild, and the house was on the small side.

"According to my parents, people didn't have stuff like we do now." Amanda stood, staring at Elvis's brightly colored rooms.

"Yeah, but was it a we-walked-uphill-to-school-both-ways story, or is there truth in what they said?" Henry asked.

"I think it really was different back then. Things were scarce. I'm sure this was total opulence back then."

We moved on to the next room.

The best part of the whole tour was being so close to Amanda. A weird tingle traveled through me each time her arm brushed mine. I tried to say funny things and keep her attention as much as possible.

We were checking out Elvis's jet, which was even more interesting than the house, when Amanda looked down at her watch.

"Oh hey, guys! We'd better get going. It's almost time to meet with the reporter."

I took a deep breath. Suddenly, I was nervous.

"It's ok, we're in this together," Amanda said. She touched my arm lightly and smiled, and it was all the encouragement I needed.

Chapter 8

As we drove over to the diner, we discussed what exactly we would tell him and what we would keep to ourselves. We didn't want to tell him anything that would make him want to come back and investigate.

I couldn't help but stare at Amanda. She had been so clever to think of calling Jay Heath. I wondered if she'd ever stop amazing me.

The Arcade looked like a classic diner, all shiny metal on the outside, not like the diner back home that was a regular, brick-wall restaurant. According to the plaque outside the entrance, it was the oldest restaurant in Memphis and just happened to be right down the street from the Lorraine Motel, where Martin Luther King was shot. We'd seen the press photos of Jay Heath on the Internet and it didn't take us long to spot him in a secluded booth near the back.

He'd aged quite a bit since the picture had been taken. His temples sported a bit of gray hair, but he still had masses of it. Rectangular shaped, wire-rimmed glasses framed his dark brown eyes and days of stubble covered his chin. He put his coffee mug down when he noticed us moving in his direction.

He must have informed the server that there would be four of us, because four glasses of ice water already sat on the table.

He stood and shook our hands once we reached him. After introducing ourselves, we took a seat, all three of us sitting on one side and Jay, alone on the other.

"Before we get to business," Jay said, "I'd really like to order. It's been a long day and I'm starving."

We nodded and picked up the menus. After we'd ordered, he said, "So, you want information about the Higby death?"

"Yes, sir," Amanda said, reaching out and taking a sip of her water.

I took the copy of the article and set it in front of him.

Using two fingers, he pushed it back toward me. "I don't need a copy of that article to remember." He then stared at us for a few awkward seconds. "I'm just not sure why you're inquiring after a death that occurred so long ago." His investigative skills shined through.

"Well, we're all in a mystery club at school and whoever comes up with the best mystery to discuss once school starts again gets this cool prize. And we want to win." Amanda said, just like we'd rehearsed. "When we saw this article, it seemed suspicious to us, so we thought we'd investigate a bit more."

"All right." He said it like it was a question.

"So, we thought we'd interview you and see if there was more to the story."

He raised his eyebrows then looked down at the table, his fingers tapping on the sides of his mug. "So, you're looking for a mystery, huh?" He looked at each of us in turn, like he was weighing and measuring us. "What if you discover there was foul play? What then?"

I couldn't help it, I leaned forward, placing my elbows on the table. "So there was foul play?"

He leaned back, shaking his head and chuckling a little.

"Well, I am a reporter, and I do see things that the everyday person might not. It doesn't mean my conclusions are correct, however."

"We only want your truthful observations. We'll come up with our own conclusions." I looked at him expectantly.

He sighed.

"Let's just say my editor edited out some of my truthful observations from the Higby incident."

Both Amanda and Henry leaned forward now.

A corner of his mouth went up in a strange smirk. "All righty, then. When I got on the scene, or rather, snuck onto the scene, I noticed that someone had tried to tidy up. The smell of bleach was pretty strong, I had to use my shirt sleeve to cover my mouth and nose.

"I had arrived only a few minutes after the police carried Mrs. Higby's body out to the truck. That was something else that was funny. Why didn't the paramedics come into the house and wheel her out on a gurney? They only appeared when the police brought her body out of the house.

"A ladder stood in the middle of the kitchen, right below a chandelier. The ceilings were high. The story was that she'd been trying to change a light bulb or something. The wall by the table glistened in the light, so I walked over to it. I could see some blood spatter and something else on the curtains, but the wall had been wiped totally clean. I don't know how she could have fallen from that ladder and cracked her head hard enough to cause that. Honestly, to me, it looked like someone had been shot in the head.

"So, I thought I'd found the jackpot. I'd investigate and uncover what really happened. Then I spotted a folded up note on pretty pastel paper that had bloody fingerprints on it. It was sitting on the table waiting for me to read it. Just as I was about to grab it, I heard the front door open and hid in the pantry. I left the door open a crack so I could see what was going on. An officer came and took the note and left."

"There was a suicide note?" I asked. I didn't take my eyes off him.

"That's not what I said. I have no idea what that note said. It could have been the officer's notes on the crime scene for all I know."

"But you thought it was a suicide note." Amanda's eyes were wide with curiosity.

"Don't officers usually use little notepads for notes, not notepaper?" I'd seen Bud pull out his little notebook to take notes a million times.

"I admit. I thought it was a suicide note. However, that very officer told me later that she had fallen on a glass jug that pierced her skull, causing the spatter. That seemed like a logical explanation, so I gave up on the case, figuring it had been a real accident."

"Which officer was it?" Amanda asked.

"I later found out it was Jack..." He pulled the copied article toward him and poked at Jack Pitt's name. "Jack Pitt. Yep. That was him."

Our food arrived and everyone started to eat. I couldn't.

"Did you ask about the note?" I asked.

"I couldn't very well ask about a note that had been on the scene and never seen, now could I?"

He had a point. I wondered if that note was in the evidence box at the police station.

"It may not be the best mystery, but you might try to uncover what that note was. I'm sure Jack is still around. He couldn't have been more than forty back then. Nice guy."

"Anything else you can remember, sir? Anything at all?" I didn't dare move from my spot.

"You should have heard the wails coming from the husband. It was awful," he said. "'This is all my fault. All my fault. What have I done?'"

"Why did he say it was his fault if it was an accident?" I asked.

"I'm not sure, but talk around town was that he never left her alone. Ever. She'd been in a bad way for a while, I guess—at least a year, anyway—probably on account of his condition, and he didn't like to leave her alone."

The article in the box came to mind. The daughter mentioned her depression. Was he afraid she'd kill herself? Is that why he never left her alone? But she didn't kill herself; that seemed obvious enough.

"Apparently, he'd gone into town to run a quick errand and when he returned, he found her dead. There was never a question about what happened. No investigation." He hung his head. "I just wish I'd been able to read that note before it disappeared."

"I don't get it. Why would you think it was a suicide note at first?"

"It had bloody fingerprints all over it."

"So you think she killed herself and then wrote the note?" Henry asked, looking completely perplexed.

"No. I think Mr. Higby came in, saw she was dead, held her or touched her or whatever and got blood all over himself and then found the note."

I had to find that note. What could it have said? Maybe that was the evidence the chief and mayor suppressed in her case. What had they suppressed in my father's case? I had to get a look at the evidence.

Suddenly I couldn't eat fast enough. I was dying to talk over everything we'd just learned with Henry and Amanda.

The reporter treated us all to sundaes before we left. We were all full as ticks by the time the checks came.

"Thanks so much for meeting us." Amanda shook his hand. Henry and I followed suit.

"It was my pleasure. This club has me intrigued. Maybe I'll stop by sometime in the fall and do a story on it. I would've loved having a club like that at my high school."

"Thanks again," I said, wanting to divert the conversation.

"Let me know what you find out."

"We will, sir," Amanda said, giving him a big smile.

We watched him saunter down the street and get into a Mercedes. He was a big-wig reporter for sure.

"What are we gonna do when he shows up at our high school and asks about our mystery club?" Henry shook his head.

"Someone like that," Amanda said, "isn't going to come and do a story on a mystery club. He's got bigger things to report about these days."

"I hope you're right." Henry brushed his hand through his hair. "My mom would kick my butt if she found out all the lies we've been telling."

"I'm right, Henry." Amanda punched his upper arm. "Besides, we're going to solve this mystery and when we do, she's going to be super proud of you. Just wait."

I wondered how my mom would feel about me when she found out what I'd been doing.

"We better head back. We'll barely make it before curfew if we head out now," Henry said. We started walking toward the car.

"Isn't Beale Street a couple of blocks from here?" Amanda looked down the main street.

"Sure is," I said, looking that way, too.

"While we're here, we oughta at least walk down the street. I've never seen it before and I heard it is awesome. Blues music, flashing lights, people all over."

"We can't, Amanda. We'll never make curfew." Henry looked worried.

"Just call your parents and ask. Please!" She twisted her mouth into a pouty frown. "Tell them I really want to see it and that we'll hurry."

While Henry called his parents, I mentally rehashed the conversation with Jay Heath. Something weird happened the night of Mrs. Higby's death, and I desperately wanted to figure out what.

"Yay!" I heard Amanda say. "Just remember, Henry. The answer is always no if you don't ask."

"Good call," Henry said.

We drove the car over a couple streets and after parking, we walked down Beale Street, even though it was really something to be enjoyed a bit later, when all the bands' music spilled out onto the street from the clubs. It was only seven o'clock and the artists and musicians were just setting up inside all those clubs.

"What do you guys think about what Mr. Heath told us?" I asked.

"I think we have a great mystery," Amanda said, as she looked at all the bright neon signs popping on. "I think someone is hiding something about Maybelle's death, and I think we should find out what."

"Jay thought it was a suicide, and the note...it had to be a suicide note. Don't ya think?" I sighed.

"The article did say she had been depressed for like a year," Henry said.

"But why would they want to cover up a suicide? More specifically, why would Old Man Jack be involved in covering it up?"

"Seriously. Why would they go to so much trouble?"

"Maybe it was really a murder."

"What?"

"Maybe Jack was being lazy and didn't want to have to do a murder investigation."

"That seems a bit far-fetched, don't ya think?" I said, giving him the stink eye.

"Look, I'm just trying to offer different options."

"He's right, Billy." Amanda spoke up. "A suicide doesn't explain everything—what about the jewelry you dug up? It's got to be involved somehow, right? It could have been a robbery gone wrong. We shouldn't rule anything out. Not yet. We need to get our hands on that note."

"What bothers me a lot is that Jack is somehow involved in both my dad's murder and Mrs. Higby's death. It seems to me he is the key to both of them."

"You can't go asking that crazy about anything. You'll never get anything out of him."

"How do you know?" I asked. "Sure, he skulks around town and talks about conspiracy theories and nutso stuff, but that doesn't mean he can't tell us what happened those two nights."

"I think we should check out everything else first. He's dangerous, and I'd like to live to see my senior year."

"Don't be such a baby."

"Look Billy, I think Henry's right. If we can do it without having to talk to a psychopath, we should."

I still didn't agree.

"And, I think we better focus on your dad's death first. He's the priority." Amanda pushed her shoulder into me as we walked. My heart stampeded.

I tried to point out all the interesting buildings that lined the street, making sure I walked right beside her the rest of the time. I couldn't help but notice a lot of guys checking Amanda out. Several older men whistled and one even said, "Lord have mercy," as she passed. I moved in closer to her.

The smells from all the restaurants gearing up for the evening crowds wafted into the air but they didn't prevent me from getting a whiff of her perfume every now and then.

"Too bad we're not a bit older. I'd love to go into some of those clubs. I've never listened to a live blues band before. As if on cue, jazz and blues music started filtering out to us as we passed a club with a line snaking toward it. We sat on a bench and just listened for a few minutes.

As we were about to leave, Amanda talked to a cartoonist and he motioned for her to sit. She waved us over. I loved her spontaneity. I wouldn't have even thought to memorialize our

Memphis trip with a cartoon drawing of the three of us. We leaned close together making funny faces. The guy told us to hold still, but we were laughing so hard it was a challenge. It took all I had to keep my wits about me while one whole side of my body touched hers. When the artist turned the drawing so we could see it, we laughed out loud at the things he'd chosen to accentuate: Henry's thick eyebrows, my slight cowlick, Amanda's pouty lips. Man, even as a cartoon character she was beautiful.

After slipping the rolled up picture into her purse, she put her arms around both of us as we walked back to the car. Heat burned me up at her touch. I tried desperately to stay cool. I hoped the sweat didn't show through my shirt.

Callers tried to get us to go into this bar or that, saying they had the best live music and food to be had. The neon lights lit up the area and the streets were filling up with hungry customers. Police officers roamed the area. We heard the sounds of several bands blast out onto the sidewalks as we moseyed by.

As soon as we were all safely inside the car with the cold air blasting on us, Henry called his parents to let them know we were leaving. We would be at least an hour late. Too bad we couldn't stay any longer. His parents thought it wasn't safe. Seeing as many cops as I had on that short stretch of street, they were probably right.

We had the music playing in the car, but Amanda took control and turned it to a popular rock station. "Now this is music. None of that twangy stuff." She eyed both of us.

Henry tried to change the station back, but she wouldn't have it. I didn't care either way. If pop rock made her happy, it made me happy.

GRAVEDIGGERS

Henry dropped me off first. I didn't want to go home. I didn't want to leave Amanda, but when I'd called my mom, she insisted I get to bed because I needed to be up early to pick cherries at Mrs. Macon's.

When my alarm sounded, I jumped out of bed. I wanted to get back over to Henry's and see Amanda. Good thing old people always got up early. I could get this over and done with as quick as possible, and maybe there'd still be a chance for me to get over and see her.

Mrs. Macon's tree was loaded. I picked the cherries as fast as I could, but it still took me all morning. She sat and talked to me the whole time. I found my mind wandering to Amanda more often than not.

She was so smart. I never would have thought to talk to the reporter—and then, she just went right out and called him without even hesitating. The girl had guts. Just thinking about her voice as she hammered him with questions made me grin.

"Are you listening to me, Billy? You seem so distracted today."

"Sorry, Mrs. Macon. I've just been thinking about... college. That's all." That seemed to satisfy her, and she went off on stories about her days in college at Ole Miss right when desegregation happened in the sixties and how it was the best time of her life. Some of her stories were so funny. Times had changed just a bit since she'd been in school. I tried to prod her about my dad—to get her to tell me some stories. I was lucky to get the two anecdotes she did tell me. The way she told it, my dad bought the land we owned from the Harrises. I had to find out if that was true. Harrises and Pitts were on the top of my list to investigate.

I rushed home at noon with enough extra cherries for about twenty quarts. My mom would flip out. She loved cherries. I put them in our makeshift cellar. I showered, then dabbed on a bit of smell good I'd picked up as a sample at a mall once, and slipped on my very best shirt, jeans, and my dad's snakeskin boots. I felt like a prince going to claim his princess.

Then I saw the fingerprint cards on my desk and paused. Whoever had dug up that box knew something about what had happened to Mrs. Higby. Those fingerprint cards could have answers. Even if I wasn't getting anywhere with my own dad's death, I could at least find answers for poor Mrs. Higby. I grabbed the cards, tucked them in my bag, and headed for the station.

Chapter 9

I'd been avoiding Bud ever since that day in the cemetery—thinking about seeing him now made me nervous. I didn't know what it all meant. Had he really just been trying to protect us? Or had he been hiding something? If only I could talk to Jack—but he wouldn't talk to me. I'd tried calling again a few more times, but now he wasn't even answering the phone.

Maureen buzzed me through to the offices. When I got to the chief's, I knocked.

"Come in," he called out. When I stepped inside, he said, "Billy, I didn't think I'd get to see you until that cousin of Henry's went home."

"Very funny," I said, trying to play it off and taking a seat on the other side of the desk. "Very funny."

Bud chuckled. "So what brings you here? More questions about investigations?"

"Actually, I found this cool ammo box, and I lifted some prints off it, hoping to find who owned it." I pulled the baggie out and put it on his desk. "I know it's been a long time..."

His lips curled into a smile. He was loving that I brought him the prints. He wasn't suspicious of anything. Why would he be?

"But I was hoping you'd want to—" I continued.

"Sure, Billy. I'll run them."

"Really?" I asked.

"Yep. Let's see if we can find the owner of the box. Where did you find it, anyway?"

Just then, the phone rang. He held up a finger, signaling me to wait as he answered the phone. "Could we finish this later, Billy? I need to take this call."

"Sure," I said, pushing the prints in front of him as he started to talk again.

He nodded at me and smiled. I smiled back and left, glad I didn't have to tell more lies about the box.

When I got to Henry's house, he and Amanda were in his room looking at something on the computer. Neither looked up at me when I entered, even though I leaned on the doorframe and tried to look casual and send out vibes that I'd arrived.

Finally, I gave up and said, "What are y'all lookin' at?" leaving my cool-pose, annoyed that no one had noticed how awesome I'd looked. I walked up behind them, trying not to let Amanda see how nervous I was to be back in her presence.

She turned to me. Her light brown hair fell over her shoulder and glistened in the light. Her opaque brown eyes flitted over my outfit and she smiled. "We're looking up funny videos on YouTube. Pull up a chair. We found some hilarious ones."

There wasn't a chair to move over, so I ran downstairs and got one from the kitchen, putting it next to Amanda's.

"You smell good," she said, taking a deep pull on the air around me. "That cologne fits you."

A fire lit in my stomach. She liked the cologne.

"You weren't wearing it yesterday, were you?"

"Nope."

Henry glared at me, almost opening his mouth to say something, but when I made my eyes big, he dropped it and grinned a mischievous grin. If he embarrassed me, I'd have to kick his butt.

"I need a drink," Henry said, standing up and walking toward the door. "You want anything, Amanda?"

"Sure, have any orange soda? I'm totally addicted to it. I think I'm in withdrawal." She laughed, still clicking through different videos on YouTube.

"Billy?"

I turned to tell him to get me a glass of water, but his raised eyebrows and the jerk of his head toward the door convinced me that I better go with him.

We stomped down the stairs and into the kitchen where he stopped short of the refrigerator. "What's the deal, Billy? Since when do you wear cologne? Last time you did that was when you were crazy about Misty. Are you hot on my cousin? Is that why you were such a dork at the airport?" His grin was enormous, and I felt my face heat up—which rarely happened.

"No way." He knew I was lying. "And if you want to talk about being a dork in front of girls, Henry, we can go there."

"You know she's way out of your league."

"Yes." I popped my head up. "But I can't help it. She's so amazing. Smart, funny, good looking, honest, trustworthy…"

"EWW! You're sick. She's my cousin. You can't crush on her."

I looked at him, the heat in my face turning to red hot fire.

"You really have lost it, haven't you?"

I just stared.

"She lives in Florida. You can't date her. Besides that, you're basically my brother. It's like incest or something."

"It is not. And we're not really related anyway…and am I glad we're not."

Henry shook his head.

"Henry, she's the most extraordinary person I've ever met. She's nothing like the good looking girls around here. She likes simple things. She's adventurous. She's bold. She has morals."

He opened the fridge and got a couple of drinks out. "The day has finally arrived and it happens to be my cousin that gets you all hot."

I punched him hard in the arm and he almost dropped he drinks. "Don't talk about her like she's just some hot girl. She's more than that. I think this is it, Henry. I've never felt this way before."

He shook his head slowly from side to side. "You really are whipped. I hate to break it to you, but I think she has a boyfriend."

My insides shook. "What makes you think that?" I headed for the cabinet to get a cup for water, trying to act cool.

"She's always on her phone, texting or laughing, like girls do when they talk to girlfriends about their boyfriends. I can just tell."

"Like you know, with all your experience and all."

"Sorry, man. Just keeping it real. That's all." He looked at me with true sympathy.

"She can't have a boyfriend," I muttered to myself. "She just can't." I filled my cup with water from the fridge.

"Who just can't have a boyfriend?" Amanda bounded into the room and grabbed the Orange Crush from Henry's hand, opened it, and then leaned on the table and took a long drink. I tried not to look at her legs. Today she wore light blue shorts.

"Uhhhh," spluttered from both our mouths. My mind whirred. What could we say?

She used her drink to point to Henry. "You interested in some hot chick, Henry? Or is it you, Billy? You thinking the girl already has a boyfriend?" Her drink pointed in my direction.

We both continued to stare dumbly. She took another sip and then said, "No relationship is permanent if the right guy comes along." She winked and then sauntered out of the room calling back to us. "Hurry up! I found the coolest video ever." We turned and looked at each other, our eyes wide.

"That was close," Henry said, hitting my arm.

"Too close for me. I can't believe you didn't say anything."

"What did you want me to say? Yeah, it's Billy. He's totally crushing on you and can't stand the thought of you having a boyfriend. You don't happen to have one, do you and if you do, is he the right guy? I could have pointed at you and everything."

I shoved him.

"We better hurry. She might just start to be suspicious—wondering what's taking so long." He turned out of the room. I followed, my heart beating a guilty rhythm.

"You guys have to see this," she blurted as we entered. Her face lit up and my knees softened a bit. Henry went to the far side of her and I sat in the seat closest to the door. She was right, the video was hilarious. Every now and then her skin would touch mine and send a fire shooting through my veins. I had this sudden urge to make sure she had everything she needed. I needed her to be happy.

I laughed at everything she said and I even felt my voice change slightly, to sound more interested, more concerned. I sounded like a total idiot, and Henry's big eyes confirmed that more than once.

"We need to make plans for the Fourth," I said, just realizing how late it had gotten. "I told Sarah Ann you'd call her yesterday. You've already missed that deadline, and you better not keep her waiting. She's expecting your call."

He gave Amanda a rushed glance, and then I noticed the sweat immediately start to bead along his hairline. I never could understand how just the mention of Sarah Ann's name turned him into a sweaty fool. Now that I'd met Amanda, I knew. Luckily, I didn't have to deal with the sweat, just other obnoxious side-effects—like complete stupidity.

"There *is* a girl, then? You asked her out already and she said, yes?" Amanda said. "That's a super good sign, even if she has a boyfriend." She smiled brightly. "Oh my gosh! You are totally sweating, Henry. We've got to get that under control. Girls hate sweaty guys."

That was the wrong thing to say. A horror-stricken look crossed his face and he stood up abruptly, knocking his knees on the desk. "Crap. Crap. Crap. I let you talk me into a suicide mission, Billy." He moved toward the door. "Why did you ever tell me I should ask her to the picnic?"

"It's not suicide, Henry," I laughed. "You've liked her since the second grade and never talked to her. It's time you make your move."

"You heard her," he said, motioning to Amanda. "She said she'd rather die than do anything with a sweaty pig like me."

Amanda looked a bit disturbed for about half a second and then said, "That's not what I said. I said—"

I grabbed Henry and dragged him out of the room.

"The only way you'll be able to get over this sweating and craziness is if you actually take the leap and talk to her—be around her." I pulled him further down the hall and lowered my voice. "I mean that's what's kinda happened to me with you-know-who." I raised my eyebrows for emphasis. "Remember me at the airport? Now I can actually speak to her."

Amanda wandered out into the hall. "Look, Henry. You misunderstood what I was saying. I can totally help you so that you don't sweat in front of that girl, Ann?"

"Sarah Ann," he corrected.

"Sarah Ann." She beamed. "I mean, look at you, now. Five years ago, I never would have believed you'd turn out so cute. You were such a nerd back then."

We couldn't help it, both Henry and I busted up laughing, doubling over.

"What? What?" she said, a slight laugh escaping her lips in expectation of a good laugh.

"We thought the same about you," Henry said, tears pooling in his eyes. "That is so funny."

She threw out her hip and said, "Are you kidding? Me? With my coke-bottle glasses, my frizzy out of control hair, and my pudgy, fat pre-puberty body? I was a knock-out back then. Really. You guys can be so obtuse." She flipped her head up in mock exasperation.

Then all three of us ended up laughing so hard we had to sit on the floor.

Henry's mom walked past us, carrying a laundry basket. "Boy, I wish I'd heard that one." Elvis, Henry's bulldog, followed behind her and sniffed at us as he passed.

That made us laugh all the harder. Once we'd laughed ourselves out, we all lay back on the carpet in the hall and sighed, over and over again.

"So where are you going on this date and what am I supposed to do while you're gone?" Amanda sat back up, leaning against the wall and bringing her knees up to her chest.

My heart raced watching her. Why was she making me feel this way? I'd never had to deal with this before. This had to be love at first sight.

Henry covered his face with his hands and then rubbed them violently back and forth over it before saying, "It's the Fourth of July picnic and dance." He spit the words out in a frantic rush. "I can't do it. I just can't."

We were back to square one.

Amanda moved over to him, extricated his hands from his face and said, "I'll teach you what to do. We can practice together. We've got over a week."

I didn't want Henry to practice with her. I wanted to be her practice partner.

"I can't. I'd need a year of practice."

"You can." She turned to me. "What are the plans?"

"Well, it all depends on Romeo here. I'm running in the 5k in the morning. Are you sure you won't race with me, Henry?"

"It's not natural to choose to run that far, Billy."

"It's for a great cause this year. Do it for me."

"Sorry. Can't do it."

"What is the cause?" Amanda asked.

"For survivors of violent crimes."

"That is a good cause."

"Anyway, I should be back from the 5k by ten or so. The picnic starts at one, so if we leave here at twelve-thirty, we should be okay."

"You're going too, hot stuff?" She swatted at my foot.

I don't know where my courage came from, but I said, "Yep! With you."

"With me? You never asked me."

I raised my eyebrows. "Amanda Brady, will you go with me to the annual Fourth of July picnic and dance?"

She threw her head back, putting the back of her hand up to her forehead and said, "I thought you'd never ask."

I wanted to grab her up in a hug and plant a huge kiss on her right then. Instead, I looked away.

Henry chuckled despite his obvious discomfort. "What else do we need to plan?"

I glanced at Amanda. "We shouldn't plan this in front of my date. We'll plan it tomorrow. I've got to go. We'll call the girls after we plan."

"I thought you didn't have a phone," she eyed me, a mischievous look on her face.

"Who needs a phone when Henry's your friend?" I stood.

Henry put his hand out to me and I pulled him up. Then I mustered the courage to help her stand, too. My hand dwarfed her small, soft one. We stood, looking at each other for a few seconds too long, too close, and she slid her hand out of mine, smiling and lifting her shoulders up and down in a nervous movement. She giggled and took a step back. I looked at the floor. There was no way she had a boyfriend.

"My mom wants me to get some fish for dinner tomorrow. You up for some fishing?" I asked Henry, hoping Amanda would join us.

"Heck, yeah. Should I ask my mom for the car?"

"Nah. Mama's off tomorrow. She's putting up cherries."

"Guess we better make sure we don't catch anything right away." Henry rolled his eyes.

I gave him a look that could kill. He wanted to get out of helping my mom.

"Just kidding. I know your mom needs help. But, don't rush everything. The fish don't like that."

I headed down the hall. Turning back, I said, "You coming, Amanda?"

She pressed her lips together and with an exaggerated nod, she said, "Yeah, I think I will."

GRAVEDIGGERS

"I'll be here at six sharp to pick y'all up. And bring a big ol' stick." I smiled and started down the stairs.

"A stick?" Amanda yelled after me. "Y'all fish with sticks? Don't you have poles?"

Henry laughed out loud and I just kept going and yelled back, "Nice that you're finally not sounding like a Yankee."

After getting everything ready including putting the twelve foot aluminum boat in the back of the truck, I went to bed thinking of Amanda wondering if she'd ever give a redneck like me a shot.

Chapter 10

My eyes popped open and my heart thudded hard against my ribs as I sat upright. Sweat dripped down the side of my face and I sucked in a deep breath. In my dream I had been running in the dark through the cemetery, cradling the green box with one arm and pulling Amanda behind me with the other. Feet pounded hard behind us, and we had just fallen into an empty grave that had no bottom. I was glad to wake up. The clock read five thirty.

Still breathing hard, I got into the shower, not bothering to turn the hot knob on at all. The box wasn't the only thing dominating my thoughts anymore. Amanda was too.

After getting dressed, I put the cooler, the bait, my pole, and tackle box in the back of the truck. I headed over to Henry's. Amanda walked out carrying a long stick and said, "Henry told me y'all had poles, so what's the stick for?"

I glanced at Henry, who followed behind her, surprised he really made her go find a stick. "Well, while I fish and Henry dips the water out of the boat, you'll get to paddle and keep the snakes back."

Her look of complete disgust and surprise made Henry and me bust out laughing.

"Oh," she said, doing her hip thing and making me want to go grab her up in my arms, "You made me go find *just the right stick* as a joke on me?"

"No," Henry said. "We really do need that stick. He was just kidding that he got to fish the whole time."

She looked at me with a what-the-heck-is-he-talking-about look. Her eyes narrowed, and her silence scared me into a confession.

"What he means is, we all rotate every half hour or so and the person keeping the snakes back also paddles, and whoever dips the water out also fishes, that's why we have two poles, see?" I pointed at the two poles and gave her a sheepish look, trying to look contrite.

She glared at me and then at Henry. "Are there really snakes and does your boat have a hole in it?"

The look on her face made Henry laugh out loud as he walked to the truck.

I gave her a pained smile and said, "Yes. That is the honest-to-goodness truth." After getting into the driver's seat, I started the truck. Once Amanda and Henry were in their seat belts, we were off.

"Why are you taking me to a lake with snakes? I hate snakes." She exaggerated a shiver.

"Ah, come on! Have you ever really even seen a snake?"

She nodded forcefully.

"I mean in real life."

She switched to a slow shake *no*.

"They're just as scared of you as you are of them—for the most part. The snakes don't really need to be shoed away until we have a couple of fish on the stringer. Then the snakes

117

want to eat our fish, so we have to keep them away. Otherwise, they're just as scared of you as you are of them." I turned away from her and mumbled, "Most of them, or we'll be swimming back to the bank."

"And don't let them in your boat," I added under my breath.

Henry took a swipe at me.

"And what's your mama gonna think knowing y'all brought me to a snake infested lake?" She smirked.

"Look." Henry brushed his hand through his hair. "We're not only getting fish for his mom. Billy and I are hoping to give the biggest donation of fish to the annual fish-fry and because of all the big, ol', nasty snakes in this lake, no one goes there to fish, so we can catch a whole mess of fish there."

She looked at us like we were crazy. She turned the music up and sang along until we got to the lake. Her voice was nice.

Henry and I popped out and grabbed the boat from the back and slid it in the water.

"Hop on in, Miss Amanda." I held the boat still for her, the muddy water lapping over my shoes. She rolled her eyes and stomped over. She put her hand on my shoulder, it seemed to burn through my T-shirt, and she climbed in.

While Henry got in with the gear, I educated Amanda on what to do with any snakes she saw and how to paddle. I paddled us out a ways and turned the paddle over to Amanda.

"I've never paddled in a lake before, only in the ocean or in a river," she said. "This is easy compared to that. I'm used to getting soaking wet while in a boat. Granted, I'm usually in a swim suit or wet suit, but..."

"Well, if you do it right, you won't get a drop of water on you today." I smiled, thinking that's what she wanted to hear.

"No drops? Huh?"

"No drops," I said.

"But what about a shower of water?" She raked the paddle through the water and doused both of us.

Henry leapt after her, reaching for the paddle. He overshot and landed in the water with a huge splash, almost sending us on our heads.

Amanda shrieked, laughing loudly, her brown eyes sparkling. She laid the paddle in the boat and grabbed the stick. "Hey, Billy," she squealed as she poked at Henry with the stick. "I found a snake. Now what do I do?"

Henry looked all around him wide-eyed, I'm sure looking for snakes. Then he sent a spray of water her way and she ducked, losing the stick to the lake. Henry lunged for it and threw it into the boat. He flicked me a mischievous look. He motioned to Amanda and then swam to the opposite end of the boat and began to act like he was climbing back in. He then grabbed her arm and tugged. She resisted and he called out, "Now!"

I did my duty, despite my reservations. I put my hands on her back and sent her flailing into the water. The downside to all of this was I was sure to be the final target. Neither would let me stay dry. At least it wasn't cold.

Amanda came up sputtering, laughing. I really liked this girl. She was no crybaby. She gave me the look, and I knew my time to remain dry was limited.

She disappeared into the water. I looked all around, trying to locate her and make it hard for her to pull me in.

Where'd she go? She'd been under a long time. What happened to her?

I looked hard in the water. Maybe she got caught on some branch. Something had to have happened.

"Henry. Where's Amanda?"

"Don't know," he said, swimming toward the boat.

"Something's happened to her. I just know it. We've got to find her."

I was about to jump in the water and look for her when Henry pulled himself up into the boat on the opposite end of where I was.

"Stay in the water, Henry. Look for her." I readied myself to jump in just as a hand grabbed my arm and pulled me toward the water. I was off balance just enough to make it impossible to regain it, and I tumbled in, hitting my knees hard on the edge of the boat as I fell in.

I couldn't help but draw water into my lungs, I was completely unprepared. I sputtered and coughed as I came up to face a giggling Amanda. She swam away from me before I could grab her, and she re-appeared on the other side of the boat and raised herself up and in while Henry balanced the boat. She was strong. It was no easy feat to pull yourself in.

With both of them balancing the boat, I pulled myself in, too, glad that no snakes had decided to join us in the water.

"I have to admit. That was good. Henry, you're such a liar."

"Nah. I'm just a great actor."

We spent the next three hours in near silence, begging the fish to bite. Sure, we caught a ton, but were hoping for a lot more.

GRAVEDIGGERS

We were all feeling a bit hungry, so Henry volunteered to go get the munchies we'd left in the car.

"Meet ya at the shore," he hollered as he jumped into the water causing the boat to rock like we were out on a rough ocean.

We were quiet for a while, just the two of us. I wanted to say something to her—something to let her know how I felt about her. I was still mulling over the perfect line in my head when she started to talk.

"Billy?" she said hesitantly. My heart beat a bit faster. "I just wanted to say—listen, we've been talking a lot about your dad's murder lately and I just realized, well, I... I never told you how sorry I am. About what happened. I'm just really sorry that happened to you."

"Oh," I said, swallowing. "Well, thanks."

"Do you mind my asking... what do you remember? About what happened to him?"

I took a deep breath. Was I really up to this? Did I want to rehash everything for her right here and now? She looked at me with such anticipation, I couldn't refuse her. As we rowed to shore, I told the story.

"I was seven." I took on a clinical voice and tried to distance myself from the story I was about to tell. "A wicked storm blew in. Terrible wind, lightning, thunder. Everything went black even though it was right before dinner. Daddy went out to get our goat. We lived about ten minutes outside of town. The goat was so loud that we could hear her all the way in the house. He had already put the horses up and had come in to get a flashlight. The goat was tied up out in the ditch bank by the street, clearing the weeds out. I told Daddy

I loved him more than a thousand tigers, and he said he thought running into a thousand tigers might be more preferable to going out into the terrible storm.

"I held the door open for him and watched him disappear when he was only about five feet outside the door—the rain was coming down that hard. Then I waited and waited. When he hadn't come back after a long time, I got really curious and wondered if he needed my help. I put on my raincoat and went out to look for him. Mama came after me with a flashlight. As we walked up the long drive, the rain pelted us and the dark clouds seemed to press down on us. When we saw our goat, Bessie, on the other side of the road without my dad, we knew something was wrong. Mama started to run. I froze, right there in the mud.

"She screamed when she got to the road. It was a blood-curdling scream that cut through my bones. I wanted to run to her. She sank to her knees, and I was still frozen. Minutes passed, maybe hours. I don't know."

I stopped talking as the memory washed over me.

"Call 911," Mama hollered.

The rain slowed. We didn't need flashlights anymore. The sun peeked through the clouds.

She wanted me to call 911? Daddy was hurt? I splashed my way back to our house and called 911.

"I can't really tell you what happened after that. It's all a strange blur. But, I do remember glass sparkling in the sun as the clouds moved out."

Amanda was quiet for a moment after I stopped talking. She looked down at the fishing pole while I wiped the tears from my eyes.

"Do you mean glass from the accident?" she asked.

As I sat there, the picture of my dad lying in my mom's arms on the asphalt with glittery glass all around them took over my mind. Somehow talking to Amanda had made me remember. "Yes," I said, realizing this was big. "I'd forgotten that." She was smoothing her shorts and gave me a hesitant smile. She looked conflicted. I reached out and took her soft hands in mine. "Do you realize what you've done? You helped me find a lead."

She shook her head and then looked at our hands. "What do you mean?"

"Whatever car hit my dad lost its windshield in the process."

"Ooh," she said, squeezing my hand. "We need to find out what cars in town replaced their windshields around that time."

"Yep. I know it's a long shot. I mean, I don't even know how to go about finding out who replaced their windshields ten years ago."

"Billy—we're going to find out what happened. I just know it. Think about it. Whatever car hit your dad, it had to have some serious damage—more than just a broken windshield. If it really was someone from your town, there has to be a damaged car."

I nodded. She was right. Why hadn't anyone found the car? "Thanks, Amanda. It means a lot to me—that you're helping me with this. I don't know if I could even have gotten this far without you."

She started to answer, but just then we made it to shore and Henry came back.

"Come on, y'all I got the car ready. Let's pack it up. There ain't no snacks in the car. We must've left the box at home and besides, these fish ain't biting anymore," he said with disgust. I smiled at Amanda and started packing up the stuff.

After cleaning the fish at Henry's and putting them in his freezer, I helped Mama with the remainder of the cherries, making jam and pie filling. After that, we made some pies and invited Henry's family over for dessert after dinner. My mom sent me to get Pastor Higby to share in the fun. When we arrived back home, all five of the Parnells were there and had brought ice cream. Pastor Higby seemed dazed, constantly asking us to repeat what we'd either said or asked him. That wasn't like him. He was always very attentive. Maybe he was getting to the stage where he needed hearing aids.

I thought about grabbing the army green box and taking it back to the church when I took him home, or even just telling him about what I'd found. Would he know something about it? That reporter in Memphis had said someone had cleaned the scene of his wife's death. Had the pastor been the one that cleaned it? What did it mean if he had? It was all so confusing. I decided it was best if I kept the box to myself for now, until I knew more. "Doing anything fun in the next few weeks, Pastor Higby?

"You might not call it fun, son, but I'm fixing to head to Dyersburg to get supplies to refinish all the benches in the church. They're gonna shine again, Billy. You wait and see. They're gonna shine."

"I'll be over to help you with that, Pastor." I offered. "I might even be able to get a few other volunteers to help, too." I looked over at Henry and Amanda who were in the middle of a conversation about surfing and boating.

"That'd be wonderful, Billy, but I don't want to take away from any of the minimal free time you have. You do need some time to look at all those books you're studying. I'm excited to see who you become. You're going to be amazing at whatever you choose to do. That, I know for sure. You're not still thinking about being an FBI special agent, are you?" A look of worry creased his brow just like it always did when we talked about it.

"Yes." I thought about getting a break in my dad's murder and felt a twinge of excitement thinking I might be able to find out the truth before becoming an agent. I lowered my voice. "I know you think the profession is too dangerous, but I can't let go of the feeling I'm supposed to help kids like me and adults like my mom never have to experience the pain of losing a loved one. I could save a lot of people." I couldn't tell him I would also be looking for daddy's killer when I became an agent, because it might slip when he talked to Mama.

His knee started bouncing and he smiled at me. It just didn't look genuine somehow. He worried about me. "I just can't imagine you leaving this town. You make it such a nice place to be. What will Henry do without you? I love having you around, and you won't be anywhere near here if you make it into the FBI. I'm sure you will save a lot of people, though, Billy...Listen, I'm feeling like I've overdone it. Could you maybe carry me home now?"

I glanced at the clock, it was already nine. "Oh, sorry, sir. I didn't realize how late it was."

He stood up and said to everyone, "It's been a great evening. Thanks, all y'all. I'm afraid I've met my quota of fun, however, and need to get into bed. My old bones can only take so much."

Everyone stood and either shook his hand or hugged him goodbye. I almost went to my room to retrieve the box. Almost.

Chapter 11

Knowing Henry had to wash all the windows in his house today, I went to save Amanda. By the time my chores were done and I headed over, he was already hard at work, up on a ladder cleaning the outside of the second story windows in the back.

"Ya gonna stay and help your best friend out?" He flicked water from the squeegee down at me.

"I have other plans." I said, moving away from him.

"You know you really owe me." He faced me now, spray bottle in hand.

I moved even further away, toward the side of the house. "I believe that debt was nullified when I called a certain Sarah Ann for you."

"Whatever, jerk." He grinned and chucked a wet rag at me.

I dodged it easily. "Is Amanda inside?"

He rolled his eyes and without answering, and continued to clean the window.

It felt weird to ring the doorbell with Henry outside, but it would have been weirder for me to go in his house when he wasn't going to be inside anytime soon. I rang the bell and Amanda answered the door.

"Billy, what's up? You come to help Henry? He's out back."

"No. Actually," I said. Suddenly finding the doorjamb very interesting, "I was just wondering if you'd like to hang out...with me."

She frowned, pressing her lips hard together.

"I was going to go around town today... do some investigating, you know. And I thought—maybe you'd like to help?"

She smiled a little.

"So, you want to go with me?"

"Sure, why not. Just let me ask Aunt Sue. Hold on."

I wasn't sure exactly where we should start, so we detoured at Arnold's Drugstore to grab a cold drink. I felt stupid having her pay for mine. She didn't even ask me before doing it, like she knew I didn't have any money.

We sat on a bench at the park and drank.

"I've been thinking about what you told us—what Jack said to the chief. I know he's your friend, but have you considered... I mean, do you think he might actually know something about what happened to your dad and he's bribing Old Man Jack to stay quiet about it?"

"Are you kidding? I can't *stop* thinking about it. Bud has been like a father to me—I can't believe he'd do anything like that. But he never told me they suspected it was someone from town. Jack was right about that. He hasn't told me anything." I couldn't keep the bitterness out of my voice.

Amanda put her hand on my arm, sending a thrill through my heart. I concentrated on breathing normally.

"I wonder what Jack could have meant... you know, when he said 'Did you tell him what we found that night?' What could they have found? I wish we knew more about the evidence."

"I've also been thinking about the glass all over the road," Amanda said. "The police always take pictures of crime scenes. There have to be pictures, and I bet there are some in the file on your dad's death."

She was right. There had to be pictures. "The only thing is, the only way we could get into that evidence room is with the chief. And I'm not about to tell him what we're up to. Not after the whole incident with Old Man Jack."

"Maybe you could tell the chief about the book you're writing and tell him you want to see the evidence so you can include it in the book or something like that."

I didn't like that idea at all. I didn't want him to know I was going to look at the evidence. What if he took something out, knowing I was going to be looking? Then it hit me. I knew how we could get into the evidence room and not be seen.

"How do you feel about lying? I mean to get to the truth?" I already knew she didn't like outright lying.

"That depends on who I'd be lying to and who would get hurt."

"No one's going to get hurt. And you'd be lying to the chief—or at least the dispatcher."

"Is it going to get us a look at the evidence box?"

"Yes."

"Then I'm in." I could see the dimple again. She was too gorgeous.

"We'll call in a fake crime that Bud is sure to go out on. Then we'll go in, and I'll tell Maureen the chief said to come to get a tour and she'll let us in."

"You are sneaky, Billy Howard. Very sneaky. What do I say?"

"Just say that you saw some poachers on four-wheelers by Westlake. That's about half an hour from here, and he has a soft spot for that land." He took me there every year to camp for a week, and he'd always talk about how pure the area was due to the ban on motorized boats and four-wheelers as well as hunting."

"What if they ask me for details?"

"Tell them you just saw them near the lake's inlet. Make sure you block your number. Tell them you don't want to be identified. That actually happens all the time. People are chicken to be witnesses."

"And here I am, being a witness to something I didn't see. I hope no one gets hurt by this."

I stopped and looked at her. I wanted to tell her no one would get hurt, but that was something I couldn't promise. I wondered, too, if it was right to involve her. If she got caught, she'd be in a lot of trouble. "Just keep the call short and sweet and to the point. Act like you're scared and don't want to be on the phone too long. It'll all be fine, you'll see." I hoped I was telling her the truth.

She dialed the number and then said everything I'd told her, in a rush, halting here and there. She was a great actor.

"No. No. Please. I just really don't want to get more involved in this. I-I-I've got to go. I'm sorry." Then she hung up.

I smiled big and couldn't help myself, I gathered her into a hug and twirled her around. Once I set her down, I said, "That was amazing. Actress here."

She stared at me and then my hands that were on her upper arms. I moved back, out of her personal space.

She moved into my personal space. "This better work." Her eyes twinkled in the sunlight.

I cleared my throat, my mouth was suddenly dry.

We watched the police department from the park, hoping Bud would go out on the call.

"What's next?"

"I'm going to ask Maureen, who'll be smacking her gum, for the chief and when she says he's gone, I'll say something like, shoot, I brought Amanda for the tour. We'll come back another time. And Maureen will say something like, 'Well, you know your way around here, honey, you don't need the chief, do ya?' Then she'll add something about me not eating enough."

Amanda pressed her lips together and exhaled out her nose in a suppressed laugh. "She sounds great. But what's her deal with food? No one in her right mind would call you skinny. You're buff."

I looked away trying to hide my embarrassment but feeling pretty great that she thought I was buff. "I think she just likes to feed people."

We watched the chief drive away. He even waved at us. Before we could rethink the plan, we crossed the street, walked up the steps leading to the entrance of the station and went inside.

"Well I'll be. If it isn't the skinniest boy in town. Ain't your mama feeding you anymore, honey? I'm making chicken fried steak today, and I'll run you some over as quick as a lick once I get home. We can't have our future disappearing into nothing right before our eyes." She winked and smacked her gum. She'd outdone herself with her hair-ratting today. I'd never seen it so high. Her tight pink dress cut low in the front to show her large chest and the chunky black necklace, earrings, and bracelet appeared to weigh more than she did.

Amanda's eyes about popped out of her head as Maureen made her way from behind the counter and pulled me into a hug, crushing me into her. When she finally pulled back, she looked me up and down once more and said, "Yes, that's what you need, some of my chicken fried steak. Don't you think?"

"I wouldn't pass that up for anything." I paused while we both smiled at each other. "I'll just go back to the chief's office." I started to move that way.

"Oh, sorry, sweetie, he's just now left on a call. Madder than a hornet, he is." She nodded her head, up and down, smacking harder than ever on that gum. I wondered how her jaw could handle all that chewing.

"Why? What happened?"

"Apparently, someone is out by Westlake, poaching away. Some anonymous caller called in the tip. Unbelievable how people just can't seem to follow the law."

"It's just awful. I hope he catches them."

"Oh, he will. One thing's I can tell ya for sure is that he won't leave that place until he's got 'em in custody. There ain't nothing he hates worse than a poacher." She continued nodding and chewing.

"You're right, of course. Well, we'll come back later. I was just hoping to show Amanda around the office." I turned to leave.

"Oh, don't you dare walk out of here. You know this place just as well as Chief McKnight, and you know that." She smiled tenderly and then made a swishing gesture with her hands to go past her desk to show Amanda around. "Now go. Show that sweet honey every nook and cranny."

"Are you sure?"

"Course I am. You're as good as a son to the chief. He wants you to feel at home. Now, git."

Guilt swirled around me but I pushed it away by replaying the conversation in the cemetery. "Alright." I walked Amanda past the reception desk and after Maureen unlocked the door to the back offices with the button under her desk, we sailed through and into the inner sanctum.

I stopped by Bud's office to get his key for the evidence room. It sat behind his desk, propped up against the wall. I felt foolish walking down the hall carrying the yard stick that was attached to the key. I hoped none of the other officers would see us. We went straight to the evidence room from there. I didn't want to take any chances that we'd run out of time. We hurried through the door and after closing it, we flipped on the light. While the room was small, it was packed with stuff. File cabinets lined one wall and then there were rows and rows of shelves with boxes on them. The boxes were labeled with dates and names. I figured the evidence of my father's death would be in a box, not in the files.

"Wow!" Amanda whispered. "Look at all those boxes. It's like that show *Cold Case* on TV."

We looked at the first row of boxes. They seemed to be filed in chronological order. We were at dates five years ago. We walked along the aisle and when we got to the end, we still had two years to go. I didn't dare speak, as if the spell that had been cast to get us in the room would somehow end if I did.

We slipped behind that row to the next. Each step I took seemed to make my body tingle more and more. Once we got to the section containing boxes from ten years ago, I held my breath and moved steadily down the line until I saw it. Nicholas Howard. I stared at it, my hands shaking. I was telling my hands to grab it, but they refused.

"Let me get that for you," Amanda said, reaching up and taking the box from the shelf. She did it slowly, carefully.

I licked my lips with cautious hope. That box had to hold answers. It had to.

A small desk sat up against one wall, and she set the box on it then looked at me, eyebrows raised in question. I nodded and she opened the lid. We looked inside. There was a mass of things piled inside, all in labeled plastic Ziploc baggies. All that is, except a large manila folder that stood up against the side of the box. She glanced at me again.

I reached in and pulled out the folder, laying it on the desk. Behind me, I could feel Amanda pulling out all the baggies. I rubbed the back of my neck, staring at the closed folder. I thought I heard something in the hall outside the room and froze. I told myself it was the water fountain cooler turning on. Feeling a new sense of urgency, I told Amanda to start snapping pictures of all the baggies.

"Gotcha," she whispered, taking a quick look at the door before pulling out her phone.

I spread the papers out all over the desk, clumsy and hurried. Amanda must've finished with the baggies, because she moved over and started snapping pictures of the papers I'd spread out. I moved over to where she had been and looked at the contents of the baggies as I put them, one by one back into the box. The last item really threw me. It was a woman's earring. There'd been a man's watch in one of the other baggies. Two pieces of jewelry—a man's and a woman's.

"Don't you think it's weird that there's only one earring?

"I wonder if it came from the killer. Maybe your dad was still alive for a little bit after he was hit and the person who hit him came to his aid and he grabbed out, you know, like in movies, and snagged her earring in the process?" She was on the last row of paper documents.

I looked hard at it.

"What about the watch? It couldn't have been ripped off the same person. Wild."

That's when I heard the door to the back rooms buzz open. I knew that sound. I'd heard it a thousand times. "Someone's coming." I threw the earring and watch back into the box and Amanda scrambled to get all the papers shoved back into the folder and then into the box.

Nausea tugged at me. I sprinted to the spot where the box belonged and shoved it back. I raced back to the desk and said in a rushed whisper, "Just pretend I was walking you through this room."

We walked toward the far wall, trying to look natural and yet not looking at each other. I didn't know if I could keep cool if I did.

"Yep," I said, a bit louder than I normally would. I heard the door click open. "This is the evidence room where everything important is kept. We can't touch anything." In my head, my voice wavered, but I wasn't sure what it sounded like to others.

"Wow! All this stuff is from crime scenes?" Amanda said with an enthusiasm that surprised me.

"Yep!" I looked up to see an officer staring at us. I sighed with relief that it wasn't the chief.

"Hey, Billy. You know this room is off-limits," Officer Olsen said.

"Yeah, but my friend Amanda is visiting from Florida, and I really wanted to show her how cool this room is. The chief wasn't here and—"

"Just having you in here could invalidate all the evidence in those boxes. Now, out with ya." He was smiling, but I could tell a deep irritation plagued him.

"All right. All right," I said, throwing my hands up into the air. "I didn't mean any harm. Just showing a girl a good time."

"You know you're free to wander anywhere else in the office, just not in here." He gave me a stern look.

"Thanks, Olsen. I guess I just forgot." I looked at my feet and pretended to be embarrassed.

He took the yardstick with key from its spot leaning up against the table. "This time, I'll keep this between you and me."

"I'd appreciate that," I said.

He waved his arm out to guide us through the door. We hurried out.

When we got out into the reception area and grabbed the door handle to exit, Maureen said, "Hold up there, mister." She stomped out toward us.

Had she somehow seen what we did in the evidence room? Had they had cameras installed recently?

"I called over to the store and had him send over some lunch for you two." Her arched eyebrows arched even more. "This might help get some meat on your bones."

I smiled, took the bag from her and hugged her, giving her a kiss on the cheek before thanking her.

Amanda said, "Thanks," as we hurried out the door.

Guilt seeped into me, the further away from the office we got. It seeped into every pore. I'd lied and put Amanda at risk. What was I willing to do to get to the truth? Was it worth endangering my friends?

Once at the city park, we sat at a table and caught our breath.

"Boy! That was a close one. I thought she'd somehow discovered what we'd done."

"I about had a heart attack. Seriously. That was the scariest thing I've ever done. I'm sorry I put you in that position. I wasn't thinking straight. I won't put you in danger like that again."

"Don't be silly, Billy. I knew what I was getting into. I wanted to take the risk. It's worth it to me. And don't spare me next time." She looked like she meant it.

"Should we go to my house to look at all the pictures?"

"Heck yeah! And next time we bring Henry to be the lookout. But why don't we eat those sandwiches Maureen worked so hard to get for us first—or did you squish them into mush?"

I looked down at my hand to see my hand clutching the bag she'd sent with us. I set it on the table and grabbed one squished sandwich and one perfectly fine one. I handed the good one over to Amanda and said, "Mush or not, it smells great!"

She laughed as she opened the paper wrapper and took a bite of hers. I had to use my wrapper to keep mine together. It wasn't a pretty sight. Several kids from school started a game of touch football and called to me to play.

"Come on, Howard, we need a quarterback for the other team."

"Another time." I was tempted, but the heat combined with the fact that it would take me away from Amanda kept me from playing.

We watched the boys play while we finished our sandwiches. Then we headed back to my house to look everything over. I pulled out some paper, and we started charting the evidence we had.

"Any one-hour photo places around here?" she asked.

"No. You'd have to go to Ripley or Dyersburg for that. We should've gotten my mom's car while we were in town."

"We'll get the actual pictures later. We can still chart them by looking at the phone."

"Sounds good."

We used several different sheets of paper and wrote out what we knew. We even made a map of my old street, what houses were there when my dad got killed and who lived in those houses.

We made a list of the evidence. Then we made a profile of who might fit a suspect list. A week ago I wouldn't have put teens or women on the list, now I had to. Crazy how your perspective can change with only a few pieces of evidence. The earring could mean a woman hit him, and the fact that Mr. Wallstrom had been hit by a teen driver made me think the killer didn't necessarily have to be a drunk male like I'd always imagined.

It was hard to read the handwriting from the interview statements. We needed the actual pictures and a digital copy to put on the computer to blow them up and study them.

"According to this profile, it could be almost anyone," Amanda said with a sigh.

"Yep. But I think we have to take into account the other things we know. We should think about the people we already suspect. Let's do Tom Harris first. Does this evidence support or exclude Mr. Harris as the person who hit my dad?" A ball of heat flooded my gut thinking about Mr. Harris running my dad down. The heat seemed to come faster, hit me harder than any ever before.

"I don't think it does," Amanda said. "That earring suggests it was a woman and the watch suggests it was a man. Or really, it could have been two people. A driver and a passenger. A girl and a boy."

"You're right. And, what if the watch or earring wasn't the driver's or passengers, but instead was my mom's or dad's?"

"I hadn't thought of that. And it will be tricky getting that information from your mom without giving away what you're doing."

"You got that right." I brushed my hand through my hair. "I think we'll be able to get more out of these pictures once we have a hard and digital copy to put up on Henry's computer." I wondered what the photo shop would think of some teenagers having pictures of police evidence.

"I think you're right."

"Besides, I'm sweating to death. Since we're getting nowhere, let's go see if Henry's done."

"Sounds like a plan to me," she said, standing up and wiping sweat from her temples.

Henry was inside eating a sandwich. "Hey, lazy jerks," he said as we walked in.

I made my voice low, so that none of his siblings or mom could overhear.

"You'll never believe what we just did."

He expelled air out of his nose and took a big bite of his sandwich. "Try me," he said with his mouth full.

"We snuck into the evidence room at the police station." I tried to whisper, but my excitement took my voice up a notch.

"Are you serious? You did that without me?" He shoved me.

"Ouch!" I said, rubbing my now throbbing arm.

He finished off his sandwich and motioned for us to follow him to his room.

We showed him the pictures and talked about the earring and the watch as well as the glass they'd put into evidence.

"Sounds like we need to take a trip to Dyersburg and get some pictures made."

Both Amanda and I nodded.

"Nothing like a little adventure."

"That reminds me, Henry, we've got to plan our date. Should we go to my house so Miss Nosy won't have a chance to overhear?"

Amanda threw a pillow at me. "So, you're just going to leave me here, all alone while you make your amazing plans?"

"Yes," I said, standing and heading for the door. "It's all about surprise." It felt like blood raced through my body. A deep hope grew in my chest. I was winning this girl over.

Back at my house, Henry headed straight for the refrigerator.

"Dude, you are a bottomless pit! Stop messing around and let's go plan our date," I said, coming around the table to close the fridge. As I did, I knocked a pile of mail off the table. I stooped over to pick it up and noticed the top one was for me. Strange. I didn't know anyone who would write me a letter. I tucked it in my pocket.

Henry pulled a Tupperware of leftovers out of the fridge. "I can't help it. I'm a growing boy. Your mom won't mind," he said as he popped it into the microwave.

"Whatever, man, I'm gonna go to the bathroom. Just come up to my room when you're done with that."

Henry grunted and I rolled my eyes at him as I headed to the bathroom. After washing my hands, I remembered the letter. Curious, I pulled it out and tore it open, wondering what it could be.

Inside was a letter from Sarah Ann. I scanned through it.
Hey Billy,

I thought I'd write you a letter telling you how excited I am about the Fourth. It's going to be fun spending a full day with you. I know I'll be with Henry, but what I'm really glad about is that I get to have time with you too. I think you're so cute and fun. I sprayed this letter with my favorite perfume for you. I'll be wearing it at the picnic. Save a lot of dances for me.

Sarah Ann xoxoxx

I looked at the door to the bathroom as if Henry could see through it. I shoved the letter back into the envelope and put it at the bottom of the stack of towels under the sink. Henry could never know about that letter. Somehow I had to convince Sarah Ann to give Henry a chance. I took a deep breath and headed for my room.

Henry was already sprawled out on my floor. I flew onto my bed like Superman, trying to hide the nervousness I felt.

"So, what's the plan, Stan?" Henry asked.

"I don't care what we do as long as I get to spend time with Amanda." I wanted to make sure Henry knew I couldn't care less about Sarah Ann.

"Hello? You're supposed to be going to help me be a normal human being and get my future wife to love me back. I never should have agreed to this. You're going to leave me high and dry, aren't you?"

"I'm not gonna leave you hangin'. And don't forget, all I wanted was for you to take Sarah Ann out. You're the one that roped me into this."

"Man, you'll forget I exist the second Amanda bats an eyelash at you."

"You underestimate me, my friend." He had no idea what circus tricks I'd have to pull off to get Sarah Ann to think of him instead of me.

He rolled over to the base of my bed and said, "Seriously, Billy. I need you to have my back on the Fourth. Will ya? This is the most important day of my life."

"Until the next one." I chuckled.

He sat up, his feet jutted under my bed.

"There won't be a next one if you aren't there for me." His gaze followed me.

"I'll be there. Good grief, man. Chill out." I got up and sat in a chair at my desk.

"You better be." Henry stood up and sat on the bed.

"So, we'll pick the girls up at twelve thirty. You have to come to my house and get me first. Then we'll go get Amanda and then Sarah Ann."

"You're not serious. Can't Amanda just come with me?"

"I totally am. You're supposed to pick up your date, not have her tag along like some kid sister. It's my first date with her, Henry. I want it to be perfect."

"Fine. We pick them up and then head over to the park?"

"Yes." I stood back up, wondering if I ought to just tell him about the note. He was my best friend, and if a girl I liked had given him a note like that, I'd hope he'd tell me about it. The problem was, Henry'd never get over it. I couldn't tell him.

"We each need to bring a couple of blankets to sit on and cover us for the fireworks, and I don't just mean the ones that will be above our heads." Henry waggled his eyebrows.

"We also need to bring a couple of card games we can play in between lunch and the dance," I said. "I'll get my mom to make a lunch. Do you want to be in charge of treats like cotton candy and slushies?"

"Sure. No problem, but, have your mom make her fried chicken then. No deer meat. I don't think Amanda would know what to think about eating a deer." He gave me a serious look.

"But a chicken—that's okay?" I laughed and tapped the book on my desk, trying to act natural.

"Everyone eats chicken." He dismissed my concern.

"I'll grab some drinks for all of us. It's supposed to be really hot. Maybe we should go early and lay out our blankets to save a shady spot."

"Good idea."

"You coming over tomorrow? Or do I even need to ask?" He lifted his eyebrows.

I nodded dumbly.

Henry huffed and left the room.

"Don't forget to call Sarah Ann," I called after him.

Chapter 12

I woke early and went on a run. I stopped by the police station in hopes Bud was already there and had gotten the results of the fingerprints I'd given him. I stood in front of Ms. Maureen at seven sharp with a gym bag on my shoulder.

"Is the chief here?"

"Sorry sugar-pie, he's with Mayor Clement ironing out the last minute details of the celebration for tomorrow." She popped her gum.

I looked at my shoes. "Any idea when he'll be back?"

"I imagine he'll be gone most of the morning. You want me to have him give you a buzz when he gets in?" She must have just had her hair dyed; it looked extra blonde against her dark orange skin right then.

I fingered the keys in my jeans pocket, thinking. I looked over to the fax machine.

"You expecting something?"

"I had him running some fingerprints, that's all. Just wondering if he got the results."

"That's all done through the computer instead of fax now," she said, taking a quick glance at the fax. "You want me to ask him about it when he gets here?"

"No. No, ma'am." I shook my head. I didn't want him to think I was that anxious to get them. He might get suspicious. "No. I'll just come back by later or something. It's no big deal. Just thought it might be fun to see the results."

"Gotcha sweetie. I'll just tell him to give ya a call." She combed her long, purple nails through her curly, ratted blonde hair.

"Thanks, Maureen. By the way, the sandwiches were great." I left, my hand in my pocket clutched around the keys. I still had a chance to find something out today. The post office opened at ten. I'd be back for the fingerprints later.

I ran back home and completed my chores. While I ate breakfast, the phone rang. Maybe it was the chief.

"Hello."

"Where are you?" It was Amanda. My heart sped up and I took a deep breath.

I pressed the receiver hard against my ear, hardly believing it could be true. Amanda was calling *me*. I was a bit tongue tied for a second.

"Billy?"

"Just finishing up my chores."

"Well, Henry and I have already collected three stories while you've been playing around. It's time to get to work. Meet us at the bowling alley?"

"Who'd you get the stories from?" My heart raced at the thought, hoping they'd found out something new.

"You're going to have to show up to find out. So hurry up. It's good."

"I'll be there in thirty."

"See ya then."

GRAVEDIGGERS

I sat thinking about my two friends collecting stories for me, giving up valuable vacation time to help me chase down leads. Henry was such a good friend. Guilt pinched at me thinking about Sarah Ann's note. After showering and getting ready, I took one final look around, making sure the room would pass my mom's inspection, and then took off for town.

Henry and Amanda were waiting in front of the bowling alley, and I stood up taller as I approached. "It seems like people talk more freely when you're not around." Henry scratched his upper arm and then reached into a sack he was holding. "But no one wants to talk about the murder."

I looked around quickly and said, "Shhh! Someone could hear you. You should say accident."

Henry rolled his eyes. "It was murder," he mouthed, giving me a dirty look.

I wondered if it was Amanda that got people talking and not my absence. "So, fill me in."

He handed Amanda and me ice cold sodas, and we walked the short distance over to the park as we drank. They began telling me about the stories they'd heard. I listened hard so I could remember every detail to record later, in private.

"Ms. Joan was in the park with her granddaughter this morning," Amanda said, her voice filled with excitement. "She gave us some juicy info. She said your dad was well liked by most, but he was hated by a few. Apparently, he got on Mr. Harris's bad side right after he got back from college. Harris used to own the land your dad bought, but he fell on some hard times and had to sell it. Later, when he found out he could have gotten a lot more selling to Coffco, he tried to get your daddy to sell it back to him. But your dad refused."

"He really didn't want that land to be developed. It meant a lot to him," I explained.

"Yeah. Harris was pretty angry about it though. Apparently he tried to claim your dad had stolen that land from him, said he'd forged documents or something."

Anger rose up like bile in my throat. "That's ludicrous! My dad would never—"

Amanda reached over and squeezed my hand. "We know that, Billy. Don't worry."

I smiled at her in thanks. "The Harisses have got to be involved—everything is pointing back to them."

"Not the earring," Amanda reminded me.

"And there's more. I got a story, too you know," Henry chimed in. He leaned forward and started to reveal his tale. "I know you know your dad was the school's star basketball player," Henry added. "But did you know he was also the MVP of the baseball team and the quarterback of the football team? He was the all-around star athlete."

I didn't know. How could I know that? I'd known he was good at baseball, but he'd never talked about football. "Hmm." I didn't want to admit I didn't know.

"Well," Amanda continued. "Apparently, he not only got the good stuff from being the star, but also all the bad stuff, too. Ya know, everyone was jealous, or totally in love with him or hated him with a vengeance—all that crap. Mr. Vela said most saw him as the golden boy who would come back to town after college and save its struggling butt—only he didn't say butt.

"Anyway, there were some that either wanted what he had or simply didn't want him to return so they didn't have to live in his shadow. When your dad came back, those against him were against him still. Mr. Vela couldn't recall all the people who never wanted to see your dad again, but he did mention Lee Clement and Sandra Classico. But, Sandra's been gone from Halls for about five years now."

"Lee, huh? But Mayor Clement said Lee had nothing to do with it."

"And we should believe him because?" Henry threw his arms into the air. "I mean really, Billy, you can be so gullible. He's the mayor's son, of course he's gonna try and protect him."

I sat in silence, taking in what he said, trying to imagine the mayor protecting his son from murder charges. It wasn't hard. And Lee was the town drunk. Maybe he was drunk that night and hit my dad. I'd ruled Lee out because he didn't have a car or a license now. I wonder if he was still driving when daddy got hit. "But in his report, Bud said it couldn't have been Lee either."

"You don't think the mayor could have pulled the wool over the chief's eyes?" Henry stood, swinging his arms out to his sides, palms up.

"But Bud would have found damage on Lee's car, right? That evidence would be incontrovertible. There would be no hiding that." I looked up at him.

"You got me there. So, what we need to know is what car Lee was driving then and if he suddenly got a new car about that time." He had a renewed look of intensity on his face.

I nodded. "Was he still driving then? When did he get his license revoked?"

"No idea. But, I bet someone remembers."

"Let's split up then," Amanda said, standing. "Billy, you go play the son-creating-his father's-history, and we'll be a bit more cunning."

"All right. Let's do it." Fire burned in all our eyes. We were going to figure this out. We were going to discover who killed my father. "Let's meet back here at, what, five?"

"Sounds good." Amanda nodded.

"Got it," Henry said.

I decided to go knocking on doors and leave the downtown area to Amanda and Henry.

I stopped at Mrs. Franklin's first. I thought she'd be good to start with. She was so nice and had lived here forever.

"Hi Mrs. Franklin," I said when she opened the door.

"Well, I'll be, if it isn't Billy Howard. You looking for some odd jobs again?"

"No ma'am. Actually, I'm looking for stories."

"Stories?"

"Well, I'm writing my dad's history, and I'm going around collecting as many stories about my dad as people can remember."

"Well, I'm sure I can think of a few. You wanna come in or sit on the porch? I could get us some lemonade."

"That'd be great. I'll help you."

After getting the lemonade, and sitting in some rockers on her porch, she started in on my dad.

"Your daddy had a kinda magic about him. Everything seemed to come together if he was involved. He had charisma that boy. Had every girl swooning over him. And he treated them right.

"You may wonder how I know that and I'll tell ya. He took my sweet Adel on a few dates and made her feel like a princess. Your mama was one lucky girl snagging him."

"Everyone makes it sound like he was an angel and never did anything bad."

She whistled. "We like to remember the dead in a positive light, now don't we?"

I nodded.

"But I guess if your history is going to be accurate, you've got to have the good with the bad. He played some pretty silly pranks while in school. I think they call it hazing now. Sure, all the boys did it, but it sure left scars on a lot of those kids who had to endure it. He was a boy after all. He did all the normal boy things. And there were the few that resented him. The mayor's son for one. Those two never did see eye to eye. Fought like badgers. And, I'd imagine some of them girls got their feelings hurt when he wouldn't go steady with them. He never did get real serious with any girls. He just dated around. Which is, I guess, exactly what he should have done being in high school and all."

"Did he ever get in trouble with the law?"

"Nick Howard? Oh goodness no. But, some of those boys on those teams he was on caused enough trouble for ten Nicks. I'd tell ya to talk to the chief about that, but I don't think he keeps the best of records. Now, Chief Huffton, he was a good record keeper. Kept track of every little thing that happened in this town. Nowadays, they don't even keep track of thefts. Two years ago someone stole my planters right off my porch and officer Olsen told me he'd take note of it. But I know he didn't. With Huffton, I would've had to sign a report and everything. Guess they don't track the small stuff anymore."

"Do you remember the day my dad was killed?"

Her face seemed to pinch together. "That was a dark day for sure."

I nodded. "When I think back to all that glass on the street, it makes me wonder they weren't able to find a single car in town that had new damage and needed a new windshield."

"It had to be an out-of-towner. It's the only explanation. They must've rode away back to whatever hole they came out of. Awful. Just Awful."

"Yeah. I think if it was someone from town, they would have discovered the car."

"And believe you me, honey, everyone was on the look-out for that car. Everyone was shocked."

I thanked Mrs. Franklin for her time and went on my way. After each house, I recorded the stories the person told me in my notebook and then moved on to the next one. After chatting with the tenth person, I started to get a little down. Sure, I was collecting all kinds of stories about daddy when he was young, but nothing about the time after he got back from college and definitely nothing about the night of his death. People seemed to clam up when I asked about those things. Only Mrs. Franklin talked about it at all. They'd be all friendly and helpful and then bam, they became as tight lipped as a turtle.

When I asked about cars people drove back then, I got all kinds of responses. I learned that Lee got new cars every few years, and no one was sure what he drove at any given time. And they weren't sure when he stopped driving. He just did. I didn't dare get too specific about the time of my dad's murder.

I hurried back to town to meet up with the others, hoping they'd been more successful than I. And they had. They got all kinds of stories about the day daddy died. Some were exaggerated and other things just completely crazy, like how Ronda said aliens came down and took daddy's soul, and that was why they couldn't discover who had hit him. But other things were thought provoking—like how the police took the body directly to the mortician instead of to the coroner, and how the police had blocked off the entire area, not letting anyone near, including the press. Maybe that's why there was so little in the papers about it.

"But why? Why will all of these people talk about my dad to you guys, but not to me?" I kicked at the metal leg of the bench we were near and picked up a rock and threw it.

Amanda put her arm around me. "We'll find the answers, Billy. Don't worry. At least people will talk to us."

I shook my head, closing my eyes and lifting my head to the sky and pleading with God to help me. Help me get justice for my dad.

"Why don't you stay right here and record what we told you in your notebook. We'll go get some more info from people." She took my clenched hand and pulled me over to the bench, sitting with me for a moment before leaving.

Even her touch couldn't bring me solace right now. I told them about what Mrs. Franklin had told me about everyone looking for a damaged car and how Lee and my dad never got along.

Now we had Tom Harris and Lee Clement as real suspects. Maybe Sandra Classico, too, but it seemed like a long shot. If Lee was involved, then the mayor could be, too. And the chief.

After a while, I pulled out my notebook, my thoughts churning as I wrote the stories and opinions they'd told me. Then, I waited, thinking about the new developments.

The sun had moved west, leaving me completely exposed to its harsh rays. I moved from the bench to the protection of a leafy sweet gum tree. I sat with my back against the trunk. Kids played on the playground nearby. Not long after that, Henry and Amanda returned, both eating ice cream cones, Amanda holding one out for me to take.

"So, we got a few more fun stories for you, but I doubt they have anything to do with your dad's death." Amanda took a dainty lick of her ice cream. One side of my lips curled up in a half smile. We stared at each other for a few seconds longer than was normal and then she said, "I thought of a few things that are interesting."

"Tell me everything." I stood up and we made our way to my house.

"Since you lived out of town and not on a road that led to anything but farms, it would be unbelievable to think an outsider did it. Seriously. Who would be traveling down your street? It had to be one of the people who lived further down the road than you guys or someone visiting one of those people. So, I think you were totally right about how you felt, Henry. There is something going on."

"There was a dirt road that cut through to the highway, but anyone not local wouldn't know that."

"We need to make a list of who lived on the farms just past y'all's house."

"Amanda and I already mapped out the street."

"Let's go look at it." We hurried to my house like fire was chasing us. I mentally took note of the preacher and his wife, the Gustavsons, Henrietta and Sam, the Coubles, the Wheelwrights, Jamisons, Hugo Mathis, and the Abernathys.

Four had moved away: The Wheelwrights, the Jamisons, the Abernathys, and the Coubles. The preacher lives at the church, now. The Gustavsons, moved into town along with us. Hugo stayed put.

"We can't count anyone out," Amanda said it with finality.

"I think we can rule out the pastor," Henry said. "He's much too good of a man to have done that. He would've confessed. He wouldn't have been able to stand himself if he didn't."

"No one gets a free ride," she insisted. "We'll get the information we need to rule them out, and then we'll cross them off."

"I'd hate for you to be the prosecuting attorney in a case I was involved in." I snorted.

She smirked. "Better not get yourself in trouble, then."

"Do you really want to be an attorney?" I asked.

"I do. Actually, I'd like to be a judge someday. Our justice system needs honest judges to sift through all the garbage going on. I won't let the guilty go on technicalities, and I'll make sure the innocent are freed without any shame shadowing them around."

"I've changed my mind. I do want you on my case." I smiled at her.

She nudged me with her shoulder. I wanted to melt into her deep brown eyes.

"I would be a fair and smart judge."

Turning on the street that led to my house, I stopped abruptly. Bud's unmarked blue car was in my driveway.

Amanda looked at me, big-eyed. Henry was a good ten feet in front of us before he realized we'd stopped.

"What's going on?" He looked in the direction we were. "It's just the chief." He turned back and looked at us. "What's the big deal?"

I couldn't speak so Amanda did for me. "Uh, we broke into the evidence room, remember?"

"Crap!" Henry shook his head. Then he moved in close to me. "You two are sooo busted. Let's go inside and see how the good ol' chief is going to punish you." He laughed.

"Let's see if you're still laughing when the two of us are in jail for tampering with evidence, and you're all alone."

We went through the back door in hopes of overhearing what my mom and he were talking about. He was telling her the story of going to Westlake to look for poachers. He knew. We were dead. I didn't want to leave just yet, though. I resisted Henry's insistent pulling on my arm. He must've thought if we ran, we wouldn't get in trouble.

"The thing that chaps my hide," said Bud, "is that the caller said the poachers were on four-wheelers. The poachers I caught don't even own four-wheelers. I hate to think someone got away."

I couldn't believe it. He had caught some poachers. I looked back at Henry and Amanda and mouthed the words, *Did you hear that?*

Amanda mouthed, *Unbelievable!* I relaxed and could see both Henry and Amanda had relaxed too. He wasn't here for us. We were lucky devils. I pushed the door to the kitchen open figuring we were safe. Bud's eyes lingered a few extra seconds on Amanda and then he winked at me—obviously feeling pleased that I was with a girl I really liked.

"Hey, Billy, Henry—and Henry's cousin."

Henry said, "Chief, this is Amanda, my cousin from Florida."

Much to his credit, he pretended not to know her name. He stood up from the sofa and gave Amanda his hand. "Nice to meet you. I'm sorry I wasn't at the station when Billy brought you around. It would have been fun to take you on a tour of the place."

He knew we'd been there?

"In truth, it was probably more interesting with Billy. I tend to tell you a lot of stuff you wouldn't care to know."

We were completely off the hook. Officer Olsen must have kept our exploits to himself. Bud had no idea we'd been in the evidence room.

"Did you go peek in on the prisoners?"

"Are there prisoners to peek in on?"

"There are now," he said with a chuckle. "If you come by tomorrow morning, I can take you to the holding cell portion of the station. You never know what dangerous criminal you might find in there." He smiled, showing all his teeth.

"That'd be great, sir." Amanda beamed at him.

Did she really want to go see that or was she just being polite?

"Well, I gotta get back to the station. I just wanted to stop by and see if y'all had heard from Old Man Jack." A suspicious look flashed through his eyes.

My heart seemed to stop, and I felt my jaw hang open.

"You okay, Billy? You seen him?"

"No. No, sir," I said just a bit too fast.

"Well, he's been reported missing, and I'm asking around. I'm sure we'll find him." He headed for the door. We all said goodbye or some form of it.

"I'm glad you're all here," my mom said. "I could use some help taking all the cherry bottles down to the cellar. Many hands make light work."

Once all the cherries were in the cellar, we headed to my room and wrote our new suspects and evidence into the charts Amanda and I had made earlier.

"Why would the chief ask if we'd seen Jack?"

"Do you think he's really missing?"

"Who knows? What if he was asking us only to see if Jack told us anything?"

We all gave each other worried looks.

"Billy," Amanda said. "With the stories we've collected so far, it's making more and more sense that your dad's death was in fact a murder. One of these people who had a grudge against your father could have just been taking advantage of a situation that fell into his or her hands. I mean, what if someone was just driving past your house and saw your dad and took advantage of the circumstances to get revenge? Maybe they felt they were finally going to get payback and acted out of pure vengeance. What if Harris came upon that opportunity? Several have mentioned him as an arch enemy of your dad's."

"It does make some sense," I said slowly. "I guess I'm just not sure if I'm ready to really believe Old Man Jack over the chief. It feels...disloyal."

"Ok. That's fair. The chief is your friend. But you can't rule out all the people who hated your dad, yet. That's all I'm saying. If you do you could miss something important. It could be anyone, but if it was someone from here, why wouldn't they stop? It just doesn't add up." She lifted her hair from her neck. "It's so hot, guys. I'm wilting." Sweat glistened on the underside of her hair as she raised it. "This is a different heat than I'm used to in South Florida."

It was a blistering day, and our house was especially hot. We didn't have air, and the open windows brought zero relief.

"We could go swimming," I suggested.

"Now you're talking," Amanda said, standing up.

While I hid the evidence books, Henry and Amanda went to get dressed for the pond. I put on my cut-off jeans and a T-shirt, the only clothes to wear in a pond, grabbed some flip flops and a towel, and headed for our meeting point on the corner.

Chapter 13

I watched Amanda walk toward me on the sidewalk, her towel draped over her arm. Her sun-kissed skin glistened with newly applied sunscreen. She was so beautiful. Henry walked beside her, his towel around his neck and frayed cut-off jeans on. Amanda had a T-shirt and shorts covering her suit. I positioned myself to be on the opposite side of Amanda from Henry.

Out of the blue, as Henry passed us, he yelled, "Last one there has to pluck old Mrs. Nesbitt's whiskers with his fingernails."

I wasn't one to shrink when a challenge came my way. I took off after him. I passed him as we rounded the corner when it occurred to me, we'd left Amanda and she didn't know the way. I stopped abruptly, letting Henry overtake me and jogged back to where we'd left her. She was sitting on the curb, hands cradling her chin, elbows on her knees, her flip flops sitting next to her, her back turned toward me. I guessed she heard my footsteps, because she looked up at me.

"I'm not that fast of a runner, sorry."

"No big deal." I gave her my hand. "I just remembered you didn't know the way. The Joneses dug the pond only about two years ago. Sorry. It's just this game we've played since we were kids." She stood up and then reached down for her flip flops. We started toward the pond.

"I remember," she said with bitterness. "Last time I was here, you guys ditched me all the time. I was reliving that horrible month all over again. Not to mention the fact that my parents left me behind for almost two months."

Blood rushed to my cheeks. We had been awful to her. I'd forgotten just how bad until she reminded me. All the terrible tricks we'd played on her flashed before my eyes. "I'm so sorry. We were stupid kids back then."

"I know, but that doesn't take the painful memories away."

She was mad.

"It also reminds me that if I didn't look the way I do now, I'd probably have received a totally different reception from the two of you."

I couldn't deny it. We'd made plans to make her time with us horrible. I felt shallow and awful. I couldn't look at her.

"Wait a minute. Had you two made more devious plans against me?"

I could feel the anger rising off her, and I peeked over at her.

"Oh my gosh!" As if my silence made it all the more real, she stopped and stomped her foot as she spoke. "Of all the low, mean, awful things—"

I went to her before she could run away forever. "I'm sorry. I admit it. We are thoughtless, stupid boys and I hope you can see your way to forgive us. We shouldn't have tortured you. Everyone deserves a fair shake, beautiful or not." I took her hand in mine. She pulled it away, but not with anger, so I grabbed it again. Something told me there was still hope.

"Just so you know," I said, trying to make the mood lighter, "we didn't care so much how you looked—you were too smart. You were a threat we had to neutralize."

She harrumphed. "And what about now?" She pushed her hip out and put her free hand on it before looking up at me.

"Now, we want a girl who's smarter than we are, to show us the way. We've discovered we're pretty dumb and need you to survive."

"And don't you forget it," she said, smiling up at me and chuckling.

"No worries there." Some instinct took over, and I pulled her to me and kissed her forehead before I could stop myself. I tried to play off the intimate gesture by twirling her around like we were in a dance and leading her down the sidewalk. I really wanted to grab her hand and tell her that she was beautiful, and there were so many other reasons I thought she was amazing, but I chickened out.

By the time we reached the small pond, Henry was already up by the tree with a rope swing, ready to fly out and drop into the water. He'd obviously been waiting longer than he'd have liked. Once he saw us, he let out a yell and swung out, letting go at the highest point to drop into the water with a screech and a huge splash.

"That looks awesome," she said, taking her shirt off. I stood there like an idiot again, unable to tear my eyes away from all her newly revealed skin. No one wore suits into the pond—it could be the end of your suit, but no one was going to tell Amanda that. She rocked a purple tankini. She crossed her eyes and threw her shirt at me before running to the swing.

After about half an hour, none other than Jeff, John, and Jamison Harris pulled up to the side of the pond with their old truck. They had never been nice to me, and now I knew why. Their dad probably told them all kinds of lies about my family and especially my dad.

They came hooting and hollering, running as fast as they could to the rope. Once their eyes fell on us, they stopped short and stared.

"Don't let us stop all y'all. The water's just fine." I stared back at them. They turned, I suppose to confer and then the oldest, the same age as we were, grabbed hold of the rope and swung out yelling "Cowabunga!" before hitting the water. He barely had enough time to pop his head out of the water before his brother plopped in only a few feet from him.

I smiled. He sneered back. After the third brother hit the water, they all swam to shore. I watched them with renewed interest. They passed in front of their beat up truck, and I wondered if it was the car that had hit Daddy. Each time I walked past it on my way up to the rope swing, I examined it quickly. A picture of the street in front of my house the night Daddy died flashed through my mind. Glass was everywhere, shining and glittering in the emerging sun. I shook my head.

The truck was all kind of banged up. It could have hit any number of things—the question was did the Harris' truck have its windshield replaced back then? How would I ever

163

know? Then I thought of our truck. We kept all the paperwork for the truck in the glove box. Did they? It had been so long. Did people keep records that far back? We sure did. Maybe they did, too. How could I get into that truck to find out?

Henry swam up to me.

"Harris's truck is over there," I said, treading water.

"Yeah. And?"

"I need to get a look in the glove box and see if there's a receipt for a new windshield in there."

Henry glanced at the truck. The front had several big dents. "Why would they have a receipt from ten years ago in their truck?"

"We keep all our receipts in our truck. Maybe they do, too."

"I guess it's worth a try. But how are you going to get in there without them noticing?"

"I don't know. Any brilliant ideas?"

"No, but maybe Amanda has one." Henry turned to watch her walk toward the rope swing.

"What are you talking about?"

Henry elbowed me as she grabbed hold of the rope. "Look at the Harrises." He smirked.

All three of the Harris boys were gawking at Amanda.

"She's the answer," Henry laughed.

I knew exactly what he was thinking, and I wouldn't allow it. Making her use her body to distract the boys was way too demeaning. "No way. I won't involve her."

She splashed into the water, and the boys still kept their eyes on her as she swam toward us. Unbelievable.

"It would work, Billy."

"I said, no."

Just then, Amanda reached us. "What are you guys arguing about?"

"Nothing." I said in a tone that should have made Henry forget about the idea.

"We thought it would be smart to get into the Harris's truck while it's here."

"Oh, I agree," Amanda said. "So what's the problem?"

"Billy doesn't like—"

"Forget it, Henry. I mean it."

He pushed himself off a little bit from us and said, "Using you as a distraction."

I went after him, but he made it to shore before I did and ran to the rope. Once there, he got right in the water. Two of the Harris boys were in front of me to use the rope. I watched helplessly as Henry talked to Amanda, I'm sure telling her his plan. I would kill him.

I swam hard in their direction after getting in the water. I dunked Henry far under the water and held him there extra-long to make my point.

Amanda patted me on the back. "Stop it, Billy. I want to do it."

I was so shocked, I released him.

"It doesn't seem right."

Henry came out of the water, sputtering and spitting and calling me names.

"You are not the boss of me, Billy. I'm willing to take one for the team. I don't normally like using my body to get what I want, but in this case, I think it's worth it." She set her jaw. She was determined. "Now, I'm about to swim over to the shore and go for the rope. It's your job to get in and out of that truck as fast as you can so that my part is as short as possible. Understand? Don't make me do this longer than I have to."

I knew there was nothing I could say to dissuade her.

She swam off, and I followed her. The boys were just ahead of us. We all climbed out and while they went to the rope, I went for the truck. I crept along the driver's side and then around the back to the passenger side. I could hear the screams of the Harris boys and hurried up. The door squeaked loudly as I opened it, and I peeked back to the pond to see if they'd heard. All eyes were glued on Amanda who was having Henry hold the rope in place while she tried several different positions to take while she swung. My insides boiled. I had to hurry.

I opened the glove box, and all kinds of papers and wrappers fell out onto the floorboard. I tried to catch some, but it all fell through my fingers. I quickly grabbed them up in a jumbled mess and headed for the bushes with them. A few fluttered to the ground as I went, but I snatched the fallen papers after I went back and shut the truck door.

I scanned each of the papers looking for the word windshield, not taking long on any one piece of paper or receipt. I found one for a windshield, but it was twenty years old. Sensing my window of time was closing, I clutched all the papers and hurried back to the truck, shoving them all back into the glove box. I slammed the door to the glove box shut, but it bounced back open. I thought of the army-green box at home and sighed. I pushed everything back in and shut it swiftly. It stayed. I quietly shut the door and walked through the woods a bit before emerging and plunging into the water not far from the group.

Amanda shrieked, not realizing it was me. "Where were you?" She asked. It was all a part of the plan.

"I was...I was..." and just as we'd anticipated, one of the Harris boys said, "He was taking a piss."

The oldest boy smacked his brother on the head and said, "Shut up, idiot!" He sneered at his brother. "Excuse him, he's an idiot. Can we try again?"

"I-I-I don't know," Amanda sputtered. "I think we have to get back."

"But nobody's won yet. That ain't fair." His voice was playful with an edge of seriousness.

"Y'all had like ten chances, it's not my fault you didn't guess right."

"Just once more," he said. "One more chance."

She looked at Henry and me for help, but Henry didn't give it, and I had no idea how to help her. I didn't know what was going on. I wanted to rearrange their faces for looking at her like they were.

"Fine, but this is the very last time. Close your eyes." They did. I didn't. I wanted to see this. "Now count to ten and then open them."

They all counted to ten and then looked at her expectantly.

"Okay y'all. Guess." They put their heads together and then said, "Yer pointin' to Jeff."

"Nope. Sorry guys." She lifted her finger out of the murky water and it was pointing at Jamison. "We've gotta go, now. See ya. It's been fun." She started swimming for the shore and we followed her.

As we reached for her towel, she whispered in a firm voice, "I hope you got something. That was humiliating." She turned to look back at the boys in the pond. They stared shamelessly. "Still humiliating," she hissed.

Chapter 14

Henry busted up laughing as we walked back to the house. I still wanted to hurt him. Once we were sure they weren't following us, I said, "I can't believe they didn't call you on that game."

She laughed, her tense shoulders relaxing. "Right? I mean, they didn't even question my veracity."

We all laughed anew.

"They were mesmerized by you. No brain power. It was crazy to see," Henry said.

She raised one eyebrow at him. "And who also loses brain power every time a certain girl's name is said?"

Henry hung his head.

"Y'all, there wasn't a windshield receipt for time around my dad's death, but there was one from twenty years ago. So, unless they threw that receipt away to hide their guilt, it looks like Harrises are clean."

"We can't count them out just yet," Amanda said. "Maybe they threw the receipt away, knowing it incriminated them."

She was right, of course.

"The truck does have front end damage. A lot of it." I readjusted my towel over my shoulder.

"Did they say your dad was most likely hit by a car or a truck?" Henry asked.

I shook my head. "No idea."

"We need to get the pics from your phone onto the computer so we can see what's on those statements."

"I know it was Harris, I can feel it in my gut," I said. "We just have to find a way to prove it now."

I felt conflicted. I should have been able to look at that evidence at the police station at my leisure. After all, it was about my dad. I really wanted to look at the evidence with Bud. I hated that I couldn't fully trust him.

By the time we made it back to my house for a late supper, we were tired and starving. Mama had fried some fish, hushpuppies, black-eyed peas, and green beans with fried onions. I could smell cherry cobbler baking in the oven. When she pulled it out after we'd eaten, she sent us with a pan to take to Henry's. We were so tired, we all fell asleep watching a movie in his great room.

I woke at one, alone on the couch. Amanda and Henry must've gone to their bedrooms. I thought about staying, just so I could wake up to Amanda and see her beautiful face first thing, but I needed time in the morning to get the results from the prints I'd given the chief. I also needed to do my chores.

The next day, I hurried through my chores and headed over to the station.

"Sorry, Billy. I don't have the results yet." He rubbed his palms together.

"I don't remember it taking so long." I fiddled with the pens in a container on his desk.

"It usually doesn't. It's my fault actually. I didn't send them in until yesterday." He rubbed the back of his neck.

That surprised me.

"I was so busy that day you gave them to me, I set them aside and then found them yesterday when I was cleaning off my desk." He cleared his throat. "Sorry about that."

The chief's phone rang. When he picked it up, he said, "Chief McKnight...Oh, hi, Sylvia. Uh huh. Sure. He's here. Just a sec."

He mouthed, *It's your mama*, and handed me the phone.

"Hi, Mom. What's up?"

"Jeb Prescott's kids have the flu, so they need some help spraying the beans. They've been without help for a week already. Even their mama is sick."

"I have plans, Mama. Can't they get someone else?"

"I know, sweetie. I think you should go and help out. Maybe Henry would like to go with you. I'm sure they could use him, too. He's offering to pay you well."

"He's not going to want to come. Even if he did, I'm sure his mom wouldn't let him. Amanda's in town."

"They'll still be there when you get back, and you'll be earning points in heaven for your kindness."

I could see the smile on her face through the phone.

"All right. When do they want me?"

"As soon as you can. I thought I'd take you before I had to go to work."

"How long are they supposed to be sick?" I rolled my eyes.

"I wish I could tell you. I just don't know."

I huffed. "I'll be home as soon as I can." I handed him the phone and he hung it up.

"Someone needing your help?" Bud scratched at his chin.

"Jeb. The flu. They need me to fertilize."

"Sounds like fun," he scoffed. "How about I give you a ride home."

"Actually, could you take me to Henry's?"

He raised his eyebrows. "Are you sure?" He knew my mom wouldn't like me making an unapproved stop,

"Yeah. I want to tell Henry what's going on before I disappear on him."

"Whatever you say." The chief stood, and we went outside to his squad car.

I walked right into Henry's house after giving a courtesy triple knock. I waved to Mrs. Parnell. "Hi ma'am. Just here for Henry."

"That boy's still asleep. Get him up, would you?" I heard someone taking a shower as I passed the bathroom. It must have been Amanda. Henry was still asleep and it was ten. I ran in and body slammed him, rolling over the bed and onto the other side. Henry only groaned. He'd gotten too used to my attempts at making him get out of bed.

I leaned up against the wall, still seated and said, "Hey man, I'm gonna be gone for a few days, maybe longer. Jeb's kids are all sick, and they need my help."

"You never should've learned how to drive those machines. I warned you." He covered his head back up with his sheet.

"But they looked so fun, so cool. It wasn't until I had to drive them all day that I lost interest."

A muffled voice came from under the covers. I couldn't understand a word.

"What?"

Henry's head popped out from under the covers. "You should learn how to say no." He gave me a dirty look. "At least I'll have Amanda to hang out with. I'd kill you if she wasn't so cool."

I was shocked, but tried to hide it. He thought Amanda was a good substitute for me. "Tell Amanda, would ya?" I said, starting to stand.

"Tell her yourself."

"She's either in bed or in the shower, and I don't want to disturb her in either place." I stood straight up.

"Not anymore," Henry said.

She stood in the doorway in a bathrobe, her hair twisted in a towel and no makeup. She looked incredibly sexy. I tried to keep my eyes on her face. I felt my face flush. A low growl tried to emerge from my throat, but I held it in. What was happening to me?

"Tell me what?" Amanda smiled.

"Billy just told me he's leaving us for a few days."

Shock hit her face but she blinked it away. "And where are you going, Billy Boy?"

She'd never called me that before. I kinda liked it. I walked around the bed. "A farmer down by Ripley needs my help. All his family is sick with the flu, and they need me to run the machines. It's time to fertilize. They already lost a week."

"You're a man of many talents, huh? Well, when you get back each night, we'll hang out. It won't be that bad."

"Actually, I'll be sleeping next door to the farm I'll be working at because I'll be putting in twelve to sixteen hours a day. It's good pay, but lousy hours."

She looked crestfallen, her shoulders slumping forward.

My heart raced at the thought she was sad I was leaving. It made me feel good, I'm not gonna lie. But, I *really* didn't want to go now. Too bad I needed the money.

"I guess Henry and I will have to hold down the fort of fun while you're gone." She kicked at the doorjamb.

"I don't have a choice. They need me."

"It's okay, really. We'll even do some PI work about your dad, too." Amanda said.

"Thanks. I'll have plenty of time to think through the evidence while I drive all day."

"We'll call ya every day and tell ya what we found out."

"I don't have a cell, remember?" The thought of them calling the neighbors for me each night was not a good one.

"Oh, right. Well, we'll have it for you when you get back."

After the first day of working on the farm, I was almost too tired to eat and fell into bed, exhausted. It didn't get much better the next night. I drove the tractor sixteen hours, two days in a row in hopes of making it home faster. The rows of beans seemed to go on forever. I had a hard time concentrating on anything but driving in a straight line. It turned out to be a good thing, because I finished on that third day before noon.

GRAVEDIGGERS

After the final field was sprayed, I drove the machine to the large barn that housed it. Jeb helped me back the machine in. Once I turned the key to the off position for the last time, I exhaled loudly, excited to get home. The dance was in two days, and I couldn't wait to find out what Henry and Amanda had dug up about my dad.

I shook hands with Mr. Prescott and he thanked me profusely, telling me he'd bring my money to me in about a week. He took me further into the barn to show me the new reaping machine he'd purchased. It was a monster. I didn't ask if I could give it a try, even though it looked like it would be fun to drive. Then I saw a couple of four-wheelers to the side of it. They looked brand new. Bean farming must have been doing well.

As we walked toward the exit, I couldn't help but see an old cream Chevelle and a red Mustang gathering dust in the corner. I walked up to the almost pristine Mustang and rubbed my hand along the fender, over the hood, the windshield and over the roof, leaving a trail in the dust. It was bad. I'd love to get my hands on that car. It did have a dent in the driver's side door, but other than that, it looked great.

"Like it?"

"Yes, sir!"

"I got that one 'bout six years back. The Chevelle, I got...oh nine years or so ago. I got a screaming deal on it and couldn't pass it up. I thought I'd fix 'er up and take her to those car shows they have. Sadly, I never made the time for it. I will one day, though. I really oughta cover both of those."

I walked around the Chevelle. It needed a lot of work. The tires were flat, there were some scrapes in the paint and

CINDY M. HOGAN

dents in several places. The worst damage was on the front right fender. The headlight hung out of its socket and the grill was busted. The entire windshield had been removed. I could see some shattered glass on the front seat.

Sparkling glass on the asphalt in front of my house filled my mind. I looked at Mr. Prescott and tried to remember when they moved here.

"Has it been here all nine years that you lived here?"

"We've only lived here seven years. Lived in Lenox on a smaller farm. When this land came up for sale, we jumped on it. It was a great opportunity for us to expand."

"So you bought the car when you lived in Lenox?"

"Yep. Nice older gentleman sold it to me. Said it had belonged to his brother in Camden, but he'd been storing it for him and couldn't any longer."

It couldn't be the car then. That town was two hours from Halls. I was getting paranoid. This couldn't be the car. I looked the Chevelle over again. I bet in its day, this car was hot. If it were mine, I'd paint it cherry red.

"Maria's made hamburgers on the grill and potato salad for lunch. Care to join us?" he asked.

"If it's all right with you, sir, I think I'd best be on my way."

"That's understandable. Give me ten minutes, and I'll carry ya home."

"Thank you, sir."

He nodded and headed for his house. I made my way to the neighbors, where I'd been staying and gathered up my things.

I called Henry's phone once I got home, but got no answer. He'd probably not charged it, so I called his house. It shocked me when Amanda answered the phone.

"Billy!" she squealed. "You're back!"

"How'd ya know it was me?"

"Caller ID, you silly."

"It could've been my mom."

"Well, I'm glad it wasn't."

I could feel her smile through the phone.

"Henry went to Dyersburg with his dad. Man time, ya know."

I looked at the calendar. Yep. It was Henry's day with his dad. They usually got back around noon, so it surprised me that he was still gone. "Hmm," I mumbled. I wondered if she'd want me to come over or not.

"So, you gonna come rescue me from complete boredom, or what?"

Without thinking, I said, "That depends on what you have for me."

"You're gonna love what I have for you, Billy Boy. Get your butt over here."

I chuckled. "Coming." She was flirting with me, wasn't she?

I wrote a note for my mom in case I didn't get back before she came home so she'd know I was back. I looked around to see if there was anything obvious that needed to get done. Seeing nothing, I showered and got all cleaned up before heading over.

Seeing Amanda was a rush. In the short time I'd been away, she seemed to have become even prettier. She ran up to

177

me and hugged me. I wasn't prepared for that and swayed back precariously on my boots when she wrapped her legs around my waist. As quickly as she'd hopped up, she hopped down. All I wanted was for her to jump right back up.

She grabbed my hand and pulled me into the family room. On the table was a stack of papers. "This is a summary of all the interviews we did." I shuffled through them. It wasn't difficult to see that the great majority were written in Amanda's handwriting. There was one that caught my eye.

"What's this?" I held the paper out in front of me.

She took it from me. "Oh, that. You'll love this. The mayor took a car in to be fixed about the time of your father's death, but the repairman was old and couldn't tell me exactly when. He would only say the end of June or beginning of July. It's a hole in the wall kind of place and they don't keep good records. The owner is as old as the hills."

"Back to the Mayor and Lee, then. What kind of damage was there to the car?"

"We don't know that. It's only another clue."

"He was probably drunk, and his daddy saved him from jail time."

"Let's not jump to conclusions. Let's stick to cold, hard facts."

This was significant. Maybe it wasn't Harris after all. "How do we find out?"

She shrugged her shoulders. "You got me. No one seems to know. But, one lady said she thought Lee hadn't been driving for about ten years now. It's quite the coincidence."

"We've got to somehow verify it. It's too bad we can't just ask Lee or the Mayor. By the way, thank you. You've been busy." I smiled at her and sat on the couch. She bounced down next to me. "How'd Henry do?"

"Uh, he, well, ya know..." She left that hanging out there.

"He wasn't very keen on spending a bunch of time on it, huh?"

"Naw, but I got more than he ever would."

"You've got that right." I turned and looked into her bright brown eyes and said, "Thanks. This means..."

"It's nothing. I think it's fun. You want to go do some more interviews today?"

All I wanted to do was kiss her, spend time with her. "We could, or we could go four-wheeling." It was out of my mouth before I could stop it. I really should be looking for my dad's killer. But right now, all I wanted to do was be close to Amanda.

"Really?"

"Sure."

"Henry took me out on the four-wheelers the day you left and it rocked. Let's do it."

We rode all over in the woods until hunger took us back to my house. After we ate, we sat out in the yard under the shade of a great big oak, sipping sweet tea and relaxing. I wanted to kiss her so bad, but I didn't know if she wanted to and I didn't want to lose her.

She set her tea down in the grass. "Interviewing people is quite revealing."

"What do you mean?" I took a drink.

"People say stuff like, 'Don't you tell Herbert I told you, but...' and 'No one but me knows this, but...' It's like everyone has all these secrets they've been dying to tell for years."

"Everyone has secrets." My hands turned sweaty and I set my tea down.

"You think?"

"Of course."

"You keep any secrets from Henry?"

I jerked my head back. Did she know? "Where'd that come from?"

"I'm a girl, Billy. I have all kinds of secrets. I was just wondering if you had any you kept from Henry."

I wanted to get the spotlight off me. I didn't want her to know my secrets, and I knew if I tried to lie, she'd see through it. "You have a lot of secrets, huh? Tell me some of 'em."

"One day when my parents were outta town for the weekend, I had a wild party at my house." She laughed. "The house was a wreck and I took all the kids' keys and told them that they better help clean up or they wouldn't see their keys anytime soon." She laughed again. "It only took about an hour to get it presentable. The next day I did some deep cleaning. My parents never knew."

"Wow! Are you serious?" I couldn't imagine trying to trick my mom like that.

"Totally."

"I've never done anything like that. My life is pretty boring, really." I rubbed my hand down my face.

"You should come visit me in Florida. I'll introduce you to some excitement."

"I bet you could." Was she just saying that or was she serious? Could I really go visit her there?

"You said yourself that everyone has secrets. What's one of yours?"

"At night, I turn into a wolf and hunt bears." I grabbed at my throat, pretending I was turning.

"Very funny. Look. If you're worried I'll tell Henry, I won't."

I thought about her telling him about the note and wondered if I could really trust her. Something in my gut told me I could.

"You have secrets from your best friend?" I asked, almost afraid of the answer.

"A few." She looked at me, turning her whole body to face me. "I'll tell you one of mine if you tell me one of yours."

I turned away.

"It must be good." She waggled her eyebrows.

"He'd kill me if he found out. He can never know and that's why I can't tell you." When I turned back, she grabbed my hands.

"Please, just tell me. I swear, I'll never tell him. Why would I?" The look on her face was earnest. I wanted to believe her.

"Because girls don't know how to keep secrets." I made my eyes wide.

"You'd be surprised, Billy Howard, at my ability to keep quiet." She looked so sincere. I didn't want to let her down.

"Tell me your biggest secret," I said, "and if I think it's big enough, I might tell you the one secret I have from Henry."

"Well...okay. My best friend was dating this college guy, and he was no good, ya know. I mean I could see it, but she was so crazy about him, she didn't see how he was bringing her down. Well, her parents didn't know about him..." Her silence told me the rest.

"You told her parents?" I jerked my head back.

She nodded. "Via anonymous note."

"You little snitch. You're terrible! Dagum girl!" I rocked back and forth.

She looked embarrassed, but said, "I still think it was the right thing to do, though."

I nodded. She was probably right.

"Now your turn." She looked at me expectantly, her arms wrapped around her knees.

I stood up and took her soft, small hand in mine. "It's best if I show you, I think." As soon as she stood, I said, "But you have to swear you'll never tell anyone, including Henry."

"I won't tell. I promise."

I turned toward my house. What was I doing? I couldn't tell her about the note. That would be the ultimate in dumb. I slowed my pace, trying to find a way to renege on my promise. She moved in front of me once we entered the kitchen. She must have sensed my change of heart.

"I'm not going to let you out of this, Billy. I swear, whatever you tell me will be locked in the vault."

I wanted to make her happy, make her smile again. I nodded, pressing my lips into a hard line and took her into my room. Amanda was in my room. Before I lost every ounce of courage I had, I pulled the note that I'd re-hidden in my closet and handed it to her.

She sat down and looked at me.

"Go ahead. Read it."

She unfolded it and read. Her eyes rounded in surprise. She then shifted on the bed and looked me straight on. "Is this Sarah Ann, Sarah Ann?"

I nodded and then shook out my hands.

"When did you get this? Do you have feelings for her?" The hurt in her eyes pierced me, but I figured it was better than the wrath that would come from Henry if he ever found out.

"I got it yesterday. And, no, I don't have any feelings for her."

She cocked her head to the side. "Are you sure?"

"Yes." I wanted to tell Amanda it was her I liked, but I couldn't for some reason. Not here. Not now.

"Well, I know you feel like you can't tell Henry, but you should anyway. It's the right thing to do."

"No way. He would be too hurt. He never needs to know."

"Really, he'll understand. Things like this have a way of getting out and when it does, Henry will be even more hurt. Be straight with him. He might surprise you."

"In the ideal world, he'd understand. Nothing about this is ideal. He's been in love with her since second grade. I can't hurt him that way. Besides, Sarah Ann is going to get to know him on the Fourth, and she'll love him. She has to."

"Well, I won't tell him, that's for sure. But, I still think you should." She gave me a stern look.

I bit my lip. He could never know. I took the note back and put it in my nightstand drawer. I needed to destroy it before Henry somehow got a hold of it.

Chapter 15

"So, you going to let me see the stuff from the box?" Amanda asked, her foot bouncing on the floor.

"Sure," I said, going over to the bed to get the bag. I couldn't believe I hadn't already shown her. "I forgot you hadn't seen it."

I poured the contents onto the bed.

She started to reach for a piece of jewelry and stopped. "Wait. Do you think the police could lift prints from these things?"

"I actually thought of that and fingerprinted everything. The bad news is that I thought to do it after I'd handled everything." How did she intuitively think of these things?

"Really? Did you find anything?"

"Well, I gave the prints to the chief. It's not like anyone can run fingerprints. No results, yet." I scowled thinking about how Bud had forgotten to send in the prints.

"The chief let you keep all the evidence?"

"No. He doesn't know where I got the prints. I told him I found an old army box and wanted to find the owner. It's been several days, so I bet he has them now."

"Let's go get 'em, then." Her eyes gleamed with anticipation.

"All right. Let's go." I slid the keys on the chain into my pocket and shoved the rest back into its hiding place.

"Oh, there's something I need to tell you," Amanda said, jumping up and down.

"Yeah? What?"

"I saw another big key like the one from the box."

"Are you serious?" I pulled the keys out of my pocket.

She took them in her hand and examined the chunky one. "I swear it's the exact same one."

"What? Where?"

"You'll never believe it." She bounced her shoulders up and down.

"Don't keep me in suspense.

"At Henry's house."

"No," I said, shaking my head. "Did you ask about it?" I leaned closer to her, afraid I might miss something.

"No. I wasn't certain it was exactly the same. But now I'm pretty sure. When we get back, I'll take this key with me and compare them."

We discussed the evidence all the way to town. The closer we got, the more nervous I became.

"Look. Is that the chief?"

He was standing just outside the library. My insides shook looking at him. I didn't like feeling that way about him. He had secrets. Scary secrets. There had to be a good explanation, though.

"Hey, Billy. Amanda," he said, smiling brightly at us.

"Hey, Bud." I decided I wanted to get right down to business. "Any word on those fingerprints?"

"Yep. The results are in."

I wished he'd have thought to call me.

"There were no hits on A.F.I.S. Why don't you bring the box in, and we'll show it around. We'll find who the owner is one way or another."

I tried not to show how disappointed I was. "Alright," I said, even though I had no intention of showing him the box.

"Well, I've gotta get going. See y'all later."

"Bye," Amanda said.

I raised my hand in farewell. We started back home, talking about what a bad break that had been.

"I don't know about you, but I couldn't stop thinking about your dad and all the whole time you were gone." And we were back onto my dad's death, leaving Mrs. Higby behind.

"In truth, I was too tired and stressed the whole time to do any real thinking on it." I admitted.

"The puzzle," she said, "is that the car that hit him had to have some damage."

"Are you forgetting Lee's car already?"

"Just listen," she said, a bit impatiently. "People in town would have noticed if someone's car had been damaged and that lady you talked to said everyone had an eye out for one. Everyone knows what everyone drives here, I'm sure. They would have noticed and remembered if Lee's car was the one."

"But what if his dad hid the car so well no one found it? After a while, he could have snuck it to some repair shop without anyone seeing."

"I asked all the repair shops around here about that. And several even let me see their records. The only car that had that kind of damage around here about that time was Lee's. I just don't believe no one would have seen it. Of course, that doesn't rule out someone fixing their car at home or in another town other than Ripley or Dyersburg, though. And, I guess they could have had it fixed at a shop that is now closed." She was crazy efficient.

"Did you ask around about who has auto body skills around here?"

"I asked, but no one's telling."

"Ya know, now that I think about it, no one ever wants to point fingers in this town. It's almost like everything is brushed under the rug."

"Like some big conspiracy in the government to keep everything hush-hush?" She spoke in a sinister tone and then laughed.

"Maybe." I said it with all seriousness.

"Bwaha ha." She laughed. "Paranoid much?"

"Maybe not that extreme, but the mayor's oldest son has a severe drinking problem. They've made a spot in one of the holding cells for him. His spot exclusively. The chief is always having to pick him up. Everyone covers for him, all the time."

"So, you're not only afraid they're going to be mad at you, but also try to sweep any information you find under the rug?"

"Actually, I'm afraid they've already done that."

"Suspicious much?"

I groaned.

"Seriously, though. Why would they want to prevent your cute family from getting justice? It doesn't make sense. Wouldn't they look better if the murder was solved?"

"If they don't call it a murder, it doesn't have to be solved. Officially my dad's death was written up as an accident. And so was Mrs. Higby's. It's starting to seem like they cover up a lot of stuff."

I could tell she was thinking hard. When we finally got to her uncle's house, she said, "It doesn't make any sense. Why would they do that? We'll figure it out. If it takes us the rest of the summer and going against the whole town, we'll figure it out. Together we can do this."

I wanted to believe her more than anything.

"It's time to find out about that key."

I reached into my pocket and pulled the keys out, still attached to the chain and handed them to her.

She held the little gold key and turned it over and over in her hand, obviously in deep thought.

"You go up to Henry's room, and I'll compare the keys."

I nodded and we went inside the house.

"It's the same key alright. I'll ask Aunt Parnell about it later. She was on the phone."

"Okay." One mystery was about to be solved at least.

She held the small gold key in her hand, the chain dangling below. "There has to be a way to figure out what this key goes to. She looked thoughtful. She walked over to Henry's computer and turned it on, a grin on her face.

I followed her, enjoying the faint smell of flowers that followed her.

"The Internet has everything, right?"

"Just about."

"Well, what if there is a key database somewhere? Maybe we could match these keys up with their locks." She continued to turn the key over and over.

"I hadn't thought of that." Why hadn't I thought of that? I hadn't thought of fingerprinting the box until probably too late and now I hadn't thought of ways to discover what locks the keys belonged to. If I expected to be an agent for the FBI, I'd better step up my game.

Amanda wasted no time in discovering a huge key database. Depending on the description we put in the search bar, it would spit out pictures of the keys and the locks that belonged to them. With an advanced search, we could find any key we wanted it seemed.

"Maybe we won't even have to ask Aunt Parnell about the key." She grinned up at me.

It took us about ten tries to put in the right information to find the little golden key. Apparently, this was a widely used key with many possibilities for locks: safety deposit boxes, post office boxes, music boxes. The list went on and on. We didn't have the same luck with the chunky old key.

She turned the chunky key over in her hand. "If this were an important key, the Parnells wouldn't leave it lying there on the hall table, would they? It couldn't go to something valuable, could it? The two keys are exact replicas."

I shook my head. "I'm sure Henry's mom can tell us."

"Yeah. I won't worry about that key anymore."

"Let's look at what we know about the other key." I pushed back in my chair and took a deep breath. "The chances of this little key going to some trinket like a music box or such, is unlikely considering the rest of the contents of the box. It must lead to something valuable. Since the contents belong to Pastor Higby, the locks are most likely somewhere here, in Halls. The two places that stick out to me are the bank and the post office."

"I agree. We should check those two places first. If the key happens to belong to a small box in the pastor's house, I might have access when I go with Henry to visit him. I think we're going there next Monday."

"No way. I don't want you searching for something like that at Higby's. What if you got caught? But, I do think we should go to the bank and the post office. Can anyone get access to a safe-deposit box with just a key?"

"Sometimes. My parents have several safe-deposit boxes, and I've been with my mom when she's taken stuff out. All she had to do was write the number down on a piece of paper. When we got into the vault, my Mom put her key in and the bank representative put his key in and we were in. I know they have other kinds of boxes that are more secure, though. I had to go with my parents when they set one up because I was on the account in case they die or something. I had to put my finger on this computer pad thing and everything. They also have a password with it. The only way we can find out what type is at your bank is to try. Besides, I doubt here in Halls they'd have anything very high-tech."

I gave her a look. She held her hands up in protest.

"I'm not dissing on Halls, it's just...you know."

I did know, but I still didn't like anyone bagging on my home town.

"Maybe I had better do it. I could tell the bank teller that my parents gave me this key to get their stuff while I was visiting here or something like that." She looked me full on, not in the least bit ashamed.

I wasn't sure I wanted to involve her in such a hands-on way, but she was probably right, Halls most likely wouldn't be all techie. That glint in her eye told me she was more than excited to act as PI. "I'll head over to the post office while you go into the bank. We can meet back up in front of the post office. Sound good?"

She gave me an intense look, the light making her eyes seem to glitter.

I kicked at the edge of the computer desk. "Are you sure you want to do this? What if you get into trouble?"

"I was born for this. Are you kidding?" She gave me her dazzling smile, stood up and said, "Let's go." She picked up the keys from the desk, and we headed out.

As we approached, Halls Bank seemed to be taller, bigger, darker than it ever had been before. Amanda didn't skip a beat, though, and she popped up the steps like there was nothing to be scared of. I hurried after her, grabbing her hand as it swung behind her. "Hey, if you smell trouble, get out of there. Of course, if you do get busted, I could probably pull some strings with the chief." I winked, but inside, I was truly worried about her.

"I'll be counting on that." She turned to go, but I still held her hand.

"Maybe I should go in there with you."

"It's okay, really. Nothing's gonna happen." She gently pulled her hand from mine.

My heart pounded as I saw her go inside. I couldn't make myself leave. It wasn't fear I felt. It was anxiousness. I said a little prayer as I moved to the side of the steps and stared at the bank doors. All stress left me, a little gift from God, yet I couldn't go to the post office. Something told me to stay.

Amanda came out only minutes later.

I rushed up to her. "What happened?"

She laughed out loud. "It's not a safe-deposit key. It's most likely a P.O. box key." She handed it to me.

"What?"

"Well, I changed my tactic a little bit when I went inside. I just had this feeling I should. I mean what if it wasn't a safe-deposit key? So, I took it to a lady behind a desk and asked her if it was. She immediately said no and then took it around to a few other workers who told her it was probably a P.O. box key. They said cheap people think it's a good place to hide valuables." She laughed. "They actually said that. Can you believe it?"

"No. But, I'm relieved."

"Why are you still here anyway? I thought you'd be long gone."

"I had a feeling, too." Guess God wanted us on this path.

"Let's go to the post office. I can't wait to see if it fits the locks there."

As we opened the door to go inside the small building, we heard a car honk and turned to see who it was. Henry was idling in his car.

"Amanda. My mom is waiting for you at the salon. She wanted me to find you and carry you over."

Talk about bad timing.

"Oh shoot," Amanda said. "I totally forgot."

"You forgot from this morning? Girls." Henry shook his head.

"Girls rule the world and you know it, so you better watch what you say." She walked toward the car. "Billy, don't do anything without me, ya hear? We'll meet up later. Should I cut my hair off?"

"Don't you dare," I said, widening my eyes in mock fright.

I went to the park and played some pickup baseball with some younger kids while I waited for Amanda. After two hours, I knew I'd have to go into the post office soon if I was going to make it there that day. I was reluctant to go without Amanda, but at the same time I was eager to find the next piece of the mystery.

Once at the post office, I discovered the numbers on the little key did match the ones on one of the boxes—one of the larger boxes, in fact. There were only twelve of them and they were attached to the outside wall and faced the wall of smaller P.O. Boxes. I pulled the key out of my pocket and looked at it one more time. I had to know what was in there. I had the key, after all. The key entitled me to open the box.

I pushed the key in, jostling it a little to make it go all the way. I inhaled deeply once before I turned it. It did its job, moving the pin that locked it tight. I flipped the door quickly open and then shut it just as quickly. There was just a big manila envelope in there. I took a look around before opening it again. Several people walked in and went through the glass door, leaving me alone. I pulled the door to the P.O. box open and then tried to find an opening in the envelope.

It was sealed tight. Maybe I should slip it into my gym bag and open it at home. I had no idea what was in there. What if it was dangerous? Whatever was in there was solid and hard. I'd just see what it was before I took it.

Without taking the package out, I used the sharp edges of the chunky key to cut it open. The cut was jagged and revealed something black. I used my fingers to rip the envelope further. It wasn't until that moment that I considered the idea that the contents could belong to the killer. I glanced around the room. A woman stood in line for the post office attendant, and her stroller was holding the glass door open. If any of the customers wanted to, they could see me and what I was doing, but no one looked my way. I pulled the package wrapping back, using my body to block the view. Did I see what I thought I saw? I scanned the room to see if anyone had entered the area or if anyone had started watching me. Noting that no one seemed concerned with me, I pulled up on the torn edges of the package and stared inside once again, my other hand glued to edge of the door.

All sounds seemed to explode in my ears as I looked at the object. With remarkable clarity, I could hear what a customer was saying to the post office employee, the opening and shutting of the door, the tapping of a waiting customer's foot, and the rocking back and forth of a stroller with a small child inside. The amplified sounds made me jerk my head from side to side. It wasn't until I heard the shuffle of feet behind me that I was able to slide the box's contents into my bag and shut the door to the box. I took off, tucking the keys into my jeans pocket. My feet took me quickly outside, a rush of adrenaline urging me on.

Chapter 16

My breath came in swift pulls and pushes until I was a good block away and could sit on a bench in front of the train caboose near the tracks. Seeing the townspeople stare at me made me realize I wasn't acting normal and needed to get a grip. My mind seemed to swing in a big arc from one place to another without rhyme or reason. *A gun. A gun.* I had a gun in my bag. What could it mean? My mind kept getting completely jumbled, but I forced myself to sit upright, exhaling loudly and rubbing my hands down my thighs. Once I'd inhaled, I was able to get a hold of myself.

Guns were a part of my everyday life, why had this one freaked me out so much? Maybe because it was a handgun, and I knew what it had been used for: to kill the preacher's wife.

Hands landed on my shoulders and pressed down. I jumped in my seat.

"Whoa, boy, it's just me. What you got whirring around in that head of yours that caused you to start like that?"

Chief McKnight. I hadn't thought about the fact that his office was just across the street. This wasn't the best place for me to have stopped. "Nothing, chief, sir." Guilt washed through me.

He looked at me like he knew I wasn't telling the truth. "You sure? You look nervous."

I took several short breaths. He was great at reading body language; I'd have to give him an excuse. "I'm just nervous about the Fourth."

"Well, that's understandable. You really like this girl, don't you?"

"That's right, sir."

"She's a cute one, that one. I could tell you liked her when I met her at your house the other day. Henry finally worked up the courage to ask Sarah Ann, huh?"

"If you call me asking her out for him courageous, yes." I bit at my fingernails.

The chief laughed openly. "I'd like to be a fly on his fried chicken tomorrow."

"I think you'd be in danger of him eating you, sir."

"You're probably right. He won't be very observant with the love of his life sitting by him, will he?"

"No, sir."

"Good." He patted me on the shoulder.

I took a calming breath. He was about to leave. He didn't ask about my bag.

"Do you have your acceptance speech ready?" Why did I ask him that? I really just wanted him to leave.

"I guess so. I'll never get used to all the attention. I don't know why the mayor insists on this celebration every year." He shook his head. "That man loves the spotlight too much."

"I'll be there to hear it."

"You better be. It's nice to have your face to focus on." He winked and turned to go.

I stood up and headed home. It was already six, and I should help my mom get everything she needed for tomorrow. I wouldn't be able to hang with Amanda or Henry the rest of the night until tomorrow afternoon.

It was the third of July. I'd have to spend much of the day helping my mom get everything ready for the Fourth. She sold homemade fudge and caramel apples at the park and we used the money for the one trip we took every year. Because Mayor Clement made such a big deal about the Fourth, combining it with the celebration of the FBI's list of the safest cities in America, people from Ripley and Dyersburg came to our neck of the woods. It was a boon to the town every year. By early afternoon, I was dying to tell Amanda about the gun and worked up the courage to ask my mom if I could go talk to her for a few minutes once the last of the apples had caramel on them.

"Of course. Everything needs to cool off before we can finish anyway."

I hurried over to Henry's and joined the two of them in his room.

"I can't believe you're here on July third, your sacred family day." Henry chuckled.

"I don't have long, but I wanted you guys to know what I found in the post office box."

"I told you not to go looking without me, Billy."

"Well, you never came back, and it was going to close. I had to go for it." I looked at Henry. "We went to the bank—"

"Yeah," Henry interrupted. "I know. Amanda told me all about it. So what was in the box?"

"A gun. A hand gun." My heart sped. Amanda covered her mouth with her hand.

"No freaking way," Henry said.

"Yeah, way. A black .38 revolver."

"Did you get fingerprints off it?" Amanda asked.

"I didn't have the chance, yet, but I will." I nodded. "I thought about the serial number, too. If the prints don't pan out, maybe the serial will."

"Yeah," Henry said. "The serial will tell us who owns it, and then we'll know who the killer is."

"Now we're getting somewhere." Amanda grinned from ear to ear.

After going back home, my mom and I finished packing everything including the food for tomorrow's picnic. I called Henry to come over so we could pack everything we could. We put the blankets, games, cards, and drinks and paper goods into a box and prepared the cooler and another box for the food. Then we headed for my room to go over the plan.

Henry shut the door behind him and said, "I'm dying, man. I don't know how I'll do this. What if she expects a kiss?" His face was going paler by the second.

I felt awkward knowing Sarah Ann liked me. I had to remind myself he'd never know. "Then you'll kiss her." I said it matter-of-factly. Would Amanda want a kiss? I plopped onto the bed and he onto the floor.

He slid closer, his legs sliding under the bed. "I want to kiss her so bad, but what if I'm terrible at it?"

I'd thought the same thing, but didn't want him to know that just then. The only girl I'd ever kissed was Emily Jean at her thirteenth birthday party during a game of spin the bottle. I just remembered how soft her lips were for that briefest second. "It'll come naturally, I'm sure."

"Amanda says I need to take it slow when I do make my move."

"She did? What else did she say?" Maybe I'd get some useful tips from what she said. I reached into my nightstand and pulled out a pen and notebook. When I did, the note from Sarah Ann fluttered to the floor next to Henry.

"Tons of stuff I'll never be able to remember." Despair covered his words.

My eyes bulged as I realized what had just landed next to Henry's hand. I had to be casual. I couldn't let on that the note was important in anyway. Why hadn't I already destroyed it? Heat flooded my face as I reached for it.

Being the good friend that he is, Henry picked it up and started to hand it to me. "What is this?"

"Nothing. Just some notes on the cases." I focused on my hand reaching for the note, making sure it didn't shake.

"Oh," he said and instead of handing it to me, he unfolded it in one quick motion.

Panic filled me. A cold chill rushed down my spine and all I could do was stare at the note in his hand.

Before I could take evasive measures, Henry had started to read. He swore and his nose flared, "What the...?"

I rolled off the bed.

"It's nothing. It's not what it seems."

"You don't really expect me to believe that do you? This is a letter to you from Sarah Ann. Why would she write you?"

"Henry, come on, just give it back. I'll explain." I didn't want him to read the whole thing. I didn't want him to get hurt like that.

"You seeing Sarah Ann on the side? Huh? You have a thing for my girl?"

"No, Henry, it's not like that. Just, let me have it back."

"You seem awful set on me not reading this note," he said, his cheeks flaming and nostrils flared.

"Look, just—"

"Shut up, Howard. Let me read it."

I didn't know what to say to make it better. I let him read.

As he finished the note, he looked up at me, eyes lit with fury.

"Why did you keep this from me?" He glared at me, his face turning red and his lips spreading into a flat line. His eyes looked fierce. "You let me go on and on all summer about Sarah Ann and all this time, you were just laughing at me behind my back."

"I didn't want to hurt you. Let me explain."

"What other secrets have you kept from me?" He fisted his hands.

"Nothing, man. You know all my crap."

With a slow hand, he held the letter up to read over it again. I watched his lips move as he read, looks of confusion, anger crossing his face.

He let the letter drop from his grasp, and it landed lightly on the carpet. His hands hung, as if suspended by chains, in the air. His mouth dropped open and his eyes closed.

"Henry?"

His eyes popped open, but he didn't speak for several agonizing seconds. Then he came after me. He got to his knees and threw a punch that connected with fury on my chin. Sparks lit up my eyes, and I landed on the carpet with a hard thud even though I'd been sitting. Blackness swirled around me but finally dissipated. I shook my head and attempted to stand up.

"You really are a piece of work, Billy. You have Amanda. Why would you take Sarah Ann from me? You have everything and you're trying to steal the one person I really care about?" He stood above me, looking much taller and bigger than he actually was.

"I'm sorry, man. I should have told you. Amanda said I should tell you. I didn't listen." I rubbed my chin. It stung and burned.

"You told Amanda about this?"

I shouldn't have said that. It must have been embarrassing to him and he wanted to contain that embarrassment. "Oh shoot, Henry, I..."

He huffed.

"Amanda just needs some time with you. She's always talking to me. She needs to talk to you. Tomorrow, she's going to discover how great you are. She doesn't really like me. It's you."

He shook his head, slow and steady, a murderous glow in his eyes and swift, short breaths pushing from his mouth and nose. "I need some time. Alone. Don't follow me."

He stalked out of my room, shoulders rounded and head down.

I rubbed my hands forcefully over my face again and again, not wanting to get up off the floor. Then I slapped my hands at my sides into the carpet, over and over again. Why hadn't I shown my best friend what I'd found? Guilt pressed on me. I was a bad person. I didn't deserve Henry's friendship. And I'd probably just ended it.

I rolled onto my side, grabbed the letter and tore it up in a violent fit.

I expected a visit from Henry, or at the very least, a phone call from him later that night. He was way mad. Feeling terrible and wanting to get my mind off of things, I started reading the book about investigations the librarian had given me until I fell asleep.

I dreamt of shadows coming and carrying me away into the darkness of hell as I kicked and screamed. When morning came, I couldn't find any joy in the prospect of going to the picnic or seeing Amanda, and it didn't even bother me that I'd slept in and missed the Victim's Advocate 5K run. I'd busted my butt to get as many donations to the cause as I could and had been one of the top five who'd brought in the biggest donations. I really wanted to be in that race, yesterday. Today, someone else could run. I wondered if Henry would call off the date or if one really even existed anymore since we never called Sarah Ann back. Had Henry? I should have at least done that, but what if he'd called the date off?

I busied myself with the chore list Mama had left me. She was already at the park helping with setting up some of the booths. She'd left me several thick slices of homemade bread, fresh honey butter and homemade raspberry jam. To the side lay a bag of venison jerky. I didn't have much of an appetite, but knew I'd hurt my mom's feelings if I didn't indulge. Once I started eating, the amazing taste of everything made me hunger for more.

I couldn't help but keep a constant watch on the clock as I worked. Would Henry ever yield? Maybe he expected me to come to him. At eleven, I made a few sandwiches and ate an apple to tide me over until lunch. I felt a twinge of guilt thinking about my mom finishing everything for us last night while I sulked in my room. I should have helped her until we were totally done. The rest of the grub was in a box on the counter along with everything to eat with: cups, plates, utensils and napkins.

Nausea overwhelmed me as I climbed out of the shower at noon, checking my message machine. Henry hadn't called. Maybe he had come over while I was in the shower. I looked for a note. Nothing was there. I fixed my hair and donned my dad's snakeskin boots, a newer pair of wranglers, my big black belt, and a Fourth of July T-shirt, hanging on to the hope that Henry would show.

It was already twenty after. Henry wouldn't be coming. Just when I was about to grab the food box, laden with all the great food my mom had prepared, and take it to Henry's for him to enjoy, I heard the doorbell ring. I raced to it and said, "Henr..." as I swung it open, but it wasn't Henry. It was Amanda.

Chapter 17

"Sorry to disappoint, but it's just me." Amanda rocked from one foot to the other, a nervous gesture.

I tried hard to erase that pang I felt and said, "You could never disappoint me." I pressed the best smile I could on my face, hoping she wouldn't see that lingering sadness I felt. I forced myself to look at her and not past her to search for Henry's car.

"Sorry, I'm being rude," I said, swinging my arm out and inviting her to join me inside. She looked out toward the street and my eyes eagerly followed. The big family van sat on the street at the edge of the sidewalk. I could see Henry's parents, sister and brother inside, smiling at us.

"Henry needs more time," she said, gravely. "But I didn't want to miss my date with the funnest guy around, and I hoped you wouldn't mind hitching a ride with his family."

"Wait a minute! Henry drove to pick up Sarah Ann? How did this happen?" Excitement and pleasure coursed through me. Henry was doing it.

"Pretty great, huh? It took a lot of convincing. I'll tell you all about it once we get to the park." She motioned with her head back out to the car full of anxious people.

"Yeah," I said. "Got it. Let me just grab the boxes of stuff and we can go."

She came with and carried one of the boxes despite my protests. I closed the door and turned to her. "Thanks for coming for me."

"No problem, big guy." She bounced down the steps and I followed, climbing into the car with Henry's family.

His mother smiled at me, a look of understanding on her face. "I don't know what happened between the two of you, but I'm sure you'll work it out."

"Yes, ma'am," I said, nodding with a quick jerk of my head.

Feeling my leg touch Amanda's sent a mad heat straight to my heart. I tried not to stare too long at her long, perfect legs, but fell short.

She pushed a long breath of air through her nose and looked at me with exasperation.

"Sorry, I-I..."

She just shook her head and frowned.

I leaned back on the bench and looked out the windows, the only way I knew I'd be able to control my eyes.

Once at the park, Henry's parents and siblings took off to do their own thing. That left me with an irritated Amanda.

She shut the doors of the van after I took out the boxes of supplies and food. She turned abruptly to me. "Look. I'll tell you what I told your bestie over there." She pointed to a spot in the park where Henry sat eating with the girl of his dreams. I smiled despite myself. "Girls don't like guys ogling their bodies. Your eyes should always be on a girl's face. Her eyes. No leg, boob, or butt staring. It's gross and makes us uncomfortable."

As she said *leg, boob,* and *butt,* I couldn't help but have my eyes take a gander at those very things.

She pressed her lips together and stuck out that mesmerizing hip.

She cleared her throat.

"What? I'm looking at your face."

"I said eyes, not lips."

What was up with her? This was our first date, and I wanted it to be perfect. We'd been getting along so well. Was she mad that I didn't follow her advice about the note and Henry and that our plans had changed? I'd make her laugh. That would do the trick. "Oh, you caught that, did you?" I tried to give her a little tap, but she moved away, annoyed with me. I thought I was being cute. "Fine, when I look at you, it will be in your eyes and nowhere else." I held up my fingers in the Boy Scout salute.

She reached up and grabbed my fingers, yanking them down. "Don't ever do that again, either." She looked around like a fox looking for the dog chasing it. Then she laughed.

I'd embarrassed her or at least did something with the potential of embarrassing her. A hot arrow seared through my heart.

"Do you have your hormones in check now or do we need to change your last name to Harris?" She had a glint in her eye, a hand on her hip. Out of the corner of my eye, I caught her biting her lip, and I worked hard not to direct my eyes to the action. I don't know why I'd lost control today. I tried to focus on all the reasons I thought she was great instead of what a killer body she had.

I nodded. I definitely didn't like to be compared to the Harris boys.

"All right, then," she said, grinning and grabbing my arm. "Let's go get a spot and have some fun."

As she dragged me, I searched for a spot with some shade potential. I found one spot, but I thought it looked too close to the tall grasses. I had no desire to get chiggers today. Instead, we opted for a spot that, at the moment, was directly in the sun, but would probably be completely shady within an hour. Henry had a great spot that would be in the shade the entire day. I couldn't help but stare. They were eating and talking. Henry was talking with Sarah Ann. Amazing.

"Sorry if I've been a little short with you today. It took all my strength to help Henry get out the door to pick up Sarah Ann. You sure did pick a terrible time to fight."

"You? Short?"

She punched me. "Really, I'm sorry."

"Don't worry about it. Thanks for helping Henry."

"He ditches you, and then you tell me thanks for helping him? You two...'"

I gave her a crooked smile. "I guess that's what happens when you've been best friends for forever."

She smiled and looked over at Sarah Ann and Henry.

"I can't believe what I'm seeing."

Amanda smiled. "You can't believe what you're seeing? You're not the one who had to help him get over his craziness. I wasn't sure I succeeded."

"Looks like you did. Good job."

"Thanks."

By the time the sun hid behind the trees, sending us into a nice, cool shadow, we'd finished our meal and cleaned it up. We walked around, checking out all the booths. When we reached my mom's booth, we could tell she was a bit overwhelmed, and we stayed to help her out. After about an hour, things slowed down and she asked if I'd go get some ice from the coolers in the main building where the dinner and dance was going to be held. Amanda stayed behind to help my mom, and I took off. When I left the building, ice in tow, I ran smack dab into Sarah Ann.

"Billy," she said, putting her finger on my chest. "You have been a very bad boy."

I did a quick shake of my head. "I have?"

"Yes...You told me you would be on this date with me and Henry and then, I discover you lied." She poked me with her finger repeatedly. I backed up and set the bag of ice on the steps.

"When I talked to you, that was the plan. Then things...changed."

"Obviously. But I'm not happy about it." She took the same finger that had poked me to run her finger up my chest and neck, along my jaw line and across my lips.

"Where is Henry?" I looked around and took a slight step back, my heel hitting into the steps. I was trapped.

"Back on our blanket. I told him I had to go to the loo and look what I found." She gave me a big smile.

I reached for the ice and said, "I've got to get this to my mom. It's melting." I held it up and water dripped to the ground.

"Did your *date* change too?" She pushed her body up to mine.

"Actually," I said, stepping to the side, "She's waiting for me at Mama's booth. Have you bought some of her fudge, yet?"

She huffed. "Billy. Are you daft?" Her chin jutted out and she tapped one of her feet.

"What do you mean?" I asked, looking at her foot.

She growled. "I only said yes to this date because I knew you'd be here. Didn't you get my letter?"

"Huh?"

"I wanted to spend time with *you*, not Henry." She tilted her head to the side and batted her eye lashes at me.

"I thought you liked Henry." I felt my face go hot.

"It's always been you." She moved closer, looking up at me.

"Sarah Ann, I'm sorry, but I don't feel that way about you."

She stiffened, eyes wide. "But, but..."

"Look Sarah Ann," I grabbed her elbow. "Henry really likes you. He's a great guy. Give him a chance." I tipped my head to the side. "Please." If Henry knew what was happening at that moment, he would die. And then he'd kill me.

She shrugged my hand off her elbow and after glaring at me, she ran away.

I shook my head and closed my eyes. What had just happened? I now had another secret from Henry. I had to push the experience away to the far back of my mind.

We spent another half an hour with my mom until she forced us to leave saying we should go have some fun. Grinning ear to ear, she slipped a twenty dollar bill into my hand as we left. We got a snow cone and some cotton candy with the money. Amanda was easy to be around. She made me laugh and feel comfortable with myself. I hardly noticed the hundreds of people surrounding us. After we'd looked at every booth a couple times, I realized we still had an hour and a half before dinner. I figured we needed about one hour to get ready, so that left us a half an hour to kill.

"Do you feel adventurous?" I asked. I thought she might like to explore a bit. Besides, it would give me the chance to spend some alone time with her. She must like me. She took my hand, after all. She must. Henry had been mistaken about her having a boyfriend. I hoped to be her boyfriend by the end of the day. What would it be like to kiss those perfect lips?

"Always."

"I thought we might go into the woods and look for some fun animals. We could play I Spy."

"Sounds good to me."

We headed for the truck.

"You have a cool truck," she said, grabbing hold of one side of the bed and springing up. "It's an '87 Chevy isn't it?"

"How'd you know that?" I crossed my arms.

"I know a lot of interesting little facts about all kinds of things." She gave me a radiant smile and threw her arms out to her sides.

"It was my uncle's baby, and when my dad died he gave it to us."

"Pretty cool. You're lucky. My parents won't allow me to have a car older than a few years. They say they aren't safe."

"Actually, this truck is probably one of the safest trucks around. It's a tank."

She laughed. The sound tinkled in my ears, sending a shockwave down my spine.

"But it's also a gas-guzzler."

"Tanks do take a lot of power to move, you know."

It was my turn to laugh.

"What now?" she asked as we got out of the truck and walked into the woods.

"I'm assuming you know the rules."

"But of course. I've known them since I was like two." She gave me a cocky smile. Then, she bounced around to face me, grabbing my other hand. "And what exactly are we going to be spying?"

I wanted the first thing to be easy so I said, "What is brown, with a fluffy tail and eats acorns?"

"A squirrel, maybe?"

"Why Amanda, you are quite brilliant."

She shook her head in disgust.

I reached into the cab and grabbed some bug spray from the floorboard. "First, we've got to put some bug spray on. We can't have you getting chiggers." I walked to the back of the truck. She was now standing behind it.

"Your woods here have chiggers?"

"Our chiggers are so big, you can see them."

"Really?"

"No."

She pushed me. I feigned falling dead on the ground. She stood over me. "You didn't know I was so powerful, did you?"

"Stay back you monster. I'd like to live to see the squirrel."

I stood up and sprayed her legs and then her arms.

"Ewww! That stinks," she said, scrunching up her nose.

"It has to be awful enough to keep them away. You smell too sweet, otherwise."

She smiled at that. I figured I had to be doing something right. I led her into the forest, hoping she'd take my hand because I was too chicken to take hers.

I spotted three squirrels before she even appeared to be looking for them. She jerked her head quickly to the side. "I think I just saw something."

I chuckled. "Was it small, brown, and scurrying in the trees?"

She punched me. "I don't know. I only saw it out of the corner of my eye. And it was fast."

"Oww!" I said, grasping my arm where she'd punched me.

We walked a good five minutes before she grabbed my hand and said, "It makes me sad that you and Henry are mad at each other." She looked at me with puppy dog eyes. "So, tell me," she said, grabbing my hand and making me temporarily lose all brain power, "Have you ever been in a fight before?"

"Sure, but nothing that's lasted more than a couple of hours."

"How long do you think he'll hold out on this one?" She squeezed my hand.

"I don't know. It was ugly when he discovered the note."

"I can imagine. I bet he was pretty mad." Her hazel-brown eyes helped me push some of the pain I felt about what happened away.

"I deserved it. I should have told him about it like you said.

"I'm guessing he felt betrayed?"

"He didn't really give me a chance to explain." I looked hard at her, her soft face calling to me to tell her everything. I pondered for a moment.

"He'll come around." She let go of my hand and made a cross with her finger in front of her heart. "You'll see."

Talking to Amanda always made me feel better. I couldn't believe how in such a short time, she'd become an absolutely essential part of my life. What was I going to do when she went back to Florida? Just thinking about it made my heart ache.

"Amanda—" I began, reaching for her hand, but the sound of a breaking branch caused us both to whip around, searching for the source of the sound.

My jaw dropped. It was Old Man Jack, crouching near a tree not twenty feet from us.

Chapter 18

The three of us froze in place, no one moving or making a sound. He looked worse than I'd ever seen him. His eyes were bloodshot, and his clothes were soiled. It looked like he hadn't had a decent meal or a shower in a month. Had he been living here in the woods all this time? Finally, Jack turned and started to run, but he couldn't move very quickly, one of his legs bent under him with every step, and he grunted in pain.

"Jack!" I called and started running after him, Amanda followed me close behind. "Wait, please, Jack! I have to talk to you."

He stopped and turned slowly to face me. The last time I'd seen him, he'd looked angry and bitter. Now, he only looked sad.

"Jack—please. I need to know what you know about my Daddy."

"Boy, ain't nothing I can tell you. I don't know who killed your Daddy."

"I heard you!" Anger filled every part of me. "I heard what you said to the chief—you know something! Tell me!"

Jack shook his head sadly. "I'm just a washed-up old addict, you just ignore me. The chief was right. I can't bring you anything but pain."

"No! What do you know? It was Tom Harris, wasn't it? I know all about it. Just tell me!" Desperation was creeping into my voice, but I tried to keep it steady, I needed to show more confidence than I felt.

A look of confusion passed over Jack's face. "Harris? You think this is about that fool Harris?"

"He wanted our land—he hated my dad. It had to be him. Why is the chief protecting him?"

"Boy, you are asking all the wrong questions. Why don't you ask who really stood to gain from your daddy's death? Ask yourself that. You'll get the answers." He turned and started to walk away.

"Jack! Wait! What do you mean? Please, tell me something! If you won't tell me about my daddy, then tell me what you saw at the Higby's!" That stopped him cold in his tracks. But he didn't turn. "I know you were there. I know what you saw."

Old Man Jack spat in the dirt. "Shoot, boy, you don't know nothin'. Why don't you go on back and listen to the Mayor tell his dirty lies."

"What do you mean, dirty lies?" Amanda demanded.

Jack just chuckled as he began to walk away. "Oh this is the safest and the best town. This is where we all want to be and live. Ain't we all just so happy happy happy. And the mayor, he's just got his fingers in all the pies. He's the happiest of all."

He kept babbling as he limped away from us. I started to walk after him, but Amanda held me back.

"He can't tell us anything, Billy. He's too far gone."

I watched him go, feeling bitter disappointment. I didn't even realize I was crying until Amanda raised one hand to my cheek and wiped away a tear.

"Billy?" she whispered.

"I'm fine," I grunted, wiping my face with the bottom of my shirt. I didn't want her to see me like this. "It's just bull, is all. That man knows something and all he gives me is that cryptic garbage." I kicked the nearest tree, sending bark flying. Amanda looked as if she wanted to say something, but I turned away from her and started walking back to the park. "Come on. Let's get back and listen to the speeches. I promised the chief I'd be there for his."

"Ok, Billy," Amanda said softly, and she slipped her hand into mine.

We walked back through the woods in silence, and I thought about what Jack had said. *Ask who really stood to gain from your daddy's death.* If not the Harrises, then who? And what he'd said about the mayor having his fingers in all the pies. What did it mean? Did it have anything to do with my daddy? Or Mrs. Higby? Bile rose in my throat, I was so angry. How could he not tell me what he knew?

"So, what are these speeches all about?" Amanda said softly. I could tell she was trying to lighten the mood and get my mind off Old Man Jack, so I smiled and tried to be light.

"Oh, well, you know—the mayor likes to make a big deal out of the Fourth of July celebration—it's the biggest event of the year in Halls, so he likes to take the chance to talk up the fact that Halls is still the number one safest city in Tennessee and on the top ten list of the national list for towns of its size."

Amanda looked impressed. "Really? That's a pretty big deal, I guess. One of the top ten cities in the nation? That's impressive."

"Yeah. Halls has been on the list for ten years now—the whole time Clement's been mayor. Putting in Bud—Chief McKnight—to run the police department was a pretty good move for him, I guess. Anyway, he likes to give a big speech, and he makes Bud give one, too. Bud doesn't really like it, but he's a good sport." I could hear clapping from the staging area. "Come on, I think they're introducing the mayor now. We can still make it to hear Bud's speech."

We pushed our way to the front, near the stage as fast as we could, and I tried hard to focus on the mayor's words, trying to figure out what Old Man Jack had been talking about. I hardly enjoyed having Amanda's soft hand in mine. We stood right next to the officers protecting the stage. Three were from Ripley and two from Dyersburg. Since people came from all the neighboring towns for the celebration, those towns pitched in police power. The mayor droned on about his dreams for Halls. Where were the lies? I said hello to one of the officers I recognized from the last few year's celebrations.

"Ah, it's Henry, isn't it?" he said.

"No. That's my best friend. I'm Billy." We had to talk loud and lean toward each other in order to hear each other.

"Oh, yeah, you're Chief McKnight's son."

"Not exactly, but it's good to see you here again."

"It's fun every year." The three within earshot of us snickered like it was some kind of joke and turned to talk amongst themselves.

"Halls is one lucky sucker," I overheard one of the officers say. "This place is packed every year. They must bring in the bucks."

Another from Dyersburg said, "How do they keep such clean records? Our meth arrests alone keep us off the FBI safest city lists."

"We have the same problem," an officer from Ripley agreed.

Mama had said she didn't want to leave Halls because it was so safe, that Bud told her meth was taking over in both Dyersburg and Ripley, and we seemed to be living in a bubble where crime never occurred.

I heard the word crime from the speakers and moved my attention to the mayor but still tried to hear what the officers were saying, too.

"A crime rate of 50?" the officer I'd talked to earlier said. "That's crazy good. We had a crime rate of 600."

As I listened, the seed of an idea formed in my mind. My daddy's death and Mrs. Higby's death had both been declared accidents, when there was enough evidence in both deaths that they should have been deemed murders. Other crimes had been ignored, gone uninvestigated or unreported. Was it all part of a plot to keep Halls' crime rate down, artificially? Is that what Old Man Jack had meant about the Mayor being the happiest one of all? Was he telling lies and hiding secrets in order to keep Halls' safety record clean? If so, why?

Another thought occurred to me. If the mayor was really hiding crimes, he couldn't be acting alone. The chief had to be involved, too. In all of it.

I looked at the mayor, stepping away from the pulpit and the chief moving forward to take over. A chill traveled slowly, steadily up my back. I didn't want to think the thoughts entering my head.

Amanda squeezed my hand and smiled at me. I smiled back, then turned my attention to Bud's speech.

"Thank you, Mayor Clement. It's hard to believe that I've given a speech on this very day for the last ten years. While I am more than pleased to accept this award, Special Agent Desoto," he said, turning and nodding to the representative from the FBI, "the real award should be given to you, the citizens of Halls." He made a wide sweep with his arms to the crowd. "Don't let the mayor convince you otherwise. That's why we've decided to use the money from this festival to directly benefit you. Of course, as always, we used some of the money for the fine fireworks you're about to see tonight." Huge applause erupted. "We are also replacing the equipment our dispatchers use. This will reduce the time it takes us to respond to your calls. So, to you! I raise my hat in honor to you!"

The roar of the thousands in the crowd was almost deafening. I looked at the mayor, who had moved up next to the chief, clapping loudly. He then raised his hands into the air and started a chant, "Halls. Halls. Halls." His eyes scanned the huge crowd, and his grin went from ear to ear. The crowd quickly caught on.

Could it be? Could they be working together to sham the FBI? The citizens? What was their motive? The chief melted into the background and left the stage while the mayor continued his chant.

Bud's eyes found mine as he exited the stage. He gave me a sheepish smile, like he was truly embarrassed. I nodded and gave him a thumbs up. I resisted the urge to run after him and question him. His speech had been short and sweet and to the point. Watching him walk away from the celebration made my gut hurt. It was the mayor Old Man Jack called a liar, not the chief. Frustration burned through me. Why couldn't he just have given me answers? A chill spread through my gut as I continued to stare at the mayor's jubilant face. The chief had been right. The mayor did love the spotlight.

"Let's get to the truck," I said. I wanted to tell Amanda about my theory. As soon as we were away from the crowd, I filled her in.

Her eyes grew wide. "Oh my gosh, Billy—You might be right! All those crimes are going unreported. The mayor and the chief have to know about them. But why?"

"I don't know, that's the part I can't figure out," I admitted.

"We've got to figure this out, Billy—what does the mayor stand to benefit from Halls having a clean safety record?"

"Reelection?" I suggested. "He wants to stay in power?"

"Makes sense, I guess. But why would the chief go along with it? What does he stand to gain? Maybe we could find a way to access his email account? Maybe there's some kind of communication between him and the chief about this?"

Amanda's eyes were filled with determination. I was hit with how astounding it was that this absolutely perfect girl was here with me, willing to do whatever it took to get to the bottom of this mystery. Suddenly, I realized what an idiot I was being.

"Amanda," I said, smiling. "Let's just forget about all this for now. Let's have fun tonight. You and me."

She grinned back. "You got it."

Chapter 19

All I could think about was holding her during the slow songs. I pushed the mayor and the chief and conspiracies out of my mind.

I dropped her off at Henry's, and I went to my house so we both could get ready for the dance. I was looking through my closet, searching for my best jeans, when I suddenly remembered the cover fee for the dance. I groaned. How could I not have thought of this before? I was just so excited to take Amanda to the dance, I forgot about how I was going to get her in.

Before I realized what I was doing, I held the ammo box in my hands. The stacks of bills were tantalizing. I could take one of the bills—no one would ever miss it, even if I did figure out who they belonged to. It was barely anything, compared to what was there.

Slowly, I closed the box. It wasn't right. Even though it hurt to do it, I put the ammo box away, and instead pulled out the money from digging Mr. Wallstrom's grave. I took three ten dollar bills and shoved them into my pocket. Mama always told me it was mine to spend how I saw fit. I still felt a pang of guilt taking it, but I had to get my date into the dance. I had to give myself a break. I changed into clean clothes and headed over to pick Amanda up.

Amanda was outside, waiting for me when I arrived. She snagged the door handle and jumped in the truck before I could get a good look at her or help her in. I didn't dare get mad at her. Instead, I said, "I'd love to get that door for you, Miss Impatient." She smelled so good. I couldn't believe I'd fallen for her in such a short time.

She looked honestly abashed and said, "Sorry. It really is hard for me to wait."

"Being here, in this town, I think your impatience tolerance will skyrocket."

"My parent's call it a sleepy little town with lessons galore to learn." She smiled.

I grunted and pulled out of the driveway.

"I didn't want to come, you know," she admitted. "I thought it'd be boring here. But I was wrong." I could tell she was looking at me, but I forced myself to keep an eye on the road.

"If I lived in Florida near the beach, I wouldn't want to come here either." Even after I said it, I wondered if it was true.

"Sorry." She sounded sincere. "I know this is your home."

"No apology necessary. I get it. It's a small town, and you're used to action."

We drove to the city park, pop music blaring. "I hope you realize the music that will be playing tonight will be mostly country." I gave her a crazy look to make fun of her.

"Guess I have to live with that. Might go home with a headache, but when in Rome, act like the Romans."

She had such a great attitude. I wondered if I'd like Florida. Would I like living in a big city? We had to park the truck a good distance away from the multipurpose room at the rec building where the dance was being held.

When I opened her door and she slid out of the car, I thought I might collapse right there on the pavement. I finally got to see what she was wearing for the dance. I took a sharp intake of air as her feet hit the ground. She wore a flirty, just-above-the-knee skirt with a silky, rust-colored, button-up that brought out the lighter flecks of brown in her eyes. A large, jeweled belt accentuated her tiny waist. I was the luckiest guy alive. I couldn't wait to spend the entire night alone with her, holding her and getting to know her even more. I made sure I made a cursory look that ended at her eyes.

"You look amazing, Amanda." I smiled, making sure I didn't look anywhere but her eyes. I wanted to make her feel like she was the most beautiful girl in the world tonight. Because she was.

"Thanks." She swung her hands in front of her and clasped them, bringing them to rest at her waist. "You don't look so bad yourself, cowboy."

I looked down at my boots and lifted the front of one, pushing my heel into the ground then nervously put my thumbs behind my belt buckle.

She smiled and I said, "The boots were my dad's."

"Cool. Why'd he give them to you?"

"When he died, I sort of inherited them."

Her face turned a bright crimson. "Sorry, I-I—"

"Don't worry about it. There was no way you could have known. It's ancient history, anyway." I pressed out a good smile and reached out in a sudden thrust of bravery to take her hand. I wanted to change the subject quickly so that she wouldn't feel uncomfortable any longer.

She squeezed my hand and gave me a sweet, toothy grin. "Let the country music play?" The inflection in her voice made it sound like a question.

"You'll recognize a few wild and untamed rock and pop songs, so don't faint. We can just go grab a treat or drink or something if you do." I smiled widely and led her toward the building.

"I was thinking, maybe we should hold our own dance out here, where we can live on the edge and choose as many of those devilish songs as possible. No one would ever know. What do you think, Howard? You up for an adventure on the wild side?"

I stopped and took her other hand in mine and said, "We could do that, but we'd have to spray ourselves with that awful bug spray again or the monster-sized mosquitoes will eat us alive. Do you remember how that smelled?"

She scrunched her nose up at the memory. "Alright, I guess we'll just have to really live it up when those few wild songs come on, to show our support."

I let go of one of her hands and then swung the one I still held back and forth as we approached the building. There was a small line and we joined the queue. After paying, we went straight for the food that lay on tables directly across from the entrance. We were starving. There was a mess of fried chicken, squirrel, okra, green tomatoes, baked apples, sliced pickled beets, and homemade macaroni and cheese. Amanda barely put anything on her plate. A few pieces of chicken and some mac and cheese. I'd seen her fill her plate up to overflowing more than once and had to ask about it.

"Not hungry?"

"It's not that." She tilted her head to the side. "I'm just not sure I'll like any of this stuff. What is it anyway?"

"What happened to, 'When in Rome act like the Romans?'"

"I guess that didn't include food. I'm a little picky when it comes to food."

I laughed. "That surprises me for some reason."

She shrugged, and we took a seat at one of the tables lining the walls.

"Maybe I can change your mind about a few things. You see, this here," I pointed, "is a fried green tomato. Mrs. O'Neal picks the tomatoes fresh off her farm and fries them up each year. They're great. You've got to try a bite." I cut a small bite and hung the fork in front of her face. Surprisingly, she moved toward it. Sure, her face was all scrunched up as she did, but then her face relaxed and she nodded her head. I guessed she liked it.

Once we had our fill, we headed out to the dance floor for a line dance.

"How are you at dancing?" I asked.

"I can hold my own."

"Ever line danced?"

"No."

"We'll stand in the second row while you learn the steps to this one. It's easier if you can watch someone."

"I'll watch you, then."

"It's hard to do if I'm beside you. If we're in the second row, you can just look ahead to know what to do."

"All right, but I don't plan to stay in that second row for long. I'm a quick learner, you know."

I laughed, thinking it was funny that she thought of it as a competition.

We got behind a few people I knew were savvy dancers. I scanned the crowd, looking for Henry. When it came to line dancing, he was always in the front row. Neither he nor Sarah Ann was there. Henry and Sarah Ann suddenly took their position on the front row. He was holding her hand and everything.

I wanted to ask Amanda how that happened, but it would have to wait. The music was roaring and everyone was starting to dance. She glanced at me before she started following the moves of the people in front of her. She did catch on. Of course I never looked at Henry and his date directly, only peeking through my peripheral vision. I found it a bit hard to concentrate.

By the second time through, Amanda knew the steps and was adlibbing her own special moves whenever possible. She was even shouting out with the rest of the crowd occasionally. I never thought this city girl would give in to country music and enjoy it. I loved how adaptable she was. I found myself checking out what Henry and Sarah Ann were doing more often than I liked. Even when our eyes met, Henry quickly averted them, acting like he didn't even notice me. It was like he was looking through me. It felt like a rock landed in my gut. I tried to ignore it and focus on Amanda instead. Whatever.

The next song was a slow one, *Best I Ever Had by* Gary Allen, "I know this song." she whispered. "At least the words. There's a pop version by Vertical Horizon. I like this version better I think."

My insides quaked as I pulled Amanda close to me, nothing separating us but our clothes. I thought I felt a tremble in her hand as she grabbed mine, and I hoped it was a good quiver. We didn't say a word as we made a tiny, almost imperceptible circle. I was transported into another world. I felt like we were all alone on a cloud in the sky and nothing would ever bring us down.

She smelled fresh and clean with a hint of ginger. Her hair smelled like strawberry pie. I breathed as much of her in as I could. I never wanted to forget the moment.

By the end of the fourth song, the room was markedly darker. The sun was going down. Soon there would be fireworks. Did I dare try and sneak a kiss? Would she want to snuggle with me under a blanket? I could only hope. Sometime later, the DJ announced that it was time to go out for fireworks and reminded us that after the fireworks, the dance would continue until three A.M. with sweet treats replacing the savory ones we'd had earlier.

We found our blanket and quickly took a seat. A second blanket sat folded at one edge. Even though it was hot, I hoped to use it later. We talked about what we did the last Fourth while settling in to wait for the show to start.

"I went to a concert in South Beach with McKay, my ex, at a stadium." She had a faraway look in her eye.

I wasn't sure I wanted to hear what she had to say if it had to do with another guy.

227

"The fireworks happened at the end. They were amazing, but I got a crick in my neck from looking straight up but other than that, it was great! Talk about a long ride home. It took forever just to get out of the parking lot."

"No worries about that here." I bumped into her arm, pretending not to care about the other guy. "We'll be home in no time." Besides, we were going to dance after the show and most left after the fireworks.

"I'm not sure I'd want to hurry home tonight." I could see her eyes sparkle in moonlight and a thrill shot through me.

The cannons boomed their warning of the imminent show of lights, power, and beauty. We lay back and she slid over to me, inch by inch until our sides were flush against each other's. The heat of her skin melded with mine like I was soldering in metal shop class. Shrieks of delight permeated the air as the first flashes of light filled the night sky.

As the show continued, her body seemed to melt further into mine, making us one. I couldn't and didn't want to fight the welling of desire for her. I turned my head with the hope she would turn hers to look at me. When she did, I moved in, slow and steady, hoping my lips would meet hers. Our lips touched, and for a moment, I thought she would press firmly against mine, but instead, she moved her head slowly away from me right after a gentle touch, and she even inched her body back. She didn't take her eyes off mine, though, and there was a sadness hidden in them. With a slow, even movement, she turned her head back to the firework show.

I wanted to crawl into a hole and die. She had full-on rejected me. I totally didn't get it. Hadn't her words, her actions showed me she felt the same as I did? I felt like a lobster with his pincers tied, hanging over a pot of boiling water. I would never recover from this. I'd lost my best friend because I was an idiot, now Amanda, too.

Just when I was going to be letting myself fall into utter despair, I felt her fingers touch mine. They slowly made their way to encase my hand. What could this mean? Was she teasing me, or was she telling me I was moving too fast? It didn't matter. My heart leapt into action, thudding like a horde of horses stampeding around a track. I didn't hold tightly, but I did let my hand hold hers. She may have rejected me, but I would not reject her. Not yet.

The show continued for another ten minutes, and then she inched back over and rested her head on my chest. I must have been moving too fast. She didn't want to kiss so soon. I could wait if I could have her this close to me all the time. I could definitely wait.

"That was amazing! Should we pack up and head for dessert?" she said, propped on one elbow.

I wanted to tell her to wait, that I just wanted to stay there, with her head on my chest a little while longer. I pushed myself up on my elbows to be level with her. "That sounds like a great idea."

She stood up and brushed herself off before grabbing the folded up blanket and pulling it to her chest. She spoke about all kinds of nonsense in rapid fire. It seemed the words she really wanted to say swirled around her, like she wanted to tell me something, but couldn't yet. I picked up the far two corners of the blanket and Amanda picked up other two, cradling the already folded blanket in the crook of her arm. Even folding the blanket with her was fun. When she moved in to give me her half, I desperately wanted to try that kiss again but held off, the sting of rejection still haunting me. She wove her fingers through mine as she handed it to me. I couldn't help but flick my eyes to hers. Those unsaid words swirled inside them, too, and I wanted to ask about them, but didn't.

Once we disentangled ours fingers. I took the blankets and carried them with one arm, firmly taking her hand in mine. She smiled up at me, her silky blouse billowing in the light wind. Outdoor lights popped on to help with the exodus. Most with small children were busy packing strollers and bundling already sleeping children in light, comfy blankets.

We stopped to pick up some of the debris and chucked it on top of already overflowing trash containers on our way to the rec center. A raging party was going on inside the building. The smell of alcohol and cigarettes wafted off the flailing bodies. Now that the majority of the young kids and parents were gone, the crowd had a more feral feel. The DJ seemed to pick up on that and played more edgy country and more pop music. While he turned the main white lights down, it seemed he'd added more rotating colored lights that bounced and jostled on the walls, ceilings and floors. He even turned the volume up. The walls seemed to pulse to the beat. Bodies danced close, hot and sweaty, swaying to the rhythm. The happy, lustful enthusiasm was contagious. No one could help but be drawn in.

Before we even made it to the floor, Amanda was already bouncing to the music. "Now this is what I call a dance party." She threw up her hands and screamed out, long and loud. I wondered how big of a party girl she really was. Was I even in her league?

She pulled me close then pushed me away all night long. We tasted every sweet treat that was offered us and drank about ten gallons of water that we desperately needed to stave off dehydration. We had pure, unadulterated fun for two sweet hours. At some point in the night, I noticed Henry, tucked away in a corner with Sarah Ann doing things I wished I was doing with Amanda.

It shouldn't have shocked me. He had laid the groundwork for almost eight years. That begged for success. But this was Henry. He couldn't even think about Sarah Ann without becoming a total river. And, only a few hours ago, Sarah Ann had come searching for me. Had Sarah Ann taken my advice and discovered that Henry really was a great guy or was she just using him?

"I can't believe that's Henry over there." I tilted my head in his direction. "Yesterday he couldn't even think of her without making a total fool of himself. What did you do? How did you get him to change?"

"First, I told him how amazing he was. The truth, by the way, and then I moved on to techniques to calm him when he got, you know, excited or nervous."

"I've been telling him how great he is for forever. It never made a difference."

"You're not a pretty girl, either." She looked at me pointedly. "You're his best friend. While he values your opinion, he knows you'd do anything to keep him from getting hurt. That's not to say he doesn't trust you. Typically, he does. Matters of the heart, however, require a woman's touch. He trusts that I know what I'm doing because I'm his target audience—a girl."

"Well, I'm grateful. The change in him is astounding."

"You may not be thanking me tomorrow as all the time you two have had together slowly disappears into nothingness."

I grimaced. "I've already lost him."

"Well, you won't be able to blame it on that letter. Now that he's with Sarah Ann, you won't have much time with him anyway. Especially if they are already going at it like they are."

I took another long look. Mixed feelings crowded my gut. Happiness for Henry tried to crowd out the cutting knives of despair of losing my best friend. I pulled Amanda close as the next slow song started, hoping to soothe the pain. Her soft skin and graceful movements lulled me into a sense of peace and security.

Despite the mostly frenzied movements of lights, sound, and bodies, by one-o-clock, Amanda and I opted to leave. I forced myself not to look for Henry, and focused on my date instead. A bit disheveled, she was even more stunning, a touch of wildness in her movements and look as we exited the building.

As the slightly cooler outside air hit us, she pushed her side hard into mine and I wrapped my arm around her waist, pulling her closer still. It was by no means cold. Tennessee was almost unbearable in July, day and night. My side heated up as if we were dancing a very slow song, and I knew I was sweating but didn't care. It was a strange sensation to want to share even your sweat with someone.

Nearing the truck, our temperatures equalizing, she pulled away. I opened the passenger side door and she slid inside. I practically skipped to my side. I thought about driving to a park and just hanging out with her, but she yawned and stretched as I started the car. The memory of her rejection earlier flitted through my mind, and I decided I should wait. The best things in life took time, right? I would be patient. I just wished I knew how she felt. Coming upon Henry's house, she reached out and grabbed my arm before I could get out.

"Wait." She shifted, moving her leg onto the seat of the truck and facing me. "About earlier..."

My face burned hot in that instant. All the feelings of inadequacy and hurt rushing there for her to see. I didn't want to hear what she had to say, or did I?

She moved her hand slowly to mine. She grabbed it and then bounced it on my upper thigh. This was not good. "I like you a lot, Billy. You've made coming here interesting, exciting, and fun, and I want it to stay that way." A few tremors shuttered through her hand and she took a firm hold of mine. "The thing is—I have a boyfriend."

My heart thundered in my chest and nausea swept through me.

"Well, I mean," she continued. "I did have a boyfriend. We broke up a few days before I came here. And the truth is, I don't know if I can get involved with anyone right now. I don't know if I can give all of myself to you or if I can even objectively say I like you."

Hot liquid seemed to spread through my limbs, turning them to a useless powdery ash. How could she deny what has happened between us? Our instant attraction? I couldn't look at her. I couldn't let her see my pain, my hurt when she felt nothing. Nothing real. I looked out the window.

"Don't," she said. "Please don't turn away. I just need some time. I'm sure you understand. It's not fair to you to jump into a relationship so soon after one ended." She tugged on my now limp hand.

Certainly, she didn't expect an answer. I didn't know if I could get my mouth to move, anyway, my teeth were clenched hard together.

"It's better that I told you, right? I don't mean to hurt you. I just wanted to be honest. To start our relationship out right. I think we have serious possibility, and I don't want to lose that...Please, say something." The tremble returned to her hand, and it made me glad.

I hoped she felt bad. I wanted her to feel what I was feeling: pain and hurt. With my teeth still clenched, I said, "Don't you think that when we met would have been the better time to tell me this?"

"What did you want me to say? 'Hey, guys, just so you know, I just broke up with the love of my life who turned out to be a two-timing jerk, and I don't know if I'll ever be able to trust another guy ever?'" She exhaled sharply.

I felt a bit of my hurt dissipate, but the pain was too great to be overcome, yet.

"You led me on." I pushed the words out with fury.

GRAVEDIGGERS

Her hand slipped from mine, and I could tell she was struggling to keep it together, but I couldn't move and go to her aide. The pain rooted me to the spot. I wanted to comfort her, but couldn't—or maybe wouldn't. I heard the click of the door and then she left. I'd never been so rude in all my life. My mother would be ashamed of me. I don't know how long I remained locked in place, feeling sorry for myself, but at some point my disappointment turned to anger again and I sped home.

Chapter 20

Mama was asleep on the couch like usual and even though I was tempted not to wake her, I knew it was what she wanted—what she expected.

She sat up immediately after I tapped her shoulder, a bleary-eyed look on her face. She'd been asleep a while. I sat next to her. She grabbed my hands. "Tell me everything." Her voice croaked with sleep.

"I'll tell you everything tomorrow."

She looked me over. I looked away. "You don't look happy. What happened?"

"I'd rather tell you tomorrow, if that's alright."

"I won't be able to sleep until you tell me." She nudged me with her hand.

I really didn't want to talk about it, but I had to. It was my mom asking. I took a seat.

She put her arm around me, grabbed my opposite arm and pulled me hard to her. Looking at my lap, I told her what had happened, the betrayal I felt, and how I didn't think I'd ever recover or be able to forgive Amanda.

"Sometimes it takes a lot of courage to forgive. But, it also takes courage to tell the truth even when it's going to

236

hurt someone. She must have real feelings for you or she wouldn't have been so honest. Give her a chance. I believe in you, Billy. You will find a way. If you don't, you'll always have bad feelings toward her."

I wished I could be as forgiving as she was, especially as I raced through the good times I'd had with Amanda. I couldn't believe she'd produced such strong feelings in me in such a short time. I hated and loved her for that.

As I undressed for bed, the scent of Amanda's perfume brushed past me several times. She was in my clothes, on my skin, and my lips. I fell asleep to an imagined Amanda in my arms, her forehead resting on mine. Sweet, but vague dreams followed.

When I woke, my mom was already gone to work and my list of chores sat on the table next to a bowl and a cereal box. After retrieving the milk from the fridge, I poured a bowl of cereal and dug in and looked of my list of to-dos. The list was long, and I'm sure she was trying to keep my mind off things. I realized I didn't tell her what was going on between Henry and me. What would her words of wisdom be? I felt helpless. I'd already apologized and tried to explain. There was nothing more I could do. Now, he needed to come to me.

Before I could do any of my chores, I wanted to go over the evidence we'd collected. Now that I was on my own, I wanted to make sure I didn't overlook anything. I could work on the solution while I did my chores.

I took out the evidence charts and wrote down the things I'd found out about the mayor and the chief and Halls' crime rate at the celebration. I also wrote down the stuff Old Man Jack said.

I pulled out the package with the gun from behind my desk. I felt alone and scared. How could I solve these two mysteries on my own? After pulling on gloves, I dusted for fingerprints, but it was clean. The murderer had wiped away any evidence. Another dead end. Leaving my gloves on, I copied the serial number down on a sheet of paper. I'd have to think of a way to talk Bud into running it for me. I'm sure Amanda would have had a great idea to make it easy. I'd have to figure it out on my own.

I pulled out the box from under my bed and fingered each mysterious piece, one at a time. The antique key called my attention: we still hadn't figured out what it could be. I wondered why there was one just like it at Henry's house and wished I could just ask him. I sighed and put it down. I'd have to figure that out at some point.

I put the ammo box away and pulled out my list of evidence from my dad's case. My eyes traveled the list, hoping some inspiration would hit. I was about to give up on that, too, when my attention caught on my description of the men's watch. The watch! Maybe it would have some initials or an inscription or something. I needed to look at the pictures from the evidence box. I hoped Amanda thought to turn the watch over. I placed everything back and went to do my chores. When I was done, I'd have a few leads to follow up on.

I hurried through the work and then headed for town just after lunch to ask Bud to run the serial number from the gun. I decided the best thing to say would be that I was considering buying a gun and needed the serial number checked to see if it had been stolen. It was a long shot and might not pass his scrutiny, but I had to try.

I sat hard on the nearest bench, the wood feeling like it was digging into my bones. A horrible headache hit me full on, and my mouth went dry. I didn't know if I could look at Bud knowing that I suspected him in covering up crimes, but it was the only way.

I saw the chief getting into his car. I rushed up to him, and he rolled his window down.

"Hey!" I said, not knowing what else to do.

"I saw ya at the celebration with that pretty little thing." He smiled.

How could he be involved? He couldn't. Bud was almost like a father to me. Back when he was investigating Daddy's death, we'd seen him all the time, and even after—he looked out for me. He'd stepped in for all the father and son activities at school and in the community, and he'd comforted me like any true father would when I was down. He was a completely decent human being, and I loved the time we got to spend together. It was sad to think it could all be over. A horrible thought struck me. Had he pretended to be my father because he felt guilty?

I shifted from foot to foot. "Yes, sir." I had to bite my cheek to keep from babbling.

"You like her, don't cha?"

"Yes and no, sir." This wasn't going how I had planned, and I really wanted to tell him everything like usual, but there were too many secrets between us now.

"What kinda answer is that?" He reached over and turned his radio down and the cool air up.

I stared at the police department now. "Well, sir. I think she's the best and worst thing to ever happen to me." The gun flitted through my mind, and I couldn't help but squeeze the paper in my hand.

"Well, that's the same thing you said a minute ago, just with different words." He waited. I still didn't look at him. "Why don't you tell me what's going on with her?"

"I'd rather not, sir." I felt my face flame at the thought, and I was afraid I'd spill my guts about the gun if we had an extended conversation. I cleared my throat.

"You know what I always say, sometimes it helps to talk it out with a friend."

Was he my friend? I wasn't sure anymore.

"Together, we might be able to find a solution you hadn't thought of before. And, as always, your secret is safe with me."

I knew what he was saying was true, I just didn't know if I could handle telling him. I was embarrassed, and I didn't know where I really stood with him. Was I a charity case, used to soothe his conscience?

"In a nutshell," I stammered, figuring the fewer details I gave away, the less emotional I would become. "We had a great time until she told me she had a boyfriend. Well, not really a boyfriend, but a recent ex-boyfriend."

"Oh is that it, huh?" he said. "I wouldn't have pegged her for taken or recently un-taken. I saw her as a girl smitten with you."

"So did I. I feel like a total idiot." I grimaced.

"I suspect she was smitten, Billy. I bet she was just afraid. Sure-as-shooting, she'll come running to ya when she comes to her senses. That girl either liked you or is a very good actress—and I'm betting on her liking ya." He patted my hand that gripped the door.

The problem was that she was a great actress. I just stared at the ground, knowing he would most likely see that I was hiding something from him.

"Look, I've gotta go talk to preacher Higby."

I popped up at the mention of his name. "Did something happen?" Was he reporting the stolen ammo case? Would Bud put two and two together and realize the fingerprints I asked him to trace came from an ammo case? Maybe I should just be out with it and get it over with. I'd confess before the pastor could expose me.

"You might say that. Apparently someone's vying for your job, digging holes on church property without permission."

My skin tingled all over. "What?" The word shot out of me like a bullet but with a pitch high and squealing. It wasn't about the box after all—or was it?

"I'm sure it's nothing. Probably just kids hoping to find buried treasure or maybe a skeleton. Don't worry about it."

I wanted to be quiet, but couldn't. I blurted, "It must be something if he reported it, though." I fought my legs, forcing myself to stand still.

"I guess I'll find out, won't I?"

I nodded, pressing my lips into a hard line, pretending not to be interested anymore. "Thanks for the advice. I hope you're right."

"You just wait. It won't take her long to come running back to ya."

I nodded, pushing air out my nose.

"Did you come to tell me about what happened or is there something else on your mind?"

"Actually, I was wondering if you could run a serial number for me. But I see that you're busy."

"Go in and have Maureen call Olsen in to help you. Okay?"

"Okay. Thanks."

I worked through the possible downside of involving Olsen. He'd always been discreet. He hadn't even told the chief I'd taken Amanda into the evidence room. Hopefully, he wouldn't say anything if he suspected something.

Maureen called Officer Olsen and then sent me back to his cubicle.

"So, you need a serial run? Looking to buy a new gun or something?"

"Yes, sir," I lied.

He punched the numbers into the computer and after only a couple minutes, the results popped up. I couldn't see the screen, but when Olsen frowned, I knew something was wrong. "Billy, who's selling this gun?"

"Some guy from Dyersburg," I said, scrambling.

"Are you sure that's the right number, because it comes up as stolen."

"Stolen?" I looked at the back of the computer, wishing I could catch a glimpse of the screen and trying to plaster a confused look on my face. I had to know what was on it. I pushed my hands into my pockets to stop the shaking. "Let me see. I must have told it to you wrong." I pretended to fish for the number. How could I get the information from the screen?

"Who was it stolen from?" I tried to be nonchalant about the question.

He shook his head back and forth. "Pastor Higby, of all people."

I stopped scrounging around in my pocket and said, "What?"

"Higby reported it stolen nine years ago. Wouldn't that be something if we just recovered it for him?"

"Wouldn't that be something," I muttered, my brain working overtime.

"You have that number in your pocket? Let's check it to make sure." He looked eager, leaning toward me in anticipation.

"Oh, yeah." I fished around for the paper and after finding it, held it up and said the number back to him, transposing two numbers in the process.

"Now that's a different story," he said after a few minutes. "That gun is clear. Amazing the difference one number makes. Good thing we double checked."

"Yes, sir," I said, my heart continuing to race. The gun was reported stolen around the time Mrs. Higby died in her so-called accident. I was more sure than ever that her death was not an accident. There was too much shady evidence—the bleach smell on the scene, the disappearing note, the blood spatter. The reporter we'd spoken to—Jay Heath—had said he expected a gunshot wound, and now I'd found the gun that must have caused it. Maybelle Higby must have been shot in a robbery gone wrong—the thief had killed her and gotten away with the jewels and the gun. But, why would the pastor allow the police to say it was an accident when his gun and property had been stolen?

"Thanks. Thanks a lot."

I got out of there as fast as I could. I needed to think.

The implications of the gun being hidden in a P.O. box in town didn't escape me. Sure, an outsider could have put it there, but it was most likely someone from Halls. I had to find out who rented that P.O. box. Was that even possible? Only one way to find out. I'd go and ask at the post office.

The postmaster said the receipts for P.O. boxes were private and he couldn't tell me anything. As I left the building, I found myself looking for alarms and cameras. I could only see one. Could I get into the main office without being caught on camera? I shook my head. Was I crazy? Did I really think I could break into the post office? The records I needed were probably in the computer, and I'd never be able to crack the password anyway. I wished people still used filing cabinets. Then I thought about Amanda and how if she had been there, she'd probably have been able to get the information out of him, and I wouldn't have to be entertaining criminal thoughts.

My mind whirled like a hurricane as I walked back home. I didn't even care that I most likely looked like a freak talking to myself the whole way. This mystery kept taking turns I wasn't ready for.

To my utter amazement, Amanda stood on my doorstep when I got home. I stopped at the edge of the property and stared. Her back was to me, and she was knocking. She must've just arrived. When she turned to leave, she saw me.

"Billy," she said.

Bud's words raced through my mind. "She'll come running to you." He had been right. I pulled myself together in one quick inhale.

"Hey!" I barked out a laugh, giving her a big grin and making my way around her to open my door, but not moving to the side to let her in. I wanted to so bad. Why was she here? I stared openly. All the bad feelings I felt for her rushed out of me, and all I wanted to do was be with her.

"Hey." She bent one knee and leaned to the side, while she fidgeted with her hands at her at her waist. She smiled brightly, with a hint of shamefacedness. "Can I come in?"

She'd asked, so I said, "Sure." I tried to make my face impassive, not letting her know how excited I was that she'd come.

We went into the living room and when she sat on the couch, I sat on the chair opposite her. I didn't think I could hold myself together if I sat right next to her.

"I've been thinking a lot about the stuff we saw in your dad's evidence box."

That wasn't what I expected. I sat back. Pressing into the back of the chair. "Really?"

"Yes." She put a large sack on the table and pulled out a stack of 8X10 pictures.

"Okay." I was starting to get mad. My chest burned, and not in a good way. Did she forget that she made a total fool out of me just yesterday? Was she trying to make amends by bringing me these pictures?

This was not going how I'd thought our first meeting after last night would go. She wasn't running to me or even acknowledging what happened between us. I tried not to glare at her but I'm not sure I succeeded.

"Old Man Jack seemed to think Harris wasn't involved, so I think we need to go over our suspect list again. We should go through and cross off everyone who had a valid alibi. We could probably narrow down—"

I couldn't wrap my head around what she was saying. A heat spread to my face and I was sure it was turning red. "Um. I'm sorry. I can't seem to understand what you're saying."

She let her head hang, her hair hiding her face and her shoulders curling forward.

"Look, Amanda," I said, not knowing where my courage was coming from. Perhaps my anger was taking over. For some strange reason I cracked my knuckles. I never did that. "You really hurt me last night. I don't know if I can pretend that didn't happen."

She raised her head slightly, and I could see splotches of red climbing her neck. My pinched expression eased a bit.

"I'm really sorry, Billy."

"That's not going to cut it." I couldn't stop myself. I had to know how she really felt about me. "Do you..." I wanted to look away, but at the same time had a perverse desire to see, so I stared directly at her. "Do you feel anything for me or was I misreading everything that happened between us?"

Her eyes met mine in one quick burst. I cocked my head and raised my eyebrows.

"You didn't misread anything. I do have feelings for you, but..." She looked back at the floor. "I'm scared."

A lightness entered my chest. She had feelings for me. The chief had been spot on. Warmth radiated through my body, and my heart drummed in my chest. I got up from the chair and crossed the room to sit next to her hoping her eyes would find mine again. She had wrapped her arms around herself.

GRAVEDIGGERS

My grin disappeared quickly as I reached out and lifted her chin up. A tear dripped from her eye and rolled down her cheek and onto my finger. She shook her head slowly, back and forth as more tears fell. She pushed past my hand on her chin and snuggled up close to me, wrapping her arms around me and sobbing. I wasn't sure what to do, so I put my arms around her, too. Her body jumped with each sob.

Soon, the crying stopped and she pulled away, wiping at her eyes and nose. I hurried over to the coffee table and grabbed some tissues for her. She dabbed at her eyes and blew her nose.

"Sorry," she said between heaving breaths, the residual of a good, painful cry. "I just don't want to get really attached, ya know?" She looked up at me then, her face red, her eyes puffy. "It's scary. What happened with McKay—it was really hard on me. He made me believe he had real feelings for me, and then he cheated on me. I was completely shocked and hurt, and then—my parents just sent me here. They always seem to pawn me off on someone else when I'm dealing with stuff. My mom doesn't know how much I want her around. And you...you live in Tennessee. It's so far away."

I pulled her to me. "I understand that you're scared. I'm sorry. Maybe we can focus on the time we have together and see where it leads. If it's something we want to continue after you go home, we'll make that happen. Come on. Let's sit down." We sat on the couch until she calmed completely down.

"Do you forgive me for being such a mess?" She took in a big breath.

"Nothing to forgive," I said, surprising myself.

She hugged me, and I gladly hugged her back. Holding her felt right, good. I didn't want to let her go.

She pulled back and smiled. The dimple showed up. I loved that dimple.

"Let's not waste another minute on my silliness. Let's get the mysteries solved."

Chapter 21

I nodded and we went to my room and grabbed the evidence charts we'd made for both murders. It felt so good to have Amanda with me again, helping me sort all this out. First we looked at the evidence from my dad's murder. We crossed off everyone that was cleared in either witness interviews or statements, but were sure to cross them off with a yellow highlighter. We weren't positive we should trust the statements and interviews considering who wrote and took them. What if they'd been tampered with? We put stars by the names Lee Clement and Tom Harris, deciding they were still our best suspects.

"Hey, did you take a good picture of the watch in my dad's box?" I asked.

Amanda flipped through the pictures and pulled out a small stack. "Yeah, I got a bunch," she said, handing them to me.

"Awesome," I said, grinning. I looked at each picture of the watch, but there was nothing distinctive about it. No inscription or anything, anyway. It was just a plain, silver men's watch.

"Anything interesting?" Amanda asked.

"No," I sighed. "Nothing new here."

"Sorry, Billy. Why don't we put this away for now, and see if we can figure out anything on the Higby case"

We pulled out the chart for Maybelle's murder. I told her about how the gun belonged to Pastor Higby and how it had been stolen. It felt great to rule out Pastor Higby as a suspect. We spent a good couple of hours organizing everything.

I stared at the pile of evidence, feeling overwhelmed. "What do we do now?"

"Well, let's think about what we know."

I sighed. "We really don't know much. We know the mayor covered up Maybelle's murder, but we don't know why. We know Pastor Higby let them cover it up for some reason. We know that Harris and Lee Clement, among others, hated my dad. We know there was an earring and a watch found on the scene. We know whoever did it probably had a broken windshield and a smashed fender. The mayor had a car with similar damage fixed around that same time, and the Harisses have a smashed up truck. That's it. "

"That's not nothing," Amanda said encouragingly.

"It feels like nothing." I threw my hands in the air. "It feels like we're getting nowhere. We need to know more, we need to, I don't know—talk to someone who was there. But no one was there except the killer."

Amanda's eyes lit up. "We do know someone who was there!"

"We do? Who?"

GRAVEDIGGERS

"The mortician was on the scene—it says so right here in the accident report." She waved one of the 8X10 pictures in front of me.

"All right, let's go talk to the mortician." I stood up.

"Hold your horses. Are we sure the mortuary is open?"

"It's J.T. Nilson. He'll be glad to talk to us. He's always open. Old as the hills and could retire, but he loves it. It's all he does, and he loves people to visit him. He's always one of the last people to leave the church luncheon on Sunday. While we're there, we can ask him about Maybelle Higby, too. Maybe he can shed some light on that, as well."

We made sandwiches before heading off to talk to Mr. Nilson. It was already past five. Once we got to his office, which doubled as his house, I rang the bell and whispered, "Just be ready to stay for a while. He loves company, and I haven't talked to him for some time."

She didn't even roll her eyes like I'd expected, but she did wink.

He opened the door. He was in an impeccably cared for dark suit, devoid of wrinkles. His teeth were stained yellow from years of drinking coffee and tea. He took a quick step forward and said, "Billy! It's been forever. Come in, come in." He stepped back and pushed the door open further, motioning with his arm for us to enter.

His parlor was decorated in the fashion of the fifties, but was neat and clean. Everything had its proper place, and he must have dusted right before we entered. Everything gleamed in the light, from the crystal to the dark, shiny wood of the furniture.

"What a great parlor," she said. "Did your wife decorate it?"

"Have a seat," he said. "She did. She had superb taste, don't you think?" He sat up straight in his chair—rigid.

"Oh, I'm sorry, I didn't know." She looked at me for support.

I smiled and put my hand on her knee. I should've warned her.

"No apology necessary. She lives on in this room. It's beautiful. Just like she was."

While it was nice that he was honoring his wife, it was also a bit creepy.

He told us a few stories about her and then described how she got cancer and died while still beautiful, in her sleep.

"I buried her under the big walnut tree in the cemetery. We actually bought adjoining plots right after we settled here. We knew we wanted to stay here together forever."

"Do most people buy plots that early in their marriage?"

"Many do, but I wouldn't say most. It's a great way to be on top of estate planning." He was selling us now.

"What about here in Halls?" Amanda asked.

"I'd say most of the old timers have already bought their plots, but I've discovered the newer generation doesn't seem to value that."

"What about cremation?" Amanda asked. "Do most people write in a will or something how they want to be interred?"

"If a person has a will, yes. Most don't have wills, though. It's quite shocking." He gave me an odd look and said, "You thinking about cremation, Billy?"

"No, sir, I mean, I don't know, maybe."

"Well at your age, son, it really wouldn't matter what you put into a will. You need to be eighteen to have a binding contract."

"It won't be long until I am eighteen."

"Well, I think it's mighty smart of y'all to think about a will at such a young age. You know—"

"Well, we wanted to do some research about that, actually," Amanda interrupted.

What was she up to? We should have talked about a plan before we came. I wished I could read her mind so I could help her. I wrung my hands.

"You'd be best to talk to a lawyer about that."

"But," she continued, "we thought you'd have the inside scoop about how wills really affect what happens when people actually die. You see firsthand what goes on with the family and stuff."

"Well," he licked his lips nervously.

What the heck was she doing?

"What I mean is, have you seen that it is better to spell it out in a will how you want to be interred or does that cause stress on the family having to carry out your wishes. And can't the family just do whatever they want?"

"Well, I, uh..."

Now I understood what she was doing. She would go through the backdoor making him think we were asking general questions about wills and work her way to the truth.

"Yeah," I said, "I mean, I heard that Mrs. Higby had a will and it wasn't followed."

"Well, I don—"

"She wanted to be buried and not cremated. But, she was cremated, wasn't she?" I kept my voice light, with no accusation, just wonder. "I'm sure I saw two full plots for both her and Pastor Higby in Higby's cemetery records."

"I don't know why anyone would be cremated," Amanda said. "Not to offend, but cremation creeps me out."

"Why not ask the Pastor?" J.T. asked, his eyes skirting the room, like he was trying to process too much information.

"I don't want to upset him by making him think of her." Amanda picked at her pants.

"It's been a long time. I bet he'd like talking about her again, although, if I'm thinking right, the anniversary of her death is right around the corner." J.T. sat up even straighter, steepled his index fingers, and put them to his lips.

"Well, you talked to the pastor, didn't you?" I asked. "It was the only way you'd know what to do with her body. Did he refer to a will?"

"No." He shook his head. "I didn't handle the cremation. Someone from Dyersburg did. Not sure why. Maybe because they were trying to avoid the middleman. I would've given him a special deal, though." He crooked his thumb under his chin and his index finger over his mouth and under his nose. "I never did understand that. In fact," He sat back up, excited about something, "I remember overhearing the chief convincing Mr. Higby to cremate. Yeah. I never even saw the body. Come to think of it, I remember hearing the chief reassuring Mr. Higby in this very parlor that he did in fact want her to be cremated when the mayor called to say the body was going directly to a crematorium. The chief said he would provide the urn her remains are now in." He sat for a moment tapping his index finger on his chin.

GRAVEDIGGERS

The mayor and the chief. This didn't sound good. I was mentally cataloguing all the information that was flooding out from J.T. making sure I didn't miss a beat.

While I sat in thought, Amanda asked him about other deaths and the procedure that had been followed. The tone in Amanda's next question made me look up.

"One other thing." Amanda glanced at me and licked her lips. I could only guess what was coming. "Billy and I were talking about his dad's death, and I was wondering if you could tell me the story. He has a hard time telling me and said you'd be the best to ask."

He looked at me, a sharpness in his eyes. "About his burial?"

"Actually," she said, shifting in her seat. "Could you tell us everything you remember?"

He took a deep breath in.

"Maybe you should ask your Mama about this, Billy, I don't..."

"We've tried, but she doesn't like to talk about it. She did say you were a great source of comfort to her. She'd trust you to tell us what she can't seem to do right now."

He looked at me, his eyes searching my face as if it held the permission he needed. I tried to look earnest.

"I'm assuming this has to do with that history you're writing about your dad?"

"Yes, sir," I said. "How did you know about that?"

"I heard you talk about it at the Sunday luncheon. Well, I'd be glad to help tell you what I know." He leaned back in his chair, and his voice changed slightly, taking on a rumbling quality. A story-telling voice. "A terrible storm slammed down

255

on us the afternoon his father was killed. It was brief, but awful. As I remember it, Mr. Howard went out to get their goat who'd been crying out in fear. I guess that goat was so afraid, she'd somehow come loose from her chain and had wandered into the deep ditch on the other side of the street. Nick went to collect her and he got hit by a car and died on the spot."

"Did they do an autopsy?" Amanda asked even though she knew the answer.

"No need. They knew exactly what killed him."

"What did Mrs. Higby's autopsy say?" I asked, unable to help myself.

"I have no idea, son. I never saw the body, remember? But, I'd bet there was no autopsy."

"Why not?" Amanda asked.

"Well, she'd fallen off that ladder. There wasn't a question about how she died."

"What if she didn't die from the fall? What if something else killed her?" Amanda looked distraught.

"We just do what we're told. If the mortician had seen something that led him to believe it was anything but an accident, he would have been obligated to report it. No report was ever filed."

"I like to watch those crime shows, CSI and stuff. I think this is all so fascinating. On those shows, it's never just a death, and they always do an autopsy."

"TV isn't real life, young lady." He shook his head. "Everything I am privy to about Mrs. Higby's death, which wasn't much, was that it was an accident. Nick Howard's death, on the other hand, left me with lots of questions." He turned to me. "I'm sorry, Billy. I just don't understand how all the leads came to naught. It breaks my heart that you never got any closure."

"Do you always—" Amanda began to say.

I interrupted her. "I didn't realize that all bodies didn't automatically get autopsies."

"Nope. Only ones where the cause of death is under question."

"TV really does make it look like everyone gets one, no matter how they died," Amanda said.

"TV portrays most things incorrectly to some extent. It's quite annoying. They make the police and coroners look like magicians or idiots depending on what suits the story. Results on most things take weeks and weeks, not minutes or even hours."

"You're right. Shows do make it seem like you guys are superhuman or something." I gave him a pressed smile.

"It's not lost on me that this must be a difficult time for you with the anniversary of your dad's death just around the corner. I wish I had answers for you, but I don't."

We sat in silence for a good minute before Amanda's leg started pumping up and down. She was getting impatient.

"I still can't believe," Mr. Nilson said, "they never found the match to that earring they found clutched in your dad's hand."

Who was the one that found the earring? I shook my head like I knew about it. "Me either." I glanced at Amanda.

"I figured that piece of evidence would break open the case. All it takes is one thing like that. Hard to imagine it was a woman, though. You'd think a woman would stop and help the person they hit."

"Maybe it means it wasn't a woman." Amanda squinted her eyes.

I needed to talk to Bud. I would make him tell me about that night. I would ask him about the earring and the lack of an autopsy. I would come right out with it. Then, I'd ask him about Mrs. Higby, too. Having this new information, I didn't want to stick around for one more minute. I stood up. "Thanks for helping us with our research. I really need to stop by more often."

"That's right. You do." He walked us to the door. "If you need more information before writing up your will, just ask."

"Thanks again," I said as we descended the steps.

Once I heard the door shut, I turned to Amanda, who punched me, hard in the arm. "I almost had him and you interrupted."

"I thought he was telling the truth. I don't think he was a part of the cover-up. But, I think I know who most likely was."

Blood rushed hot through my body, and I wanted to go see him right then. Fury raged in my brain. It registered that Amanda was there and talking to me, but I couldn't seem to make anything out. I was on autopilot and ended up at the gate to Bud's walkway. I reached out to grab the gate and open it, but Amanda's hands clamped down on my arms and pulled me back.

She came into focus, and her words started to make sense. "It's late, Billy, and you can't go talk to him now. He's probably in bed and we don't want to tip our hand. We want him to tell us everything. That's not going to happen if we go in accusing him. We need to think this through."

I relaxed my handhold on the gate. She was right. It was almost ten. The chief was known for his early-to-bed-early-to-rise lifestyle. If I had any hope of getting to the truth, I'd have to calm down and not ask him directly. I needed to be able to hide the betrayal I was feeling.

My hands shook as I turned to go home. I would have to go behind his back to uncover the proof of his dirty deed. He had the power to suppress evidence, sway me. And he had. He would pay for what he'd done.

It was dark as we walked home and my anger boiled inside me. I had to think of something else or I'd explode.

"How's Henry?" I asked.

"A little lovesick." She frowned.

"Huh?"

"Sarah Ann."

"What about her?"

"Well, she won't return his phone calls or texts, and we saw her in town today and it looked like she turned and went the other way after she saw us."

I thought about her totally making out with Henry at the dance last night. My eyebrows pinched together thinking about it. The note and meeting her outside the ice house filled my mind.

"I think she's a skank. I could kill her for doing this to him." She was totally serious. "If she hurts him more than she already has, I won't be able to control my temper."

Could she have really used Henry last night? "You have a temper?" I teased, hoping to lighten the mood. I hoped she was just busy this morning and he'd been able to reach her this afternoon.

"I think she made out with him to make you jealous." She raised an eyebrow and stared me down.

"Huh?" I said, hoping she wasn't right.

"You heard me. Did something happen last night that I didn't know about?"

I didn't dare tell her the truth but I didn't want to lie.

"I was with you all night."

She smiled. "Maybe she suddenly got cold feet or something. But it still doesn't excuse her behavior. She should tell him she has cold feet and doesn't want to go out with him if that's it." She stopped and turned to me, squishing up her face. "He's really hurting, Billy. You should go see him."

"I'll just make him mad."

"No. He totally needs a friend. He misses you. He needs his best bud." Her hand reached for my arm, but then she drew it back.

A painful stab went through my chest. I pushed down the emotion creeping up inside me and thought how great it would be to have him to talk to about Amanda. I wondered if she'd told him what she was thinking about me. Had they laughed about it? A twinge of hurt reached out and punched me. We turned onto Henry's street, and I walked her to his door. I wanted to go in the house but couldn't make myself. I'd told him everything. He wouldn't take it well if I, out of the blue, showed up. I knew him. He needed to work through everything before he could forgive me. Sarah Ann ignoring him was complicating things.

"Just come in," she said, giving me a pouty look.

"Not happening. I know Henry, and if he hasn't come to me, then he's not ready. I'm ready, but he has to be, too."

She nodded, her lips pressed hard together. "See ya tomorrow, then."

"See ya tomorrow."

I hurried home, eager to fall into my bed and pass out. When I got there, however, Mama was waiting up for me.

She smiled a sad little smile. "Billy, you got another job."

"What do you mean?" Did another neighbor need my help? Sure I was thankful, but all these distractions were getting exasperating.

"Another grave to dig. Jack Pitt was found dead tonight. They think he drank himself to death."

Chapter 22

I swung the shovel over my head, tossing the dirt onto an already two-foot pile behind me. I'd arrived before it was even light to start the grave. Maybe I could finish it before Henry arrived as a sort of peace offering.

Much to my surprise Henry showed up just after dawn. We glanced at each other and then he looked at his feet and kicked at the dirt at the rim of the hole, shovel in hand. I moved to the side and he threw the stepladder in the hole and then jumped in.

There were so many things I wanted to say, I just didn't know how. I felt a strange mix of excitement, fear, and anticipation. I held my breath, and my mouth turned dry. I wanted my best friend back.

He hit the shovel into the dirt and then turned. "Look, Billy. You should have told me about the note." He looked at the bottom of the grave.

My head bobbed in a furious motion, hope seizing me. "You're right. I just—"

"Hear me out." His eyes lit on mine for the briefest moment and I stopped talking. "I think you kept it from me because you thought I would freak out. And I probably would have. But, stuff like that...we have to tell each other—no matter what."

My head was still bobbing and when Henry raised an eyebrow at me, I stopped.

"We shouldn't let some stupid girl get between us, ever. I mean she's not stupid, but we've been friends our whole lives."

"Yeah, man, you're right."

That ended the longest fight we'd ever had. Two long days of misery.

We laughed and joked on our way to town. Everything was right in the world at that moment. My best friend was my best friend again and the most amazing girl with looks and personality to match, had a crush on me—or at least I hoped she still did. And they were both helping me as I tried to solve not one, but two murders.

Amanda met us at Pig-n-Out for ice cream.

"I didn't want to say anything at the cemetery," Henry said, "with the dead so close and all, but don't ya think it's a bit suspicious that Old Man Jack turns up dead right after he was threatening the chief and after his run-in with you two?"

"I don't like it." Amanda said before licking her ice cream.

"Yeah. I bet your bullets, there wasn't an autopsy done," Henry said.

"Actually, there was," I said. "My mom said the autopsy showed death by overdose."

"I just have a hard time believing anything anymore." Henry finished his cone.

"I'm with ya on that one. I wonder who did the autopsy."

"That's the real question," Amanda said biting into her cone.

"On another note," I said, "we haven't gotten any closer to figuring out what happened to Pastor Higby's wife. All we know for sure is that huge efforts have been made to cover up what really happened to her. The reporter and the mortician were both barred from seeing her body. Her remains were cremated almost immediately, no one saw her after she died."

Henry squinted at me. "Where are you going with this, man?"

"I think I need to get back into that evidence room. I need to find out what they're hiding. Especially now that we know the gun was stolen. Someone must've broken into Higby's house."

Amanda drew a sharp breath. "Do you really think that's a good idea, Billy? We almost got caught last time."

"The chief is typically doing his welfare visits right now. I have about an hour to go in there and photograph everything in the box. Should I go now?"

"We should all go! We want to back you up, man!" Henry insisted.

"No, if we all go, we're more likely to be caught. I have to do it alone."

They grumbled about it, but they both had to admit I was right.

Amanda gave me her phone and told me to keep it on while I was in the evidence room and talk while taking pictures so that they at least felt like they were there.

GRAVEDIGGERS

I had no trouble convincing Maureen to let me go wait for the chief in his office. She said he'd be back within twenty minutes or so. I quickly made my way to the evidence room with the yardstick and key and located the box. I wanted to have all the pictures and everything in five minutes so that I had no chance of running into the chief or one of his officers. I called Henry and left the phone on.

"Alright, there is a bunch of stuff in Mrs. Higby's box. More than was in my dad's." I snapped a picture so they could see. Then I took out each item and set it on the desk, just like Amanda and I had done with the evidence from my dad's box. I told them what each item was, but quickly. "I'm going to take pictures of each thing right now." As I took the pictures my heart pounded hard and my hands shook slightly. It was so unlike looking through daddy's box. I felt a whispering that I should hurry, so I set the phone down on the table after I'd taken a picture of each item.

I heard soft footfalls. Were they coming closer to this room or going down the side hall? I couldn't tell, but I wasn't taking chances. I shoved the lid on the box as soon as I'd put the last object in it and picked the box up to run it back to its spot when the door to the room swung open. My chest hurt and my belly seemed to go rock hard. It was the last person I wanted to see. Bud McKnight, his eyes wide with anger.

"What do you think you're doing, Billy? What box is that? Your father's?"

"No, sir. I-I."

He grabbed the box and opened it. "Mrs. Higby's evidence?" He looked at me sharply. "I don't understand."

"Well, sir." My eyes darted to the phone that was still transmitting. His eyes followed mine.

"Is this on?" He grabbed the phone. "Whose phone is this?" He shook it at me and then said, "Hello? Who's there?"

They must not have answered because he said, "Who was that?"

"Amanda and Henry." I put my hands behind my back to hide my shaking.

"Amanda and Henry?" he roared, holding the phone out in front of me. "What in the devil!"

I said in a quiet whisper, "We thought we'd open the case and find her murderer."

He closed his eyes, lifting his chin to the ceiling and exhaling and inhaling loudly through his nose. "Murderer? Do you have any idea what you've done?" His eyes popped open and his stare lasered through me.

I dropped my mouth open. "Uh..." I wanted to tell him I didn't trust him—that I thought he was somehow involved in my dad's death, but I couldn't. The look of betrayal on his face stopped me cold.

"All of our evidence and cases have been compromised now. If a defense lawyer found out about this, all of our pending cases would be thrown out. I know I've let you in here with me, Billy, but this?"

My face flushed. I knew I had done something terrible, but I was only trying to help. "I just wanted to help."

"You should have asked me, Billy."

Anger flared in me. All the times I'd asked to look at the evidence on my father's death raced through my mind. "And you would have shown me?"

"Maybe."

"That's a no." I couldn't help acid leaking into my comment.

"You're probably right, but that doesn't excuse what you've done."

I harrumphed. I wanted to tell him what I'd overheard and that I couldn't have gone to him because I didn't trust him anymore. I couldn't find the words. I stood, defiant.

"You feel no remorse for what you've done. That much is clear. I'll have to try and make you understand. Hopefully a night in the cage will make you see how utterly stupid this was." He grabbed my arm.

I'd messed everything up. Now, I'd get no information from him. He was too mad. I was lost.

I sat in the sterile, cement cell with nothing to do for the rest of the day. Bud had confiscated Amanda's phone. I wondered if he knew I'd taken pictures. I wondered what my mom would say when she found out. One thing was for sure, she'd be madder than a hornet. I'd be grounded and have loads of jobs and service to do. She'd never let this slide even if I explained everything to her. She wanted me to forget about my own father's death, what would she say when she found out I was looking into someone else's death, too? Lying on my back, I punched the thin mattress pad over and over again. How could I have let myself get caught? Stupid. Stupid.

"Cut it out!" a small, crackly voice said. "I have an awful headache and your pounding is making it ten times worse."

I hadn't even noticed when the chief brought me in that the mayor's son, Lee, had been in the cell next to mine—

sobering up, I'm sure. I stopped punching the bed. At some point I slept, waking to Lee making all kinds of loud noises with his mouth as he stretched. "Awww. Rrrrhh. Mmmmmh."

"And you wanted me to be quiet?" I said. "Please, I'm trying to sleep."

"It's noon. Any self-respecting person should be awake by now, you lazy bugger," Lee said.

I huffed and turned over, facing the wall and pulling the tiny, thin blanket up around my neck, exposing my feet. I hiked them up, pressing my knees into my stomach, trying to fit them under the blanket but failing miserably. Frustrated, I threw the blanket toward Lee and rolled up into a ball.

"Testy aren't we? Not Chief McKnight's favored son anymore, eh? Is that why you have your panties in a wad?"

I ignored him.

"Ignore me if you want, but it can get downright lonely in here. You'll see. As soon as lunch comes, I'm outta here."

"Good riddance," I said in a huff. "Why wait?"

"No food at home. Maybe you know a little something about that, huh, with your daddy gone and all. You're Nick's kid, ain't ya?"

I sat up. "Can't you see I'm trying to sleep here?"

"Dagum shame what happened to your dad. Even if he was scum."

I turned my head away from him. I felt sicker by the minute.

"I remember that night, clear as day."

I jerked up.

"You do?"

"'Course I do. Only once in a lifetime I gots ta witness a crime under the rug—and I gots ta witness it, I did."

"What do you know about it, Lee," I hissed, springing up to the bars of the cage and pressing my body against them.

He backed quickly away. "Apparently, more'n you." This time he cackled and rubbed his bald head, rocking back and forth in front of the little slot food came through.

I needed to take a more gentle tact. "Lee, you're right. You do know more than I do. I didn't mean to sound angry." My mind went to the box filled with cash and jewelry, still hidden under my bed. I was willing to do anything to get him to talk. "I'll make it worth your while if you tell me what you know."

"I only know what I overheard. Didn't see a thing, no. Not a thing." He rocked back and forth, back and forth singing *Twinkle, Twinkle Little Star*.

Had he gone mad? There had been rumors of that very thing going around town. I figured it was really the alcohol. I hung on the bars, my face pressed up against them, hoping and praying he'd give me something, but he gave me nothing. After what seemed forever, Officer Olsen came with a meager lunch tray. Lee continued singing, but a hard rock song this time. He methodically ate the granola bar, and apple, and drank the milk, not leaving a scrap—not even the core of the apple.

He had to be mad. Singing all crazy and then eating an apple core? Who did that?

He stood up. "I'm ready to go now!" he yelled through the bars. He folded his blanket in a nice square and set it under his pillow, which he picked up and fluffed before setting it back down. He smoothed out the mattress pad and then looked around the small box of a room. He sighed as Officer Olsen unlocked his cell and let him out. I kept my eyes averted, ashamed of how I'd deceived him when I looked through my dad's evidence.

I knew we had our own Otis-the-drunk cell, but I didn't know Lee got to come and go from here as he pleased. "Wait, Lee, please, tell me what you know about my dad's death." By the time I said, death, I was whispering, pleading.

"Why'd you think I'd know anything about that?" His voice was forceful and sounded as if he'd regained his awareness.

I wouldn't let it go that easily. "You said you overheard a cover-up."

"I say a lot of things, boy, but look at me. What do I know? I'm just a good-for-nothing drunk." He seemed completely aware now.

"But you said..." I let the words hang in the air.

"Look. For all I know, I did it."

Surprise filled me.

Then he walked out of his cell and down the hall.

"Did you do it, Lee?" I yelled after him. "Did your dad cover it all up? I'll get you, you coward." I could feel deep heat spread through my body.

We were right. The mayor had covered it all up. His son was a drunk. Lee liked to drink at the bar down the road from our old house. He had been the town drunk even back then. The mayor would never have allowed his son to be found guilty of killing someone. And they had had a damaged car fixed. The car that hit my dad. It was all so clear. I knew what

GRAVEDIGGERS

I had to do. A drunk or not, Lee'd killed Daddy, and I would make him pay as soon as I got out.

I spent the time I had left plotting, scheming—coming up with a fool-proof plan to get justice.

Chapter 23

My mom picked me up the next morning. I knew she had to be extremely upset about the whole thing because she hadn't even come to see me during the night. She didn't normally avoid confrontation; she hit it head on but in a calm, understanding way. She was anything but calm standing at the end of the hallway that led out from the holding cells. The chief gave me an envelope with everything that had been in my pockets when he discovered me in the evidence room—including Amanda's cell phone. I wanted to grab it out and call her, but one look at my mom, tapping her foot, her hand on her hip and her eyebrows raised, lips pressed tightly together, I knew I better not show interest in anything but her. She didn't speak when I reached her, nor did she speak in the truck. She didn't even speak to me when I went into the house. She motioned for me to sit on the sofa and I did.

She paced in front of me until I could barely stand it a moment longer. I stopped following her with my eyes and looked at my shoes. As if on cue, she started to talk.

"I can't believe this, Billy. How could you do such a totally and completely asinine thing? Your father would turn over in his grave if he knew."

He would know soon enough once I faced Lee. My dad would finally have the closure he needed to move on and be happy in the afterlife.

"And to think you compromised all that evidence." She shook her head. "You know I love you, Billy, but right now, I'm having a really hard time figuring out how you are going to make amends for this."

Silence reigned.

"This isn't going to be one of those things that you do a few things and find yourself in the clear. You're almost eighteen, and if it had been anyone else that had found you, you'd be facing charges. I can hardly even think about it."

She started to pace again.

I'd never seen her so angry.

"I'm sorry, Mama." I decided I would just play stupid and sorry. I'd have to throw myself on her mercy because I intended to take care of my father's murderer ASAP, and I couldn't do that sequestered here.

"Mrs. McCreary needs her house painted."

I couldn't believe my luck. I would be out of the house, and not too far from Lee Clement. The McCreary's lived on the same street.

"She has the paint and we have the supplies. You start in the morning. After that, you will be scrubbing and doing maintenance on the police department from top to bottom until the whole place is like new. There's nothing you can do to fix the damage you've done, but this can help bring you back into the graces of God at least."

The punishment didn't seem that harsh. I nodded my head, acting contrite, and stood up to leave.

"Oh no, you are not going anywhere." Mama held me in place with her steely gaze.

I sighed. "What do you want from me, Mama?"

"What do I want? How about an explanation? I can't understand what you were doing digging around old evidence boxes? Bud told me you were looking at evidence for cases long closed! What could you have been thinking?" She looked into my eyes, searching for answers I couldn't give.

How could I explain to Mama what I knew? Mrs. Higby's death wasn't an accident, it was murder—and the chief and the mayor had covered it up, just like they had Daddy's murder. There was a connection there—and now I knew what it was. Lee. I didn't know how he could have been involved with Mrs. Higby's death, but it didn't matter. Obviously the mayor was covering up his son's crimes, and had gotten the chief to help him. Lee had all but confessed to me that he'd run my dad down in the street. And he was going to pay for it. Soon. As soon as I could get my mom off my case.

"Mama, I'm sorry—I thought, I thought maybe if I could solve an old case, the chief would see how good I was at investigating. He'd see I was ready, and he'd let me help with Daddy's case." It sounded hollow, even to me.

"That is the stupidest thing I have ever heard, William Nicholas Howard," Mama said, her voice no longer angry, but filled with a deep sadness. "I have told you again and again, your father's death was an accident. It was the most awful thing that ever could have happened, but baby, it was an accident. Don't go borrowing trouble and looking for evil that just isn't there. Your dad wouldn't want to see you like this—destroying your life, chasing after nothing. Let it go, forgive. Live your life and leave this demon behind you."

She looked so helpless pleading with me. She truly believed what she said, but I knew differently. My insides burned with hatred for Lee. I would see him dead, but my mom could never know.

I channeled all my anger and hate and made myself cry, for her. For the show. "I'm trying, Mama. Believe me, I'm trying to give away all the dark, black sadness. I'm trying."

It worked. She came to me and hugged me.

I didn't like to manipulate her. I hated doing it, but I had to see this through. After our nice long hug, she pulled away, mascara ran down her face.

"You don't know how much that means to me." She shook her head and exhaled through her nose. "I'm so glad you are finally looking for a way to move on. But don't you ever do anything like this ever again. If you ever get a crazy idea like that again, talk to me about it before you act."

I nodded.

"Promise me, Billy."

"I-I promise." I crossed my fingers hoping it really would spare me the regret that was sure to come for defying her.

She pulled me into another breath-taking hug and then laughed a nervous laugh. "Did they feed you in there? You must be starving."

"They fed me, Mom. I'm fine. I've got a lot of work to do. I'll go get all the painting stuff and get over to Ms. McCreary's house and get painting. It's going to look great when I'm done, but tell me she chose a color other than yellow this time." I wanted to lighten the mood even more.

"She did. Peach." She grabbed the envelope Bud had given her and gave it to me.

"Oh, man, and everyone is going to think of me when it's done."

She tousled my hair as I stood and I after putting the envelope in my room, I went into the shed to gather the supplies I needed to paint the house—and confront Lee. I would finally find peace. My mom gave me a lift with all the painting supplies to Mrs. McCreary's house on her way to work.

It was a good thing it was a small one-story home. I scraped off any flaking paint and sanded those areas before taping off the windows and miscellaneous things jutting out from the walls on one side of the house. It was hard work. By one, I'd finished the hardest side of the house, the front, and would paint it after lunch. I moved on to the back, sanding and scraping. It was sure to have almost as many areas that needed taping off.

I kept my eye on the clock. I was watching out for Lee. I wanted to document his movements today. Mrs. McCreary's house was only four down from his, and he'd for sure pass by. I had no idea what the man did with his time, but I would find out so I could time his reckoning perfectly.

Sure enough he climbed out of a bed of an old farm truck. He must've been hitchhiking and some nice old guy had pity on him. He walked into his house with hunched shoulders, head hanging. I couldn't let his apparent misery change my mind.

I sat and ate my lunch, watching his house. Then, I got back to work, painting the front of the house, checking every now and then for movement at Lee's. At some point he came outside and sat on a wicker chair on his porch and slept. Must be nice not to have to work and have his dad pay all his bills. I let anger seep into my bones, and I probably would have stood there, transfixed, staring at him, if Mrs. McCreary hadn't come out and given me sweet tea and butter cookies.

"That Lee Clement sure has had a hard life," she said, shaking her head and sitting on the steps next to me.

What did she know? He was a monster. A monster that kills and doesn't face up to his punishment or admit his guilt.

"I just hope he lives to overcome his battles." Her gray-blue, faded eyes peered softly into mine.

Did she know what I was planning? No way. No human can read minds. Only God knows what's inside my brain. But I guess he does work through his servants. Did he whisper my plans to her? I sat stone still thinking of the many times I'd felt prompted to go help someone and when I arrived, I found them in dire need. I'd never known why I was going somewhere or saying something until I arrived or said it. No. She didn't know, but maybe the Lord was trying to tell me to give up on my plans—that justice was his.

I shook my head. I couldn't let sentimental thoughts get in the way of what must be done. A deep pang settled in my gut, and I felt a bit ashamed for some reason. Was God mad at me?

"Now, you," she continued. "You are a good boy who would never let a substance or a person control him in a bad way, right?"

I nodded, but very slowly.

"You've always been such a kind and giving boy. Whatever you do, don't ever touch alcohol or let a bad person influence you in any way. You may feel tempted, but run the other way. Nothing good ever comes from alcohol consumption or peer pressure." She smiled broadly and patted my hand before standing and taking my empty glass and plate with her into the house.

I got to work again and quickly finished the front before it was time to go home for supper.

I knocked on Mrs. McCreary's door. "Hi. I just wanted you to know that I'm heading home for supper. But, I'll be back to clean up and prepare for tomorrow. I know it's a mess right now."

"No problem, Billy. I sure do appreciate you helping me out. You're doing a beautiful job."

"Thank you. I'll see you in an hour or so."

"Sounds good."

I wanted a chance to track Lee's movements in the evening when he went to get drunk and all chaos broke loose in his wake. In a few days, no one would have to worry about getting in his drunken path again.

At home, I noticed flowers on the table. It meant one thing, the anniversary of my dad's death was tomorrow. In all the craziness, I had almost forgotten.

I kissed Mama goodbye and headed over to the church. The preacher was out back again, holding an urn. I didn't mess with knocking on his door, I went straight to him. He startled and I lunged for the urn afraid it would drop to the cement and break, but it didn't. Preacher Higby held it solidly. His eyes were rimmed red and he looked worn out, but he tried to hide it, giving me one of his classic smiles.

"You know it's a dangerous thing to sneak up on an old man." In truth, he wasn't that old, but at that moment, he looked about ninety. "What if I'd been holding my shotgun instead of this fragile thing?"

"I'm sorry, sir. I saw you out here and thought we could talk."

"Hold on just a minute," he said. "Let me put this up and then we can talk."

I put my hand on his arm. "Is this your wife?" Once I'd said it, I felt stupid, ashamed I'd said it in that way.

He nodded and continued to stand.

"Wait, sir. That's what I wanted to talk about."

His face paled.

"I mean I wanted to talk to you about my dad. His death. His murder. I-I didn't realize until just the other day that my dad and your wife died exactly a year apart on the same day. I thought maybe you'd understand what I'm going through— that I'd have a friend in you to talk it out."

Some color returned to his face, and he took his seat again.

He nodded, but didn't speak.

"I know you had more time with your wife than I had with my dad, but I figured it must be the same type of loss. A deep one. One that's almost unbearable."

Tears welled in his eyes and mine burned.

He reached out and took my hand, trying to speak, but unable.

We cried for a good while together, saying nothing, sharing our grief. It felt good. It felt right. Once the tears ended, I wanted to let him know about my plans, what I was doing.

"I'm going to help you." I paused and took a deep breath. I wasn't sure how he would feel about what I was about to say. "I know your wife didn't fall off that ladder. I know she was murdered."

His eyes shot open as wide as puffy, red, cried-out eyes can get.

"I will help you find peace—bring her killer to justice."

His hand darted out. "No, son. No."

"Yes. I'm going to, no matter what you say. I want to help you. I'm pretty sure that it was the mayor that covered it up. I think he also covered stuff up when my dad died."

"No. I don't want you to, Billy." There was a panic in his movements, in his look. "I laid all that pain and sorrow to the side long ago, and dredging it up won't help anyone. And certainly not you."

"But I want to. And besides, the mayor shouldn't get away with what he's done." I was about to tell him about the box when he stood up, set the urn on the table next to us and said,

"Billy Howard. I forbid you from looking into her death." There was a forcefulness to his words—almost a threat. "I will not allow you to go down that path of hate and regret."

"But, sir, I'm going to do it for you."

"I'm telling you," his voice was a growl, a menacing rumble. "Look at me, young man. I cannot and will not relive the death of my wife. I couldn't take it. It would be the end of me. Do you want me gone, boy? Because that is what would happen if you reopened wounds that have long been sealed up. I am old and weak. Let God seek his vengeance." His body shook as he picked the urn back up and scurried toward his back door. Once there, he turned. "Forget, Billy. Let it go. Churning things up will only make things worse. Promise me, boy. Promise me you'll let it go."

GRAVEDIGGERS

His face was so earnest, so urgent; I had to acquiesce with a simple nod. I'd told two big lies today. I would not let this go. Pastor Higby would discover that the truth would lessen his load and help him find peace. He may not see that right now, but he would. He opened the door and went inside. I watched as he set the urn on the mantle and then put one hand on its edge and hung his head.

I hurried away, feeling ashamed and inflamed at the same time. Maybe I shouldn't go digging around his wife's death. Maybe I was doing more harm than good. I made my way back to Mrs. McCreary's and painted until it was dark and time to go home. I made a show of taking a book into my room so my mom would think I was going to bed.

A little after ten, I snuck out my window and walked to town. I watched from Mrs. McCreary's front yard as Lee walked down the street toward Silotti's Tavern, the only bar that still allowed him to drink there. They reasoned that if he was to drink, it would be the best place for it. They would be able to keep an eye on him and call the chief or his dad to pick him up when he got wasted. Truly, it was just a way for the bar to get all his dad's cash.

The thing about Silotti's was that it was on the same road as my old house, just in the opposite direction. If Lee had turned the wrong way after a drinking binge at Silotti's, he would have driven right past my old house. That must have been what happened the night that he had hit Daddy. Heat spread through my chest thinking about what Lee had done.

I couldn't wait another minute. I knew where he was going. I'd put my plan in motion to end the pain tonight. I went to his house and checked to make sure the door was unlocked. I brought rope over from Mrs. McCreary's to tie him up and make him talk. I sat down on a chair that stood on the same wall as the front door and fingered the rope. I'd surprise him, and since he'd be drunk, it shouldn't take much effort to tie him up and make him talk. I eyed the shotgun hanging over his fireplace mantle, and worry built up inside me.

What if he resisted? Maybe I hadn't thought this through well enough. Maybe I should have brought something that would force him to submit to me, like a gun. I should have brought my rifle. Did I have time to go back and get it? What if Lee came home while I was gone? I couldn't chance it. I eyed the shotgun again.

I stood up to check it out. Was the gun even usable or just for decoration? I'd never seen Lee with a gun in his hands. I bet he was no hunter.

The gun felt solid, heavy in my hands. I opened the action and shut it and opened it again. It was loaded. Unbelievable. Lee Clement, the drunk, had a loaded gun in his living room. I clicked the safety on and off a few times. There was really no way to know if the gun would even fire without testing it, which I couldn't do. I carried it over to the chair I'd picked to sit in. It came down to the fact that I felt safer with it than without it. And, I probably wouldn't even need to tie him up to get him to talk if I had this gun pointed at him.

I thought about the gun I'd gotten out of the P.O. box. That would have been the gun to have in this situation. The shotgun was a bit cumbersome, after all.

Something vibrated in my pocket. I pulled out Amanda's phone. I'd totally forgotten to take it back to her. Henry's name flashed on the screen. I answered it.

"Hey," I said.

"Billy, is that you?" It wasn't Henry, it was Amanda. "Where have you been all day? We've been worried sick."

My heart jumped at the thought of her worrying about me. "Didn't you hear what happened? The chief caught me. I thought you knew."

"We knew that, you stupid idiot." It was Henry now. "What we didn't know is what happened to you. Your mom won't answer the phone..." I heard a shuffle and then Amanda spoke again.

"I'm so glad you're alive. We thought maybe your mom lost it and killed you or locked you up in the cellar or something or the chief locked you away for good in his creepy jail."

"Exaggerate much? Like anything like that would ever happen." My voice was even, tempered.

"Are you home then?" Amanda asked. "Did you get pictures? Can we come and see them?"

"That's not a good idea. My mom would kill me if she knew you'd come over, and I'd be grounded for the next year instead of the next few days."

"We'll just tell her I came to get my phone. It's no big deal."

"No-I-I-mean—"

"We'll be right there."

"No. Wait. I'm not home." I sighed deeply.

"I thought you said you were grounded."

"I was. I mean I am. I snuck out."

"You're grounded and you snuck out?" I heard two loud gasps. "Your mom will really kill you now. Are you on your way over here or what?"

"No!" I almost yelled. "I'm not headed over. I'm sorry. I'm doing something else. I have to take care of something. When I'm done, I'll come over."

"Tell us where you are. We'll help you."

"This is something I have to do on my own."

"Does this have to do with your dad?"

I heard footsteps on the walk outside, dragging, sliding steps, and I hung up, stuffing the now-vibrating phone deep into my pocket. I breathed shallow, even breaths. The door knob shook like someone was trying in vain to get a locked door open. Finally, after several failed attempts, Lee staggered inside. He bumbled his way to the sofa and sat heavily down without shutting the door. Why hadn't he shut the door? I couldn't face him with the door open. Someone might hear. He hadn't turned on any lights, so I couldn't tell if he was looking in my direction or if he was asleep.

"If you've come to rob me, I ain't got nothing for ya."

He was looking at me. My throat seized, and I couldn't breathe for several beats. Then a heat spread from my gut out. This man murdered my dad. I would not be afraid.

"Are you a ghost, come to torment me? Speak ghost. Speak now," he drawled, his voice slurred and unsteady. It was a perfect segue into this whole mess with my dad.

"Yes! I'm a ghost," I said. This would be easier than I thought. Maybe I wouldn't even need to point the shotgun at him. "You must feel the pain both my wife and son have felt for all these years since you took my life."

"Took yer life? I ain't taken nobody's life. No sir."

"But you did. Remember that night ten years ago when you turned the wrong way on my street after drinking too much at Silotti's? Instead of going home, you turned out toward my house, and you hit me while I tried to save my goat." My chest ached pretending to be my dad and I aimed the gun at him. Grief, anger, hatred bubbled inside me.

"You Nick Howard's ghost?"

He did do it. My hands trembled, and I felt spit build up in my mouth. Even though I hadn't planned it, I stood. I couldn't help myself. I clenched my teeth and spit, "You remember now, do you?" I clicked the safety off.

"No. No." I could hear him shake his head and a streak of moonlight lit up half his face now. "I weren't anywhere near here the night you died. I was in rehab in Chicago. Go haunt my father, he'll tell ya who it was that killed ya. He knows. He told me not to tell. It was a secret between the two of 'em."

He was more lucid than I thought he could be. Was he telling me the truth? Was he really out of town? How could I be sure? How could it not be the truth? Like an electric current that was severed, my body seemed to drain of all its energy. My hands shook thinking, about how close I'd come to hurting an innocent man.

"It's my old man you want to haunt, not me. I'm just a tired ol' drunk that needs to sleep. Leave me be, ol' spirit. I've done some terrible things in my life that deserve hauntin' but ya can't claim me for that one. No siree."

I lowered the gun and lay it on the floor by the chair. I stood, making my way to the door and feeling like an idiot.

"If you're telling the truth, then I'll be able to pass you by without my spirit attacking yours. Hide your eyes and pray for your soul."

I heard him move and then start reciting the Lord's Prayer. I slipped around him and out the open door. I walked with slow, even steps down his walkway to the sidewalk and then I ran as fast as I could in the direction of the cemetery—adrenaline pushing me. What had I almost done? I didn't get far before hearing my name called out in a loud whisper.

I stopped. "Henry?"

"Yeah, it's me," he huffed, totally winded. He bent over and then Amanda came to a stop beside him, huffing, too.

"We-We-We were totally scared you'd figured out who killed your dad and were getting revenge."

"How'd you find me?"

"My cell phone," Amanda chirped.

"Your cell phone?" I reached into my pocket and pulled it out, staring at it.

Amanda snatched it from me. "It has GPS. I looked it up, and we came running.

"Were you just in Lee's house? The map showed you at Lee's house."

"I need to go see my dad," I said, turning to go.

Henry grabbed my arm, eyes wide, sparkling in the light of street lamp. "What did you do, Billy? Was it Lee that killed your dad?"

I shook my head. "I didn't do a thing and no, it wasn't Lee." I shrugged my arm from his grasp and walked down the sidewalk. I could hear their whispers, but I couldn't make out what they were saying. They caught up with me and without a word, followed me to my father's grave. They stopped several yards away.

I sat down, my back resting on the gravestone, and I cried silent tears. What was I doing? I had been sure it was Lee, but it wasn't. I could have killed him. I hadn't intended to, but when I thought he was about to tell me he'd killed my dad, something mean and awful and forceful took me over. I had lost control. What had I become? Was I a monster like Mama had told me I'd become if I didn't forgive and forget? I thought I'd get so much satisfaction in pulling the trigger and killing the man that killed Daddy, but maybe not. I felt empty, spent like a broken down Ford.

"I know I have to avenge your death, Daddy, but I thought it'd be different. Easier. Now I don't know what to do. He said the mayor was keeping a secret about that night. How could I ever get that information out of him? I'm sorry Daddy, I'm failing you." I lay down and cried my heart out, not caring that my two best friends looked on.

I woke up to a mosquito buzzing in my ear. Amanda was lying on one side of me and Henry was leaning against a different gravestone. It was still dark out, and I had to get home before my mom discovered my absence. I sure hoped we didn't get chiggers. Pastor Higby kept the grounds well manicured, but there was no knowing when the chiggers would strike. I knew the mosquitos had gotten their fill. I scratched a bite on my forearm.

"Hey, Henry," I said, shaking him. "We've gotta get back home."

"Huh? What?" Henry shot up like an arrow. "What happened?"

I repeated myself. He rubbed violently at his eyes.

I gently nudged Amanda. "Amanda, wake up. We've gotta get back."

She opened her eyes and said, "Okay," in a small whisper. She shifted onto her elbows and then sat upright. I offered her my hand to help her up and she took it. She wobbled a little from sleep when she got to her feet, but quickly regained her balance before stretching her arms out to the stars.

We walked in silence until we were off church property. "Do you think revenge solves things?" Amanda asked.

They both looked at me for a quick second and then away.

A scratchy unwelcome blanket seemed to fall over us.

Henry said, "Are you going to tell me what happened at Lee's house or am I going to have to beat it out of ya?"

"I thought he did it," I said. I had to turn away from Henry to stop the sob that sat in my throat.

"But why? What happened to make you think he did it?"

"It was something he said in the holding cells. But I was wrong. He was gone. In rehab in Chicago. He said I needed to ask his dad—that he had the answers."

Silence.

"I almost shot him. Oh my gosh, I almost shot him. I would have done it. It was crazy. And he was innocent."

"Providence stepped in for you, then," Amanda said with all seriousness, taking my hand.

"What do you mean by that?" I asked.

"It wasn't the right thing. Didn't you feel that in your soul? Killing isn't right."

"Honestly, I felt nothing but murderous hate," I spat." I wanted him dead. And I wanted real justice."

With those words, she stepped back. "You can't be serious." Her eyes flicked to Henry and he looked away, telling her all she needed to know. "I knew you were angry about your dad, but murder to avenge him? That's just nuts."

"I didn't think I had it in me either. But, standing there, facing the man I thought killed my dad, the man I thought took everything from me—I wanted to take everything from him." My hands shook and that heat spread through me. She dared put a hand on my arm, but I pulled it away. It didn't deter her.

"Billy. You've got to let it go. This hate, this anger, it only damages you."

I turned from her and crossed my arms over my chest. I knew she was right, but I was so upset.

"I had no idea it was this bad. You've got to let yourself heal." Amanda pleaded with me.

"And what do you know about it?" I turned my head to her and shouted. "You have your father. Your mother. Your big house and fancy cars. I have nothing." Sweat slid down the side of my face.

She shook her head. "You're right. I've never lost anyone, but if you stay on the path you're on, I will."

I turned quickly away from her, trying to pretend what she said had no truth. "Just leave me alone. You don't know what you're talking about."

"Let's go home." She touched the back of my arm, and I shrugged it violently away. "Come on." I could hear the swishing of Henry's pants and the patter of his shoes hitting the cement as he started away. "Please, Billy. Let's go."

I didn't move. A stubborn rage had taken over and I wouldn't back down. I just wanted them to leave me, so I could go to the mayor's house and find out what he knew. My senses were on high alert again and I could feel Amanda breathing behind me. Slowly the sound left and I heard her whisper. "When you're ready to forget the vengeance and go for justice. I'll be here for you."

Hot tears pricked at the back of my eyes, but I denied them, stalking in the direction of the mayor's home.

Chapter 24

The night had turned inky black, now; a thick cover of clouds doused any light from the heavens. God had abandoned me that night my father was killed and now he turned his back on me again. A cat hissed at something. A lone dog barked. Something scuttled up a tree. An owl hooted, but no human sounds followed my path. I was an animal on the prowl. Focused.

The mayor would tell me what he knew, and then I would go to the chief and find out what he knew. I still had such a hard time believing Bud could have done what I thought he had. He had acted like my father, the whole time hiding my father's killer from me. I would claw and fight my way to justice. Before I knew it, I stood outside the mayor's door. I knew he would be asleep with his wife by his side, his youngest son, Mikey, in the room next door. Did the mayor sleep well at night? Would he hear my knock? Would he feel me coming for him?

I didn't even get to knock. A horn honked. Not any horn, but the horn from my truck. I turned swiftly. Had Amanda and Henry gone to get my truck? Impossible. But it wasn't Henry and Amanda. It was Mama. She had parked the truck and was stomping my way.

How was I going to explain this and who told her I was here? It must have been Amanda and Henry. They were on my blacklist now.

"It's three A.M., young man. Have you lost your mind? Did you already ring the bell?"

"No ma'am."

"Well, get your butt down here and climb into our truck. We're going home."

She was silent on the way there. She didn't lecture me or anything, she just sent me to bed once we arrived. What was up with that? It turned out that I was totally tired, exhausted, really, and I went right to sleep.

My mom was gone when I woke. There was a note for me.

You are under house arrest. You may not go anywhere today. Don't test me. We'll talk when I get home. I love you more than a thousand humming birds.

Like that was going to happen. I was already in so much trouble, what would adding a few extra things to the list do to me? The phone rang. I answered.

"Billy, it's Amanda."

I didn't feel the joy I usually felt when I heard her voice.

"Billy?"

"I'm here." I hadn't changed my mind about going after the mayor, and I thought she didn't want to talk to me until I had.

"Come over to Henry's. We've found something big about Mrs. Higby's death. You've got to see this."

"I'm not supposed to leave my house." I was mad at them. They'd turned me in.

"Your mom won't care if you come over here. You want me to call her?"

What if they had found something that would break the case open, and I could solve the Higby murder today, on the anniversary of her death? Angry as I was, I couldn't pass that up. "No. No. I'm coming."

I didn't bother to shower or put clean clothes on. What was the point? When I got there, I could see they were both extremely excited about something. I didn't feel like being excited. I wanted to go question the mayor.

"You'll never guess what we found." Henry stared at me wide eyed.

They beckoned me over to the computer, and I peered over their shoulders trying to understand what I was seeing.

"It's a restraining order," Amanda explained. "Against Tom Harris. Your dad filed it. We found it in the county's online database."

"And look," Henry pointed excitedly. "It says here Harris threatened him."

I leaned forward and read the line he was pointing to. "Harris on three occasions has threatened harm to my person, once claiming if he had the chance he would run me down with his tractor."

"See? He threatened to run your dad over!"

"Yeah, but with his tractor."

"So, this practically proves it."

"I don't know—Old Man Jack didn't seem to think the Harrises were involved."

"Old Man Jack was nuts. I'm telling you, it was Harris."

"Maybe we should go out there," Amanda cut in to our argument. We both stopped and stared at her. "What? It's not the worst idea ever. Maybe we could find a clue, learn something we haven't thought of yet."

Henry started to shoot her down, but I held up a hand. "Why not? Maybe she's right. We could learn something. Let's go."

We piled into Henry's van and drove out to my family's old land. It was strange to see the fields empty, nothing planted or growing. Such a waste. There were signs all over it, announcing that it was the future site of Coffco's factory. Daddy would have been so disappointed.

When we got to the property line between our land and the Harrises', we parked and got out of the truck. I really wasn't sure what we should even be looking for. We walked along the fence, waiting for inspiration to strike. Off in the distance, we heard the high buzz of four-wheeler engines. Before long, Tom Harris and his three sons had pulled up next to the fence.

"You'd be trespassing right now." Harris said, his voice devoid of humor. "Your daddy doesn't have claim to that land anymore." His kids stared hard at Amanda.

"We know, sir," I said. "I guess I was just feeling nostalgic. Today is the anniversary of my dad's death." I felt a hard lump form in my throat, but I fought through it, wanting to concentrate on Harris's response.

"You know your dad and I never got along, but I'm sorry for your loss." He seemed sincere and he brushed his hand through his hair. A silver watch gleamed in the sunlight. I took a step closer to the fence and the Harrises, trying to get a better look.

"Th-thank you," I said, not taking my eyes from his wrist.

"Whatcha looking at?" Mr. Harris asked.

I had been too obvious. But if he was wearing the same kind of watch that was in my dad's evidence box, it could clear him.

"Sorry. I didn't mean to stare. I think my dad had a watch just like that one you've got on." I had just made it up, but as I said it, a picture of my dad sitting at our table working on farm business came to my mind. He had owned one of those watches. In fact, he'd been buried with it. I remembered it catching the light as I placed a rose in his coffin.

"I didn't steal it if that's what you mean." Mr. Harris growled.

"No. No. That's not what I meant—"

"Every farmer in Halls got one of these watches from the co-op one year. Everyone got them. Ask around."

"Everyone got one?" I repeated dumbly.

"That's what I said." His voice was harsh.

"Thank you. And I'm sorry you and my dad didn't get along. I hope you don't hold that against me."

He snorted and the three of them drove away without replying.

"That silver watch may have just cleared him."

"What? How?" demanded Henry.

I told him about the watch in the evidence box. If someone had lost his watch on the scene, it couldn't have been Harris. He still had his. He wasn't there.

"Can we rule him out now?" Amanda said.

"Not yet." I wanted to get a look at the land dispute files. "Let's get to town and see if the recorder's office has any info on it."

"But you think he is innocent?"

"I'm pretty sure."

The Lauderdale recorder in Ripley was more than happy to help us look up the dispute. I figured he must be bored most of the time. He pulled the records up on the computer, and we looked them over. "Yep, your dad had cause to dispute the land. It was his. And when the mayor bought the land—"

"Wait a minute," I interrupted. "The *mayor* bought my dad's land?"

"Sure did. Here, I'll show you...Your mom sold the property to Beau Baker, nine years back, and then look here, the property was sold to the mayor two years later?

"Oh, but look here at the record. It's in the process of being sold. The mayor is under contract with Coffco." He made a low whistle. "Wow. Looks like he's going to make a killing on it."

Fire licked my throat. "Does the mayor own any other land in Halls?" I asked. Amanda and Henry looked on saying nothing, looking lost.

"I believe so. Let's look it up."

After a few minutes, the computer spit out a huge list of properties the mayor owned. When I saw my address on the list, I couldn't believe it. I felt queasy. "He owns the house I live in and all those rentals on my street. Look at all the land he owns. Does he come from a rich family or what?" I asked more to myself than anyone else. I opened and closed my hands several times.

"I'm not sure about that, son, but it looks like he comes into some money every July. That's when he seems to buy all his properties."

Amanda said, "Maybe he has some kind of a trust fund inheritance that funds each July."

"Maybe," I said, unconvinced. He must own half the town. It didn't sit right with me. Something was not right.

"Thanks for all your help," I said and turned to go. Henry and Amanda followed, wondering what just happened.

"Hey guys," I said as we left the recorder's office. "I need to get my work done before my mom gets home. Besides, I don't want you around when she yells at me for last night. Thanks a lot for turning me in by the way."

Amanda blushed, and Henry wouldn't look at me. I shook my head. "On the other hand, maybe I should make you come with me for the bawl out."

"No, no, that's all right. You'd better take us home," Henry said, winking. "I'm pretty sure we're late as it is."

After I dropped them off at their house, I went home and made omelets for dinner, hoping to help my cause with Mama. When she did come, she was in a rush.

"Listen sweetie, can you hang on for a few more hours? Mrs. Ellison fell and broke her hip this afternoon. I need to go over and make her husband dinner and do some cleaning up. Maybe we can visit your dad's grave together later. What do you say?" She smiled at me in a harried way.

"Would you mind if I went over there after I eat? I'll wait for you?"

She took a deep breath. "Are you sure you want to go alone?"

"Well, I kinda wanted to read him the stories I've been collecting."

"That sounds like a good thing. I'll meet you there, then. I love you more than a thousand butterflies." Sadness hit her face. It was what I'd said to her the day before daddy died. It held all kinds of meaning. She wiped a tear from her eyes as she walked out the door.

"I love you more than a thousand tigers," I whispered.

Chapter 25

By the time I made it to town, it was past nine. This time I was prepared. I had the gun from the post office tucked in my back waistband, and I carried my rifle. I knew the mayor and his family went to bed early, but I wasn't sure just how early. The cremation, the earring, the land, our house, the celebration, and Lee's words all swirled around in my brain. The mayor must have killed my dad. There was no other possible answer. He wanted the land, so he could sell it to Coffco and make a killing. It was all about greed.

Just as it got dark, I arrived on the mayor's porch. I opted for knocking on the door instead of ringing the bell. I waited. Waited for God to tell him to come and face me. When he didn't come, I knocked again, harder this time. I waited again. I didn't want to rouse the entire house. I only needed him. I sent out a mental invitation to him, beckoning him to me. I knocked a third time, and I heard feet on the stairs.

The mayor looked out the sidelight and, seeing me, narrowed his eyes. The rifle hung on the opposite side of me, pressed up against my leg, hidden from his view.

"Billy," he said in an urgent tone when he opened the door. "What are you doing here? Has something happened to your mother?"

With a minuscule shake of my head, I said, "I came to talk to you, sir." My voice was flat. Was it even me talking?

"Son, it's after nine, can't this wait until tomorrow?"

"No, sir. We have to talk right now."

"Let's go call your mother. I bet she has no idea—"

I raised the rifle and pointed it at his heart. He lifted his hands in the air and stepped back as I stepped forward into the house.

"Now, Billy, I don't know what this is about, but if you lower that rifle and go home right now, I'll not speak a word of it to anyone. It will be as if it never happened."

"Is that what you said to the person who killed my dad ten years ago? Did you tell them it would be your little secret?" Venom filled every word. My chest ached with a deep heat.

He continued to back up.

"What are you talking about, son?" Despite his alarm, he had whispered. A sure sign of the guilty.

I waved the gun in the direction of the parlor. He made his way there without taking his eyes off me.

"Sit," I said once fully in the room. I used my leg and hip to close the French doors that led inside.

I stood far enough away from him that if he decided to do the foolhardy thing and lunge for the gun, I would be able to get off a shot before he reached me.

"Now, start from the beginning. Who did you get to murder my father?" I spoke in a firm tone, trying to keep calm enough not to shoot him right then and there.

"I-I-I don't know what you're talking about. I don't know who killed your father. Honestly, I really don't know."

"Liar." My voice sounded strong, like it wasn't even my voice. "Lee told me you know who it was. Share the secret with me, now or die." I was losing it.

His neck and face were splotchy red. "I told you, I *don't know*." He trembled. His whole body convulsing. I narrowed my eyes. Could he be telling the truth?

"So you didn't order my dad's death, but you took advantage of it. He died and you bought up our land for pennies."

The mayor swallowed hard, not even attempting to deny it. Rage burned through me, and I had to fight hard not to drop the gun and beat him with my bare fists.

"But you do know something." I cocked my head to the side.

"W-W-what do you mean?"

"What's the secret you and the chief are keeping about the hit and run?"

He opened his mouth, but no sound escaped.

"Old Man Jack and Lee both told me, there's something you two are hiding. Tell me. Now."

He shook his head shortly from side to side.

I nodded in big, broad sweeps. "One...Two..." I clicked the safety off.

"Fine. I'll tell you what I know, but it's not much."

"Good. On with it."

"It was someone from our town. That's all I know. I swear."

"That's not good enough. Who do you think it was?"

"Someone who drinks," he blustered. "I thought it was Lee at first, but then remembered I'd sent him to rehab. He wasn't even around."

"So tell me, who back then had a drinking problem?" My knuckles began to ache from clenching the gun so tightly. I loosened my grip.

He shook his head violently.

"Who. Had. A. Drinking. Problem?"

"There were several people in town who did at the time, but Bud cleared them all. I can't remember who they all were. We were at a dead end. No leads, why report it? Why keep looking?"

"What do you mean? *Why report it?*" I took a step closer to him. Had he just given himself away? If so, how?

"I-I-I..."

That's when it hit me. "I get it now. You didn't report the crime so that you could win your stupid little award. Is that it?"

He stared at me and kept glancing down at the papers scattered on the coffee table in front of him.

"Is it?" I said in an even voice.

He nodded. "You mean you've been lying and cheating just so you could get that award?" I laughed a bitter laugh. "You hid evidence in my dad's death and Mrs. Higby's, too, leaving us without answers, letting killers roam free—and all for some stupid award?"

"Don't be naïve, boy."

"I saw you at the celebration on the Fourth. You love the spotlight. You love all the praise."

"Think what you want." His eyes kept looking at the papers on the table. He was sweating, and I suddenly noticed he was wringing his hands.

I quickly snatched up one of the papers, and he lunged at me.

"Don't even think about it." I re-aimed the gun at his face and he sat back down.

"It appears you're more worried about me seeing these papers than you are about me discovering you covered up my father's murder." I picked them up, keeping the gun pointed at the mayor so he wouldn't get any ideas. It only took me a second to realize what the papers were. They were letters and documents addressed to and about Coffco Company. I read them quickly, trying to understand. They were dated going all the way back to eleven years ago, when the mayor had first been elected.

Ensure the long-term viability of our company...If Halls' safety record continues to improve, we see no barrier...Coffco to relocate to Halls, pending location of new factory...

The final paper was a bill of sale, the one for my dad's property, now in the hands of Coffco. Suddenly everything was clear.

"You've been falsifying the crime statistics. To get Coffco to relocate to Halls. You orchestrated the whole thing so that you could even sell them the land to build their filthy factory. My father's land!"

"Billy," the mayor swallowed and croaked hoarsely, "I swear I had nothing to do with your dad's death. It was just fortunate timing for me—"

303

"Fortunate timing? You bastard!" He flinched, apparently terrified I would shoot him. I still wasn't sure I wouldn't.

"How did you even get the money to buy our land, and all the other properties—we saw your records at the county recorder's office. You come into money every July."

He looked down, finally showing some shame.

"The festival. You've been embezzling funds from the festival every year."

He paled. I had my answer.

"Look. I'm not hurting anyone doing what I'm doing. Can't you see how much Halls has benefited from appearing so safe? Coffco will bring more business to Halls, good jobs. Eighty percent of the people that will be working at Coffco intend to move here. They don't want to live in Dyersburg or Ripley because their crime rates are much higher. Look at all the money I'm bringing here, to this sleepy little town that would be disappearing if it weren't for me. Business is booming and everyone is benefitting. Even you."

"But mostly you, right?"

He was silent for a moment.

"I bet Jack Pitt would disagree."

He pursed his lips.

"Did you kill him? Or are you just covering up his death like all the others, to keep the town looking clean and safe?"

"It's not like that, Billy. You don't understand. I only leave the ones off the list that are complete dead ends, like your father's hit and run and Mrs. Higby's murder. If there were any leads..."

He'd confirmed it. Mrs. Higby had been murdered.

I glared at him. "From now on you're going to be honest in your reporting, aren't you?"

"Come on, Billy. You have—"

"Aren't you? Because if you're not, I'll be sending a note to the city council about your scheming."

"You can't!" he crowed, triumphantly. He thought he had me. "Coffco will back out—the citizens of Halls will be the ones to suffer. Sweet little Billy Howard would never let that happen."

"You don't know anything about me," I spat. "Just test me, and I'll tell everyone what you've done, and damn the consequences. I'll keep your secret for now—let Coffco move to Halls and bring their money and their jobs. But you and the chief, you're going to change your ways. You're going to do everything in your power to actually make Halls a safe place to live. Or everyone will know what you've done. You'll go to jail for the rest of your life."

Mayor Clement clenched his jaw and narrowed his eyes at me, but finally he nodded.

"One more thing. The money you make from the sale of my dad's land—that goes to help survivors of violent crimes."

I jerked on the curtains on the windows and used them to tie him up. He'd be able to escape; I just wanted to slow him down.

I backed up to the door, opened it and went out.

Chapter 26

My feet knew exactly where to go. I stepped evenly up to the chief's house and rang the doorbell. He was the only one I would be disturbing. He lived alone.

"Billy," he exclaimed as he opened the door. When he saw the rifle in my hand, he gasped. I looked down—I hadn't even realized I still had it. I dropped it.

"Billy, what's going on? What did you do? What happened?"

Tears streamed down my face, and my shoulders quaked with noiseless sobs. I was spent. Everything I had learned from the mayor seemed to weigh down on me. I couldn't hold it anymore.

"How could you, Bud?" I whispered. "I thought you were my friend, my dad's friend. And you just buried his death like it meant nothing."

"Come in, Billy. We need to talk."

He led me into the house and sat me down at his kitchen table. It hardly registered as he heated up some tea in the microwave and handed it to me.

"What's going on, Billy? Start at the beginning."

My eyes were dry now, and I leveled my bloodshot gaze at him. "You know who hit my dad, don't you? You've been hiding that information from me all this time. Why would you keep that from me? I don't understand. I've always treated you like a father, and you betray me like this."

"Billy, I don't know who did it," he said gently. "Where did you get that idea?"

"From the town drunk. Better be careful who you put me next to when you lock me up. It's not me who messed up the evidence, it was you. Who was it? Who?"

"I'm telling you that I don't know," he sighed.

"I know about your deal with the mayor. You helped him cover up crimes. Did he give you a cut of the money? Is that why you did it?" I searched his face, trying to find the truth.

"Billy—you didn't?" his eyes were wide with horror.

"He's alive. I had my rifle with me when I went over there, got him to tell me the truth. But I didn't hurt him. I'm not that despicable. I'm not like you."

His jaw hung down. "Now, wait just a minute, son. It's not what you think. There was no evidence to follow."

"How many crimes haven't gotten the attention they deserved because you were selfish and wanted money?"

"It was never the money for me, Billy. The mayor would have fired me if I didn't go along with his plan. But even that... Look, Clement promised me that Halls would benefit. Once Coffco moves here, we'll have so much tax money—we'll be able to get new officers, new equipment. Everything I've needed for years, we'll have it all and more. I couldn't pass up that opportunity. You have to believe me, though, Billy. We never would remove a crime that we felt had the potential to be solved. I swear it."

"Then what was Lee talking about? What is it that he says you are hiding? Tell me."

"I don't know. The only thing I can think of is that he overheard us talking about our record-keeping secret."

"Did you fire Old Man Jack because he wouldn't go along with your schemes?"

He looked at his shoes. Guilty as charged. "Jack went along with us for a while, but he didn't like it. After Mrs. Higby—he couldn't get over it. Leaving an unsolved murder like that. The guilt ate at him and he started drinking, doing drugs to take the edge off. He got so bad, we couldn't keep him on the force any more. The mayor agreed to keep paying him a portion of his salary for the rest of his life, if he'd only leave the job and keep his mouth shut."

So that's what I had overheard—what had started this all. "Did you kill him?"

Bud looked stricken, as though I had actually hit him. "No, son, I would never...that you'd think that just kills me. No, the drugs finally caught up with him. It was an overdose."

I believed him. I could never look at him the same way again, but I believed he was telling me the truth.

"What did he see at the Higbys'? What happened to Maybelle?"

"We couldn't figure it out, Billy. She'd been shot with Charles's gun, but there was no way he could have done it. He had an alibi, gone at the store during the time frame when she died. He called in the crime, and when Jack found him he was blubbering over her dead body, completely incoherent. He hadn't seen anything. There was no sign of forced entry.

Nothing there to tell us where to look. We chose not to record it. You know why."

"What about the note? The one the reporter saw?"

"I don't know anything about that."

"So you convinced Pastor Higby to cremate the body, and go along with the story of the fall."

"Yes. We all convinced him."

"Fine, I believe you," I said, tiredly. What did it all mean? Why had I ever found the box in the first place? It had led me to this—finding out about the mayor, the chief, all of it. But I still didn't have any answers, not for Mrs. Higby and not for Daddy.

"You know daddy's been dead for ten years now?" I whispered.

"I know."

"Tell me what you remember."

"Billy, you don't want to go over that again."

"Tell me," I insisted. I needed to hear it.

He began with the moment he came on the scene, arriving right after Jack. The ambulance arrived shortly after he had. I remembered my seven-year-old brain not understanding what was really happening. I didn't understand why Mama was screaming and yelling and grabbing at her hair. I was scared. Even though I saw my dad dead on the street, I thought the paramedics could make him live again. Rain poured down on us, making it all the more unbearable.

I remember with crystal clarity the words of the paramedic with the buckteeth and tiny eyes, "He's gone. We'll take him to the mortician."

I remembered it all—nothing was missing—with Bud telling the story, it was easy to recreate it. It was awful and beautiful all at once—almost freeing.

I said, "Who did you think it was? Who?"

"I had no idea." He shook his head.

"You had to have an idea." I shook my head in a slow, even motion.

"Everyone was cleared, Billy. There's no reason—"

"Just tell me who you investigated."

"We investigated everyone. Everyone was a suspect."

"But who did you think were your best suspects? Come on, Bud. I need this."

He took a deep breath. "At first, I wondered if maybe it was Lee. But Lee was at a rehab that day. He'd been gone several days already. He'd gotten drunk and run into a cow the week before. That was the last straw. I revoked his driver's license against the mayor's wishes and his dad sent him to rehab. Then I thought Devon Macon. He moved away a few years back. He was at work. It seemed like we questioned every stinking person in town. We looked at hundreds of cars. There were no damaged cars and no good suspects. I did everything I could to find whoever it was. Believe me."

That's when I decided to tell him what I knew. "I overheard you and Jack Pitt talking in the cemetery. He said you found something that day. That you knew it was someone from town. You didn't deny it then, don't deny it now.

He sighed. He was busted and he knew it. "After checking everybody out, we couldn't imagine how it could have been a local that killed your dad. No cars had any damage, and they would have had they been involved. We immediately concluded it had to be someone that didn't live here. But, your street was a dead end. Why would some out-of-towner drive down your street? It never felt right to me, but we couldn't prove anything."

"Why keep that from me?" I leaned back.

"Are you serious? Your mom wanted you to have a full, rich life, one free of any more pain or heartache. I knew if you had any inkling that it was someone from Halls, you wouldn't be able to let it go and you would seek vengeance."

"That's just stupid."

"Look at yourself, Billy. Look in the mirror behind you. Your clothes are dirty and your hair's crazy. You look like you haven't slept in days—and why? Because you got the idea that someone you knew killed your dad. Someone in town. I know you better than you think."

"You lied to me. You are a cheat and a liar. I'll never trust you again. I hate you." I said it, but I didn't feel it deep down. It just seemed like the right thing to say. It seemed like the thing to say that would free me from the deep ache that sat on my chest.

"Do you want me to show you the files on it?" Bud asked.

"It's a bit late for that, don't you think? Besides, I've already seen them." I said it to hurt him. I knew it would.

"So, you not only looked in Mrs. Higby's box, you looked in your dad's too?"

"Yes." I thought about the evidence and how the chief had cleared everyone that lived on our street.

"Well, then you know, I cleared all your neighbors."

I remembered the witness statements of all of them. The

Higbys had been sound asleep when the police came to question them. And there was no damage on their car. In fact, it was broken down. They had it in the shop.

The Coubles drove a big truck and the injuries weren't consistent with what a large truck would have done. Nor did their truck have any dents or signs of an accident.

The Gustavsons and the Abernathys were out of town.

Henrietta and Sam were cleared. No damage to their cars.

The Wheelrights' and Jamisons' cars also cleared them. Hugo Mathis didn't even own a car.

"Please don't let this change our relationship." Bud pushed his hands through his hair.

"Too late. It's hard for me to even look at you. I can't believe you gave into the mayor's demands."

"We all make foolish decisions. Granted, mine is bigger than most, but I never meant to let it get so out of hand. Everything I did was to help Halls."

"You never should have stopped looking for my dad's murderer."

"I only stopped when your mom insisted that I do. She said she had made peace with what had happened and wanted me to move on. I did. She asked me to never discuss it with you. She made me promise. She wanted you to forget. She wanted you to find peace and feel the love of Jesus who sends the peace. I tried to do as she wanted. I tried to honor her."

I was cut short. Mama made him stop? He didn't know what really happened. It was freaking me out. I needed air. I was feeling crushed.

GRAVEDIGGERS

"I have to go," I said abruptly, pushing away from the table. He called after me as I ran out, but I couldn't stop. Mama. She was trying to protect me, but keeping me from the truth was killing me. This was too much. I needed my dad.

Chapter 27

I walked in a daze to Daddy's grave. I was surprised to find Mama still there. She sat, leaning against his gravestone. She looked beaten down and lonely.

She reached her arms out to me as I approached, thinking I wanted to be comforted. But I didn't. At least I wouldn't admit it. When I didn't immediately fall into her arms, she wiped at her face with her sleeve and then said, "What is it, honey?"

"You asked Bud to stop investigating Daddy's death? How could you do that to me when you knew how desperate I was for answers?"

"I was protecting you, son. I wanted to help you get free."

"Did you tell the whole town to keep quiet? Is that why I couldn't get anyone in this stupid town to tell me anything?"

"I'm sorry. I thought it was the best thing. I really did."

I knew she believed this. But it wasn't right.

Only a minute later, the chief showed up. I could feel him behind me.

"I will never forgive you for this, Mama. I needed that information. I needed to get closure in my own way, not yours. And you," I turned to the chief. "You are a traitor in the worst way. I trusted you all my life and I can never trust you again."

I ran away. I couldn't even sob. Anger filled me. I would not take this. I couldn't take this. I didn't have to take this. I would never trust either of them again.

I ran for Henry's, but stopped at my house and gathered all the evidence and notes I'd collected and took them with me. I threw pebbles at his window until he motioned for me to go to the front door.

"You look awful," he whispered.

I don't know if it was my appearance or all the stuff I had clutched in my hands that signaled him to keep his distance, but he didn't ask me any questions and let me go to his room and crash.

I didn't wake until noon the next day when Henry slammed me to wake me. Payback from the other day, I'm sure. I couldn't laugh, although he did.

"Look dude, you stink. Shower. Your mom brought clothes and other stuff. In the bathroom. My mom made BLTs and fresh lemonade, so don't take all day." He left.

I ambled into the bathroom and showered. I did look terrible. I needed a shave bad. I smelled my pits and they reeked. I opened the window and turned the water so hot it almost scalded my skin. I scrubbed and scrubbed but it seemed I couldn't get clean. When the water turned warm, I took that as a signal I'd been in too long. I shaved and dressed.

Much to everyone's credit, no one asked why I was there. I assumed Mama had told them something when she brought my clothes over, I just didn't know what.

I would never know who hit my dad. We would never find out who killed Mrs. Higby. It was over. I had to accept the reality of the situation. The cases were truly cold, and no one would ever be able to solve them—and not because there was a plot against me or the dead people, for other reasons entirely. The cases hadn't been solved because they were unsolvable.

I would take the box to Pastor Higby today and wash my hands of it. I would confess and take whatever punishment he had to mete out. I hated to admit it, but Mama and Pastor Higby had been right. My path to vengeance had hurt not only me, but all the people I loved. Sure, they had been in the wrong, but they had only wanted to protect me. Looking back at my actions, I felt ashamed and embarrassed. I had let vengeance cloud my purpose.

Mrs. Parnell put us to work, sorting through all the DVDs and putting them in alphabetical order. It was wicked hot outside, so we stayed in and watched *Nacho Libre*. Amanda had slowly found her way next to me. That familiar hum started in my chest and spread through my body, reminding me how special she was and how lucky I was to know her.

"I've missed you in a weird way," she whispered in my ear and even took my hand. It felt good to have her small, soft hand in mine. Her voice made me feel warm inside. I stared at her and she stared back, sympathy and care in her eyes. I should tell her what happened. I took a deep breath and let it all fly, Henry joining us once he realized what I was saying.

They listened in complete silence, jaws gaping more than not. When I was done, the silence hung in the air until I broke it.

"I vote for a bonfire. Let's get rid of all the poison upstairs. I'll take the box to the pastor tonight and beg for his forgiveness."

"We'll come with you." Amanda patted my arm and grabbed my hand.

"No. While I appreciate that, this is something I have to do on my own." It felt good to say it. "But, you can help me burn it all."

We rifled through the things in the box, making sure there wasn't anything we wanted to keep. Amanda mentioned several times that it was a shame we couldn't solve the murders. She seemed to look at everything, trying to find something that would help us to solve the crimes. I stared at the jewelry all lined up in neat rows, fingered the chunky, shiny pieces. I looked over the copies of the pictures I'd taken of the evidence in Mrs. Higby's box.

When I got to the chunky key, I asked Amanda and Henry about it.

"I totally forgot to ask," Amanda said. "But, there's no time like the present." She bounded out of the room. We continued to sift through the charts until she came back.

"It's a key Mrs. Higby made one year for Christmas gifts. It was supposed to be a key to unlock the true treasures of life. It was symbolic of the key to salvation and happiness. The key that unlocked treasures beyond this life or something like that."

"That's pretty dumb," Henry scoffed.

Yesterday, two days ago, a year ago, I would have thought the same thing, but not today. I knew there was something to that. The key for me right now was forgiveness. There could be no happiness without it. Easier said than done.

"It's not dumb," Amanda said, punching Henry. "It's beautiful. She said there was a poem that Mrs. Higby wrote to go with the key, but it had been lost years ago."

I silently wondered if the bloody note Pastor Higby retrieved was a poem she had written about him. I would ask him about it. I hoped he would tell me.

"Your mom wants to take us over to get some ice cream." Amanda flipped her hair over her shoulder.

I stood up. I never turned down ice cream. We put Henry's blanket over all the evidence and charts, and we left. We sat in the park eating our ice cream and playing on the equipment. It felt good to play around.

I walked down to the caboose by the police station and someone honked at me. It was Jeb Prescott riding in his partially fixed up cream Chevelle. The tires had air and the windshield had been replaced. It also looked like the car had been cleaned and waxed.

"Wow! Mr. Prescott. It already looks great!"

"Thanks, Billy. You reminded me what a great car this was. I'd really like to see it in some shows. I decided after all this time, I'm never going to get around to repairing it myself, so I'm taking it to a body shop in Memphis that specializes in restoration. They've promised me they can fix the front and make it look like the original." He fished around on the seat and handed me a check for my work spraying his fields.

"Thank you, sir."

"Do you happen to know where Mr. Higby lives these days?"

"I sure do." What did he want with the pastor?

"So he does still live here? I went by the address Higby's brother had written on the bill of sale, but it seems like it's the future site of Coffco." He had a merry glint in his eye.

"Yeah. He's the pastor at the Methodist church over on Tigrett. He lives there, too."

"Great. I needed to see if he had the original manual to this baby tucked away in his house somewhere. I thought I'd get it to complete the restoration if possible."

My insides squeezed. "Oh. Is he the one you bought the car from?" The words seemed to stick in my throat.

"Sure is. Thanks for your help the other week and tell your mama hi for me."

He drove away and I stood there, frozen, a buzzing noise taking over my mind. Next thing I knew, Mrs. Parnell drove up next to me with the van and had me climb in.

It couldn't be true. It couldn't be what it looked like.

"I know we did it a bit backwards, today," Mrs. Parnell said, "having dessert before dinner, but I thought it would be fun to make pizzas and watch a fun movie together tonight." Henry's little brother and sister squealed with delight.

When we got back to the house, I still couldn't think right. Mrs. Parnell gave us each a piece of dough to flatten out and top with whatever toppings we wanted. I hurried so that mine would get into the oven first. I had business to take care of. I went up into Henry's room and stuffed the box, its contents, along with Pastor Higby's gun and the articles about Mrs. Higby's death into my bag. I set the bag by the front door before returning to the kitchen. Both Henry and Amanda were helping the other two kids get their pizzas just right.

Mrs. Parnell came into the kitchen holding three different movies. "Everyone gets one vote for the movie tonight. Majority rules."

I couldn't even taste the pizza, but I scarfed it down as soon as we were all seated in front of the TV and the movie started. It was just starting to get dark outside.

"Mrs. Parnell, the pizza was great. I wish I could stay for the movie, but I think I need to be heading home."

"All right, Billy. You go right ahead." Relief was painted on her face. She wanted me to forgive my mom.

Amanda met me at the door. She looked amazing, and I hated to leave her.

"You're not going home, are you?" Did she know me that well already?

"No. I need to go see the preacher."

"Are you sure you're okay? You look—"

"I'm just kinda nervous about this." I knew she thought I was going to get a different kind of closure with Higby.

"Yeah. Right. Understandable. You sure you don't want me to come—moral support and all?"

If she only knew what I was really going to do. "I'm sure. Hopefully I'll be back soon."

She shoved her phone into my hand, her soft skin touching mine. "Take this just in case you need us. We'll be there for you, no matter what." I grabbed her small hand in mine. How I wished I could stay with her. "We'll have the bonfire when you get back."

I nodded. She was so close, I could feel her breath.

"Amanda," I said softly.

"Yes, Billy?" Her eyes met mine, and she was so beautiful, so perfect, I had to touch her. I raised my hand to her cheek. She leaned into it, and the feel of her silky skin sent a shock of joy through me.

"I just...want to say thank you."

"Then, you should," she smiled softly and leaned in, her lips only a sliver from mine.

I closed my eyes, and our lips met. For that moment, all the turmoil of the last few days fell away, and everything was right with the world. The kiss lingered, slow and perfect. Then, the moment was over. She pulled away and sighed softly. I pulled her in for a tight hug, and lay my head on her shoulder. It took me a minute to recover and remember what I was doing before the kiss.

She whispered in my ear, "You're welcome."

I laughed softly. "I could never thank you enough."

"I'll be thinking about you, sending you good vibes. By the way, I'm not scared anymore."

I touched her face. "Me either." Was I really going to leave her?

Her smile was bright, encouraging.

From there, it was like I was on auto-pilot. I grabbed the bag and headed out.

I would get the answers for at least one murder tonight.

Chapter 28

I stood at my father's grave.

"What should I do?" I asked him. "I loved that man and I find he is your murderer?" Hot tears spilled down my cheeks. A light flipped on in the preacher's living room. I thought of him holding that urn, how we had cried and mourned together and all along, he kept this secret. There were too many secrets in this town. Too much pain.

As I walked, my encounters with Lee, Harris, the Mayor, the chief, and my mom flashed through my mind. Then Old Man Jack's face stared at me from an imagined coroner's office. Pastor Higby was the cause of all of it. He should have owned up to what he had done.

I knew what I had to do. I would get the truth even if it meant I had to force him with his own gun to tell me. I continued on my way to his door and opened it, only slightly surprised it wasn't locked. He stood by the mantle, looking at the urn.

"I wondered when you'd come." He turned to me. Eyes red with tears.

"How could you?" I asked, shaking my head. "How could you?" I yelled this time, my whole body quaking. "You've been my friend all these years. You knew I was searching. You knew I needed to know what happened to my dad, and yet you said nothing. Why? Why?" I cried.

"I was selfish. I was wrong." He turned and looked at the urn, stroking it lightly with his fingers. "I was a drunk. I-I—" He put his head in his hands and sobs wracked his body.

Tears of his betrayal swept down my face and neck and into my collared shirt. He had done it. Not only had he done it, he'd hit my dad and run. He'd kept it a secret and lived while daddy died. Boiling heat spread through my body, and blood pounded in my ears.

Extreme anger overtook me, and I pulled the gun out of my bag, papers spilled to the floor. I wanted him dead. He didn't even flinch. This is what I'd waited for. Wasn't it? Why couldn't I just do it? I held the gun in my hand at my side. I couldn't raise it.

"I know I don't have a right to request anything, Billy. But if you could, see that I'm cremated and mix my ashes in with my wife's. Bury us together under the pecan tree."

"First," I said. I felt strong. Invincible. I couldn't see anything but him. "You are going to confess and tell me exactly what happened that night you killed my dad and ran like a coward."

He pulled the urn down from the mantle and when he did, a folded up paper with bloody fingerprints fell to the floor next to the newly printed copy of the article about his wife's death.

"What is that?" I asked, knowing full well it was the note Jay Heath had seen on the table after the murder.

"It's nothing," he said. "Just a note from my wife to me."

The look on his face played Judas on him. He didn't want me to read it. I had to.

I motioned with the gun toward it. "Pick it up and put it on the table." I brushed my eyes, hoping to be able to see what was written through my tears.

"It's nothing. Just some poetry."

"Then it won't matter that I read it, right? Pick. It. Up." Anger flared within me. Maybe I could kill this man.

He did, and when he made a motion to tear it, I dropped the gun and lunged at him, wrestling it away from him. He curled into a ball. "No. No. This is all my fault. It wasn't her. It was me." What was he talking about? Higby picked up the copy of the article.

I stood and opened the note, the gun lay a foot away between Higby and me. The sticky blood had glued the pages together, and they were difficult to separate without tearing. He hadn't opened it since that night. I looked at him, a ball of misery.

"Did you kill your wife too, because she refused to keep your secret? You sold the car to hide your first crime, but how? How did you hide it from the chief that night?"

"We parked it in the barn, where we kept the animals. It belonged to my brother. The next day I took it to Lenox and sold it. Our car was at the garage."

My hands trembled while he told his tale, making it harder to accomplish my task, but deep in my soul, somehow, I knew this small note held all the answers.

Dearest Charles,

I tell you first how much I love you. I am proud of you and how you've changed your life. I, however, can no longer live knowing what

I have done. Guilt eats at me, but my dear, I won't tell our secret. But I need to tell God, in person. I think he works in mysterious ways and by me hitting that poor man that night, he enacted change on yours. You are a beautiful man with much to offer. Continue to do good, and I will see you in the next life if my maker can find forgiveness for a wretch like me. I go to my maker seeking forgiveness and a calm mind.

Live a long, loving, and caring life, my love. I wait for you. But don't join me anytime soon.

If my maker will see fit to forgive me, we will be together again. I miss you already, but this life offers nothing for me and I offer nothing to it.

Goodbye my love. I die in sweet happiness knowing you have overcome and overcome well.

Maybelle.

The tree. Higby named the tree Ol' May. It was for his wife, Maybelle. The box. Higby had buried it, and he'd dug it back up. He was honoring her with the contents of that box in some way. He must have been crazy with worry over where it went.

I couldn't see again, and I swept at my tears. The only movement I was able to accomplish was the result of the sobs that welled up in my chest and exploded out my mouth.

"It wasn't you. It was your wife?" I rocked on my heels.

"No. It was my fault. I'm telling you, it wasn't her fault. She picked me up from the bar. I was totally drunk. Our car was in the shop, so she used my brother's. Remember the rain? We argued in the car. I wasn't ever supposed to go to the bar after work. I grabbed at the wheel. It was stupid. That's when the car hit your dad. She got out of the car—we both

325

did—we tried to help him, but we were too late. She was never to blame, but in the eyes of the law she would have been because she was driving. I couldn't allow her to go to jail. I came up with a plan to save us and it worked."

"Except she couldn't live with the deception." My heart ached. He had only been trying to spare his wife.

"She got so depressed. She wasn't my May Sunshine anymore. I tried everything and didn't dare leave her alone, but that night I had to. I wasn't gone long at all, and she took advantage of it. She'd planned it all out. My sweet flower is dead. I am the one responsible."

"What about the jewelry? And the cash? Why did you bury it?"

"I couldn't let people know she'd killed herself. They'd think differently of her. I tried to make it look like a burglary. Besides," he looked down, shame washing over his features, "if her death was ruled a suicide, I couldn't collect the life insurance we had on her."

"That's despicable," I shook my head in disbelief.

"I'm dying, Billy. I've been dying for years now—my liver. Without Maybelle's insurance, I couldn't pay for the treatments. When I found her, I called the police, but before they got there, I hid some cash and valuables to make it look like a burglary. Then Jack came and convinced me it would be better for Maybelle's memory if they told the town it was an accident. That Maybelle'd fallen from the ladder. I tried to make it right! And that stuff in the box. I couldn't make myself open that box once it was closed, so I buried it—burying my guilt." He gasped now, obviously in pain. "I tried to talk to them and explain, but they kept telling me not to worry, they'd take care of everything. They helped me take care of her body, make it sound like an accident, so no one would know, no one would suspect. That shame burned in me...I turned to the Lord and gave my life to Him. I've tried to make it right. Every day since that day all the way up to when I dug that box up, I've tried." His breath was coming in ragged now, pained and uneven. "I'm sorry about your Daddy, Billy. I'm so sorry."

"No. No." I whispered it through my sobs, desperately wanting to find the strength to complete my task, the whole reason I was here today. "Why did you have to dig it up?" I looked for the gun and my eyes lit upon it, resting in the space between the Pastor and me. I knelt down, but instead of reaching for the gun, I collapsed to the floor, giving in to my grief. I could not kill this man.

"When you and Henry got so close to digging it up, all the memories seemed to crash into me, more forceful than ever before. I figured it was God's way of telling me it was time to atone for my sins. I planned to confess to the congregation that Sunday, but then...then the box disappeared."

I rocked in my misery. I wished I'd never picked up that box. Something was happening inside me as I cried. A pity for the man who was by all accounts truly culpable for my father's death found root. I pushed at it, not wanting to allow any hint of forgiveness to enter me. I'd wanted this too long. The pity changed to something warm, something that I hadn't dared think possible. Was this love springing up inside me for this wretched man who ruined my life? I attempted to open my swollen eyes to look up at him. He held the gun that had sat on the floor between us in his hand, aiming it at his temple.

"No, Pastor!" All I'd wanted when I'd come here was to make him pay. It was different now.

The warmth that had begun to grow turned to a deep comforting heat, it filled my soul in an instant and I freed myself from my anger and hurtled myself at him. He must live. He must. He couldn't die with the same gun that shot his wife. I hit at his arm, but I wasn't quick enough. A shot pierced the air and screams followed it. Were they mine? Was I shot? Hands grabbed at me, pulling at me. They were Pastor Higby's. I would not let this man go. This man I now loved more than I had ever loved anyone before. The pain he must have endured all this time, solely to protect his wife's good name.

Blood slicked my hands, and I could feel his body limp in mine. Blood oozed from his chest. What had I done? Why had I brought the gun here? I released him slightly so I could look in his eyes. He stared back at me. He was still alive.

"It's good, boy."

Blood peeked out from the corners of his mouth and I choked on a sob, pulling him to me and yelling, "I forgive you. I forgive you. Don't die!" I raised my head to look up. "God, save him. Save him. I need him. Please God." God's name became a whisper on my lips.

I could hear and feel commotion outside. Voices, movement that needed to go away, and in front of it all, the whispered words, "I love you, Billy, like you were my own son. Do good like you've always done. I go to my dear wife who waits for me. Who needs me." Higby's voice choked out several times. "Your father would be proud of you. Don't feel bad about this today. It is good. I forgive you, son. I forgive you. Make sure they know it was me. It was me. I should have been honest. You are a good boy to look for and find the truth. The truth sets you free. I will finally be free."

I pulled him to me hard. "No. No." I cried into his gray hair for what seemed forever. "You can't go. The new preacher will get a backhoe ..." His body went limp in mine, and I moaned as hurried feet and arms pulled me away and men—paramedics—said words I couldn't make out and worked on him, jabbing him with needles and moving him to a gurney. Where had they come from? I tried to go to him, but strong arms held me back. I tried to pry them loose and another set grabbed me and held tighter still. Why were they keeping me from him?

He was gone. I felt it in my bones. I felt the bloody note clutched in my hand, and I shoved it into my pocket. I glanced at the spot the urn had sat. Maybelle looked down on me from her picture, familiar dangly earrings hung from her ears. The matching one was in his father's box at the police station.

I became aware of the arms holding me. It was Amanda's arms. She pulled me to her, not shushing me or telling me it would be okay, because she knew better. We rocked, there on the floor in my misery together as they wheeled Higby away from us and out of the house.

Mama's face appeared in front of me. My eyes burned and I lunged for her. The hands holding me fell away. She cradled me, shushing me. She told me it would be okay, because she knew it would be. The burn of love I'd felt for that man burned still and a sweet peace joined it, a mercy from God? Why would he have mercy on me, a boy with a murderous heart? Peace overtook even that thought, and I realized that God's goodness was intended for me, too. He loved the sinners as well as the faithful. He was there to bring me forgiveness. He wanted me to find forgiveness and peace, just like Mama had always said.

And the peace was all encompassing, rich and enduring, even when the police led me away.

The whole time Henry and I dug Pastor Higby's grave, we told stories of the good man we'd loved so dearly. We laughed. We shed a few tears. We made the perfect grave for him and his wife under the pecan tree in the spot where I'd first seen the army green ammo box. Ol' May would protect them and create a place for them both. A place they could both rest in peace knowing I'd never tell their secret—knowing I was okay and finally had closure. A place I could rebury the box along with a bloody note.

A big orange backhoe sat back by the shed. The new pastor was progressive. This would be the last hand-dug grave in the cemetery. It felt right somehow.

Amanda kept us company, the girl who listened to a small whisper to come find me when she found the gun on Henry's bed was missing and brought help with her. A girl I adored. She leaned up against the tree and recorded the stories Henry and I told as we dug.

Everyone would know how an imperfect man could affect many lives for the better and that forgiveness could free us from pain if we allowed it.

About the Author

Cindy M. Hogan is the author of the best-selling Watched series. She graduated in secondary education at BYU and enjoys spending time with unpredictable teenagers. More than anything, she loves the time she has with her own teenager daughters and wishes she could freeze them at this fun age. If she's not reading or writing, you'll find her snuggled up to her awesome husband watching a great movie or planning their next party.

To learn more about the author and the books she has written, visit her at cindymhogan.com or on Facebook at watched-the book.

Acknowledgements

Huge thanks to my husband Bill, for the great idea for this book. While it's miles from his original idea, it never would have been created without him.

Thanks to everyone that made sure I got the food, speech, and setting of a small southern town right: Lisa Pennington, Bill and Sylvia Hogan, Cindy Mashburn, and Marilyn Clement.

Thanks to Carolyn Wheat for writing the book that made me understand the difference between mystery and suspense. To my many beta readers and those in my critique groups.

And to those integral in getting the final product out: Charity, my editor, Steven Novak, my cover designer, my cover models: Gabrielle Hutchinson, Jason Anderson, Justinryan Penrod, Chelsey and Dane Money, Cara Krebs, Marly Peterson, Hensley Hogan, Jason Tebbs, Kyle Mollinet, Hannah Hogan, Danny Wenzel, Addy Nichol. To Rachel Hert for her help with back copy and Heather Justesen for formatting—Tons of thanks.

Writing a mystery is so totally different than writing a suspense novel. I hope you all love the final product.

Visit Cindy on her Blog:
cindymhogan.com

For series trivia, sneak peeks, events in your area,
contests, fun fan interaction, like the Watched
Facebook Page: Watched-the book

Follow Cindy M. Hogan on twitter: Watched1

If you loved this book,
Jump into the exciting adventures of the *Watched Trilogy*
Up the stakes and suspense with *Adrenaline Rush*
Laugh with Brooklyn in *Confessions of a 16-Year-Old Virgin Lips*